CATBOAT ROAD

KATE ROUNDS

Bywater
BOOKS

2022

Bywater Books

Copyright © 2022 Kate Rounds

Print ISBN: 978-1-61294-245-2

Bywater Books First Edition: September 2022

Cover designer: Ann McMan, TreeHouse Studio

Bywater Books
PO Box 3671
Ann Arbor MI 48106-3671

www.bywaterbooks.com

For my sister Andrea Rounds.

CATBOAT ROAD

KATE ROUNDS

*"What we see there are not giants but windmills,
and what seem to be their arms are the sails
that turned by the wind make the millstone go."*

—*Sancho Panza*

From *Don Quixote* by Miguel de Cervantes

1

From our position on the stairs, Sawyer and I could see Mrs. Forest sitting on a stool in our kitchen, sobbing.

Our mother—Willamena "Bill" Ragsdale—had a dishrag on her shoulder, as if Mrs. Forest might projectile-spit, like a baby, onto her shirt. Bill removed it to dry a wineglass; it squeaked and sang as she wiped the rim. Mrs. Forest watched like she might as well be dead.

"It's so cliched," she said.

Mrs. Forest's husband Lee was cheating on her with some chick in his office.

Mom motioned Mrs. Forest to come to her side of the butcherblock island. Now it was a desert island: our mother alone with Mrs. Forest, her incarcerated breasts and the spoon-curve ass you could cup in your hand while you slow-danced in the living room, the way we'd once seen our parents do after they'd been smoking weed on the couch, making no effort to keep the smoke from drifting up the stairs.

I don't think I knew it then, or understood, that passion is like a painting that could fall off the wall and still be beautiful.

Bill held Mrs. Forest's head to her chest. "He's a good man," Mrs. Forest sniffled.

"In the beginning, maybe. Now he's kind of an A-hole."

"Brett and Levi like him."

Mom laughed. "Our kids used to like us, too."

Mom was just trying to make Mrs. Forest feel better. We still liked our parents, mainly because they were hard to piss off, unless we did something unethical, like ghosting or canceling. When it came to smoking pot and body art, they were like, whatever.

Sawyer was eighteen, I was seventeen. We were Irish twins, occasionally the same age, and old enough to make our own decisions.

Mom leaned her elbows on the butcher block and stared up at Mrs. Forest, whose feet clutched the rungs of the barstool, her sequined ballet slippers dangling from her toes.

My mother's most distinctive trait was her laser focus on the person she was talking to—like no one else existed. Today it was all Mrs. Forest.

There were no kids on the stairs; no husband Rags Ragsdale selling ads for our local paper the *Horton Frigate*; no philanderer at the Bowsprit, running his hand up the thigh of his mistress, Ethel, instead of hard at work at Medical Arts.

Bill and Mrs. Forest were drinking red wine, joking about the sun and the yardarm. Were you supposed to wait until the sun was over or under it to start "cocktails"?

It was noon.

Our dog, Crack, hung around the kitchen in hopes of licking up some crumbs. Tracking the conversation with his eyes, he pricked up his ears at key points, occasionally letting out a little squeal. He was a small mixed breed whose defining features were his intelligence and that he was a loser as a guard dog.

"Ace," Sawyer hissed, passing me the butt of a joint. It was hard to imagine that the ladies couldn't smell it. We watched a perfumed river of perspiration run into Mrs. Forest's cleavage.

Reading my mind, Sawyer offered me a Starburst from his pocket. "We could, like, totally touch her ass," he exhaled.

"I suppose you found out the usual way," Mom was saying.

"They always want you to know; otherwise why not delete

their texts?"

"You're a lovely woman. You can do better than Lee," Mom said. "So what are you going to do?"

Mrs. Forest sighed, breasts rising toward her dimpled chin. "And this Ethel? She's not even an admin; she's a coworker at Medical Arts."

Our mother pulled strands of hair away from Mrs. Forest's eyes, stroking her face with the back of her hand. "Two physical therapists."

Professional touchers! People who know how to massage and manipulate.

"Shit!" I said.

Luckily, my mother and Mrs. Forest were too buzzed to hear me. They took turns pouring from the bottle, which stood like a little sentinel between them. I knew the wine would be reddening their teeth. Mrs. Forest's often had a whisper of lipstick, as if de Kooning had started a brushstroke and then thought better of it.

At some point, Mom had laid out a plate of the plainest Carr crackers. Mrs. Forest got up to get another bottle from the rack by the sink, hauled cheddar cheese and bread and butter pickles from a Shaw's bag. She plucked cracker crumbs from her sweater.

Crack licked them off the floor. He weaved between the stool legs, looking hammered. "When they're not screwing, they're probably *practicing* screwing, like it's some kind of maneuver," Mrs. Forest said.

"Which it is." Our mother sometimes made blanket statements about sex, as if she were an expert.

Maybe she was. She wasn't my idea of sexy: small, skinny, put-together. When she laughed, she squinted, which made her look vulnerable and blind. She wore glasses as a fashion accessory, adding "dashes" of color with knockoff cell-phone cases dangling from her wrist. Men loved a woman who took care of herself—not one with loose, wild lines, all the perfect imperfections, that make art, art.

3

"What do you mean by that, exactly?" Mrs. Forest turned her head to the side, the way Crack did when he wanted to understand human words.

"If you're not in love with someone, maneuvers are everything."

"Are you trying to make me feel better?"

"Sometimes all you want is good sex." Bill turned sad suddenly. "Those kind of secret, special things that people do." She was waiting to be wrapped in Mrs. Forest's arms; it was her turn.

I could take a lot of things from Bill, but not vague, unnamed desires that hovered like something alive in the room.

After Mom walked Mrs. Forest to the driveway, Sawyer and I headed for the kitchen. Sawyer sat on Mrs. Forest's stool, as close to her ass as we could get.

"Sawyer," Mom said, returning to the kitchen. "I want you to do something with that Christmas tree that's still in the driveway. We're the only family on Catboat who still has a tree. It's January 2nd, for Chrissake. And it could start a fire. It makes us look . . ." She was like a browser, searching. "Haphazard."

"Spontaneous combustion?" Sawyer draped his long arm over Mom's slender shoulder, leaned down and breathed, "We love you, Mom." I was slightly taller than Bill, which gave me a heart-stopping glimpse of her undefended scalp, but Sawyer was the only one in our family who was actually tall. (We often accused our mother of having had sex with any number of available males. Including Dr. Lee Forest, who was a hot bro— which might explain, though not excuse, his fooling around. Sawyer was also the only one with dark hair.)

My hair could be anything: I dyed it, spiked it, streaked it, highlighted it, what Bill called "frosting."

"Yeah, we love you, Mom," I said

"When you call me by my given name, I know something's up."

4

"'Mom' is your given name?" I said.

"Candace," my mother said, using my real name, "You may discover this someday. When you become a mother, your name in that baby's mouth is so precious and so *forever*. The name your parents give you or any pet names your friends or partners give you, they don't mean anything. The *M* sound for mother is universal in any language, did you know that? Doesn't matter if it's Urdu or Russian; it's all the same. And it breaks your heart, the way your kids eventually will."

"Wow, buzzkill, Mom . . ." Sawyer pulled the shirt cuffs from his jacket sleeves like a gangster. He often wore incongruous dress shirts.

"No need to be dramatic." Our mother looked at Sawyer as if she were shocked by her own DNA. His hair shone black. He had summer-sky eyes and pink cheeks; he was adventurous with facial hair. He was thin, but surprisingly buff, considering he did almost no exercising. A T of chest hair ended at his belly button. He was a chick magnet.

"Anyway," Sawyer said. "for someone who flunked out of high school, that was a brilliant speech." Our mother had a degree in sociology from NYU.

Mom was an art therapist at Horton High. Sometimes the art was more successful than the therapy. We never made fun of her "clients," like other kids; bullying was against our principles. We were friends with one of her students, Chippie Holbeck, who was good at things we were not, like sports and driving.

"*Le Forest* is a shit," Sawyer said, eager to get to the dirt. You couldn't do much to mangle the name *Lee*, but my brother and I tried.

"We were listening on the stairs," I said.

"Why bother to hide, if you're going to tell me everything anyway?"

"You have no boundaries, Mom." I tossed an empty wine bottle toward the recycling. It hit the rim, rolling toward the refrigerator. "You would have just invited us to get tanked with you and Mrs. Forest."

5

"You can call her Susan, you know."

"You call her Suzie," Sawyer said. "That's quite intimate, Willamena."

The landline rang. No one had a landline anymore. Grandma Gretchen had given us the Felix the Cat wall phone as part of her "cleaning house" process. She was a political activist who spent much of her time on the road.

"Declutter," she'd said.

No one used old Felix. Mostly we got robocalls and scammers. This time it was Grandma Gretchen.

When Bill hung up, Felix's tail moved back and forth like a metronome. "Your grandmother was arrested," Bill told us. "In New Jersey, of all places."

"What this time?" Sawyer tipped the plate upward, letting the rest of the cheese and pickles fall into his mouth. Crack waited expectantly, but no go. "Pipeline? Pythons?" It would be news if Grandma *hadn't* been arrested.

"Turbine. When they spring her, she's coming up here."

Our town was in the middle of a battle over a wind turbine. There was a shitload of comments on the *Frigate* website. Right-wing climate deniers claimed that among the turbine's many drawbacks was "a force field that gives rise to sexual excess and experimentation."

Even if they were right, we supported clean energy, wind in particular, and the way the turbine could produce it out of thin air.

"Grandma is going to live with us?" I asked.

"Your dad thinks she will be safer here on Catboat Road."

"Awesome, Grandma rocks." I returned to the subject at hand. "I can't believe you just let Mrs. Forest go like that. Friends don't let sex objects drive blotto. You should have had Le Forest pick her up."

"Lee was probably shagging Ethel on a massage table," Mom said. We thought this was a scream, but Mom said it with a straight face.

"You don't really think I'd let her drive in her condition. She walked down to the rec center and took the Hop Along."

"He's a cunt!" Sawyer said.

"*Language.*" Bill almost never censored our speech. "Sawyer, I don't think men should use that word."

"Le Forest is a cunt," I said.

"Fair enough. That's a word women should reclaim. Like the 'N' word."

"Only women can use the 'N' word?" Sawyer bowed, his torso at a right angle to the floor.

Bill ignored him.

"Mom, were you coming on to Mrs. Forest?" I asked. "It looked like it from your body language."

"Of course not. You kids are just projecting. Mrs. Forest was making me exhausted."

"You just called her 'Mrs. Forest.'" Sawyer grabbed the second bottle and drank the dregs.

Bill tried to throw Sawyer's wine bottle into the recycling, but missed by a mile. It spun the bottle, then died in the middle of the room.

You could say my involvement with my mother's best friend started with my eleventh New Year's Eve. It wasn't the first time I'd laid eyes on Mrs. Forest, but it was the first time I'd *seen* her, felt her entering the room. That night I watched her tongue-kiss Dad's friends under the mistletoe.

There's no way she would have kissed a kid the way I'd seen her kiss just about every male in the room, except for her own husband, Dr. Lee Forest. She even kissed my father, Rags, who'd squandered the opportunity with a beery air kiss.

She'd caught me watching. She winked and let the word *honey* escape on a contrail of booze and smoke. She was like weather coming in a window. Winter air clung to her coat, thrown on Bill and Rags's bed. I hid my face in its magenta wool, bleeding as the zipper cut my cheek.

My mother was watching Mrs. Forest too. They were friends, but the way they interacted was alien to me. Sawyer was my best friend.

People often thought Sawyer and I were real twins, since we were born the same calendar year. But he was tall, dark, and handsome, like they say in bad books. I had my mother's compact build. I had my father's coffee-colored eyes.

It was how we acted. We read each other's minds; we'd rather be with each other than anyone else. Even if someday we had spouses, we wanted to live together like one big happy family.

The New Year's when Sawyer was twelve, Dad had "hired" him to hold trays of champagne over his head like Atlas holding up the world, and bend at the waist to serve flirty women with their fierce lipstick and bare arms. Sawyer loved dressing like a real waiter: black shirt, black pants, napkin tucked in his belt. We were both waiting—as if real life happened all of a sudden like an accident—and watching.

Back then I'd been a watcher, not yet a voyeur.

That night I'd watched Mom gesture to Mrs. Forest with an empty champagne glass. "Suzie," she said. "Help me in the kitchen."

"I can't."

"Why not?"

"My dress, what if I get red wine on it?"

"Champagne is not red wine." Mom sometimes spoke to Mrs. Forest as if she were an exasperating member of our nuclear family.

"Salsa?" Mrs. Forest ran her hand over her front, coming in casual contact with her own chest.

Mom threw a tablecloth at her. "Cover your precious dress in this."

Mrs. Forest was as much a goddess wrapped in linen fabric as she'd been in her clingy dress. Soon she and Bill were laughing and working side by side, Bill rinsing, Mrs. Forest bending to put plates in the dishwasher, the men and the making out forgotten, the last guests drunk and uninteresting. Under the tablecloth

I knew Mrs. Forest was spilling from her low-cut dress as she leaned into the dishwasher.

The men and their kissing, and the hungry way they ate women with their eyes were one thing, but Mom and her friend—I wanted to break them apart, like sentences, to understand them.

"You know, Billy baby, you could wear something a little more fetching yourself," Mrs. Forest said. "That moo-moo or whatever it is, we could have used *that* for a tablecloth."

"I don't need to look fetching, and neither do you, by the way."

"Oh, but I do."

Bill flicked a dishtowel at her friend. "I like you just the way you are."

Mrs. Forest grazed the down of my mother's cheek with her glossed lips. "And I you, kiddo."

When Mrs. Forest left, a hint of her stayed behind.

2

Blowin' in the wind

By Chuck Butten
Frigate staff writer

It looks like an alien spacecraft come to rest in the marshes near the transfer station. The 400-foot tower is Horton's new wind turbine. With a power of 1.5 megawatts, the $6 million dollar turbine is expected to save the town some $300,000 a year in energy costs.

Built by Zephyr Industries and powered by Blow Job software, the turbine has an innovative, patented generator with permanent magnets and a specially developed and optimized control system.

The blades are 252 feet in diameter.

Dad loved the bullshitting at the *Horton Frigate* newsroom on Scrimshaw Street. He especially liked it when a writer looked up from her keyboard and yelled, "Hey Rags!"

My father also loved running around town persuading shop owners that their businesses would tank if they didn't take out an ad in the *Frigate*. The paper didn't have much of an online presence, outside of a few breaking news items about the bulb that had blown at the lighthouse or the ducks living in the belfry at Star of the Sea.

Dad stood behind me smiling, as if I'd accomplished something. My brother and I were not star students, but we didn't text nude photos or bring assault weapons to school.

"Ace!" the reporters called out. They hadn't seen me since my summer internship.

"How was your Christmas?" This was Becky Fuller, who "covered the waterfront," praying for wrecks and red tides.

"It was nice visiting with relatives," I said.

Dad's frown stuck to his face like a band-aid. Grandma Gretchen only showed up for protests, not for holidays, and Rags and Bill had no siblings, so who were these fantastical relations?

We retreated to Dad's "office." Editor in Chief Honor Allerton believed that salespeople should be "on the road," so she gave them the worst digs.

Chuck Butten, the reporter who covered the turbine, stopped in, slamming me so hard on the back I almost fell over. "Good to see you."

"Likewise."

A slavery apologist, BLM basher, and closet Trump campaigner, Chuck didn't trust anyone under thirty, pontificating against political correctness, "litra-chure," the phrase "the takeway," and feminists. His sexism inhabited him like a bacteria. The bitter word *Hillary* erupted from the slit in his scraggly beard on a daily basis.

Chuck looked like he might be terminal; gray skin and bald disks like Communion wafers in his thinning hair. He was round-shouldered, which gave his torso a *C* shape, but he was able-bodied. He preferred handball to reporting and sometimes appeared at work smelling of the rank little glove he was still wearing.

Chuck opposed the turbine because it was supported by people like the Ragsdales who had no problem with sexed-up gender-benders. The public restroom used to be a bastion of separateness—like Horton itself, which had been settled by Separatists. Now it was a never-ending twilight.

"Listen." Chuck leaned against Dad's desk, crossing his ankles. "I could use a research assistant." He looked at me.

"How much?" I was cheap but not free.

"Whatever Honor usually pays you, but I was thinking we could get Prower down at the Board of Ed to approve some kind of extra credit deal."

"No writing. Writing's not a core collaborative."

"Not a what?" Chuck said.

"Not a deliverable."

"Ace." Dad looked embarrassed. "If you're getting paid, you need to do what Chuck tells you to do."

"Basically, writing's *my* job," Chuck said. "I'm talking research. I know you kids are like, up-the-wazoo Googlers."

Bill had a Kindle she'd bestowed on us as a kind of homeschooling. Sawyer and I clicked on enormous fonts, so that we could lie on Sawyer's bed, reporting content errors and using the highlight function to underline self-improvement passages. We knew exactly how many days of school you could miss without flunking out.

For his part, Chuck had written a mimeographed collection of bigoted doggerel, impaling himself on the sacred altar of free speech. The slipshod geography of his face was revealed in his author picture, dorky chin in hand.

Honor was waiting for him to die at his desk.

Dad's parental antennae went up. "You have a lot on your plate, honey."

"What plate?"

"Homework, maybe?"

"Interdisciplinary, Dad, this is project-based."

"Yeah," Chuck said.

"Can I research whatever I want?"

"Turbine stuff, mainly," Chuck said.

Sawyer and I liked research. We were the only ones who'd actually read *The Voyage of the Speedwell: A History of Horton, Massachusetts* by Catherine P. Rounds, published by the Horton Historical Society. Apparently not one but two ships had been headed for North America. Twice the *Speedwell* set sail from Southampton and twice turned back because of a leaky hull the crew had reportedly caused. They were reluctant to voyage to the Hudson River.

Had they known that they'd actually be landing in fun-filled Provincetown—a brief voyage from Horton—they might have been more willing. The hardiest Separatists boarded the *Mayflower*, salvaging from the leaky *Speedwell* their precious crockery, linens, and cutlery, some of which would one-day find homes in the IKEA cabinets of Horton.

"Turbine stuff?" I repeated. "Okay, no-brainer."

The windmill stood by itself on a stretch of marshland, next to the "transfer station," a fancy name for the dump. Grandma liked to remind us: before the internet was the dump.

Those who wanted to remove the windmill claimed its blinking lights and whooshing noise caused insomnia, headaches, nausea, vertigo, fatigue, anxiety, allergies, tinnitus, cramps, substance abuse, flight of ideas, NPR pledge drives—and nymphomania.

It was the last that seemed to have freaked out Horton. The town, named for the mistress of a *Speedwell* passenger, had come to be known as Whore Town. The apparently bodacious Ms. Horton had gone on to birth numerous "bastards," who'd come in handy as farmers and fisherpersons in the new land.

While the Ragsdales and our left-wing cohorts may have been suffering from some of the conditions the windmill was accused of causing, we fought to preserve it. Clean energy placed us solidly among sane, farsighted people.

That's where we wanted to be.

Dad's phone rang, as if on cue. He still had an old flip phone, better than a smartphone for cutting off conversation.

"Deal?" Chuck stuck out his hand and exited with a shoulder slap.

Dad had hung framed photos of me, Sawyer, and Bill in his office. Their wedding picture showed bare feet on the beach, intimate and exposed. The best photographs signaled what was happening just before and just after the click of the shutter. That was where the narrative lay.

Had they imagined their joined lives would somehow be amazing?

The photo of Sawyer and me showed us leaning against the split-rail fence across from the seawall.

"That wisecrack in the newsroom?" Dad started in. "Visiting with relatives? I know your mother and I haven't provided you kids with an adequate family narrative."

"You've been hanging around with the writers again," I said. "Everything's a narrative." A Silvio Sub wrapped in thick paper sat on top of Dad's files. Rags loved taking a break with Silvio, who took out a quarter-page ad every week.

Dad cut the sub in half, taking a big bite. He looked like the herbivorous stegosaurus in kids' books, with tiny sprigs of vegetation peeking from their terrible maws. It was weird that the vegetarian dinosaurs had grown bigger than the ones who ate their friends and families. Hard to believe they'd been destroyed by a single meteorite.

"Aunts, uncles, cousins, they weren't part of our family narrative," Dad persisted.

"Well, there's your mother."

Grandma Gretchen would soon be up from New Jersey. She responded to our texts with ever more eccentric emoji.

"And everything's a 'community,'" I went on.

"Honor needs to talk to the writers about that." Dad daintily wiped his mouth.

"The five-ingredients-only community, the serial killer community."

"The e-cigarette community," Dad snorted, spraying crumbs.

14

"I actually heard that."

"And everything's a conversation!" I raised my voice. "We don't need a conversation about gun violence. We need a law!"

"A conversation is when you're chatting over the fence about the recycling schedule!" Dad yelled back.

"Tell Silvio thanks for the sub." I wiped my mouth. "Maybe I'll go with you on some sales calls."

Dad's elation was like one of those acute pains your body delivers: if it went on too long, you'd die.

But tagging along might help with the startup Sawyer and I were working on.

Dad was secretly hoping that my being Chuck's research assistant might "net results," but I had no eyes to be a journalist. I envisioned myself as a house husband, with Brett and Levi Forest, blushing behind their pulled-up T-shirts, exposing their fat little clam bellies. My brother and I often babysat for Mrs. Forest's identical twin toddlers.

I fancied myself too butch for the word *wife*. I didn't want to be male or trans; I just wanted to inhabit the gaps, passing through walls like an avatar.

Our mother, meanwhile, prayed that we wouldn't be like Haley Goodman, who in middle school had crashed her mom's Outback into the seawall.

From our vantage point, on the day she did it, you could see the hood of the Outback, its silver metal glistening against the concrete wall. Why had Haley chosen the middle of the day in broad daylight?

Rags, Bill, Sawyer, and I had joined the rubberneckers behind the yellow tape. It seemed like everyone in Horton had gathered at the scene, the highest and thickest section of the seawall, near the lighthouse, the lighthouse keeper's cottage, and a few summer homes on their dusty plots.

Haley's mother was screaming that it was her fault because she'd left the keys in the car. Her husband covered her mouth as if he were trying to chloroform her. "Do you have people?" a pretty EMT with gloves in her back pocket and scissors on her belt asked them.

Weren't we supposed to turn away from Haley's unbloodied arm, sticking straight out the window like a signal?

I did turn away, just for a second. Mrs. Forest was in the crowd, burying her face in Le Forest's lapel. He rested his chin on her head, his eyes glued to the ocean. At that point Mrs. Forest didn't have kids, so she wasn't projecting.

People love to appropriate tragedies for themselves. They make great conversation-starters, as long as they're not happening to you.

Our parents hustled us to a more respectful position on a bench overlooking the harbor, where everything seemed normal: boats swaying on their moorings and our familiar landmarks across the water.

Dad spoke. "I can't imagine you guys would ever do something like that."

"We don't know how to drive," Sawyer said.

"Driver's ed is not necessary for that kind of driving," Mom said. "And just so you know, your dad and I always leave the keys in the car."

"Don't tempt me, Mom," I said.

"Ace, this is a serious matter," Dad said.

"I know, Dad, I'm upset is all. There'll be a grief counselor at school tomorrow."

"Of course, you would come to us first if you were even contemplating such a deed," Dad said.

"Yeah, Dad," Sawyer said. "Don't wait up for me! I'm off to the garage for some carbon monoxide!" Sawyer held back tears with the heel of his hand. "Scratch that. I'm way not handling this correctly. I feel really bad that she went and did what she did."

Haley always wore what Bill called "jumpers," sleeveless dresses with jerseys underneath; they made us feel sorry for her. Sawyer had tried to help, telling her she'd look cool with big bicycle chains looping around her waist.

"Nobody at school liked *or* disliked her," I said. "Maybe

that's what made her do it." Kids who were hated sometimes clung to the hyper-aliveness of it. And people who were loved just let other people cling.

Sawyer sniffled. "It was probably the baby cows."

Haley was a cow activist, I explained to Rags and Bill. "She once told me at the beverage station that it was because calves were wrenched from their moms to provide milk for *homo sapiens* that cows were anxious and depressed."

"Still, she shouldn't have gone smashing into a wall," Sawyer said, "a utility pole, anything, really. It's so final. You need to have a Plan B, an escape valve. That's what they teach you in driver's ed."

"You guys said you didn't want to take driver's ed," Mom said.

"Yeah, well, Dunky Rasmussen told me, and he should have told Haley Goodman," Sawyer said. "Fuck him!"

"Was she a friend of yours?" Mom asked him.

"No!"

The Forests stopped by on their way to their car, and Mom and Mrs. Forest collapsed in each other's arms. Le Forest shook hands all around. Bill and Mrs. Forest disengaged liked ripped Velcro.

Mrs. Forest put her arms around our waists and walked Sawyer and me halfway to her car. "Your parents are so lucky to have you," she said, kissing each of us on the cheek.

I quickly kissed her back, which made her wipe away a tear. Her perfume seemed almost illegal. It would hold me captive for the rest of the day, complicating my feelings about Haley's deed.

When we returned, our parents were still on the bench, quietly holding hands. "We shouldn't be so oblivious," Dad said.

"Mrs. Forest was crying," I said. "That wasn't oblivious."

"Suzie Forest isn't us," Mom said.

"She practically is," Sawyer said.

"Seriously," Dad said. "This Haley Goodman business isn't in the cards for either of you, right?"

"No," I said.

"Why not?"

"If you *want* it to be in the cards . . ."

Mom slipped her arm though Dad's. "Rags, honey."

"Sawyer?" Dad said.

"I have everything to live for, Dad."

"Like what?"

Mom stepped in. "Our kids are well adjusted, Rags."

"Fuck this shit," Sawyer said. "Dad's right, I keep sounding wrong. I need to go to a grief counselor."

"We need to honor Haley's memory," Dad said.

"How can you honor the memory of someone who was in my French class, like, just two hours ago?" I said.

"We could have a moment of silence," Sawyer suggested.

"Okay, let's start," Dad said.

"I'll time it." Sawyer tapped the face of the secondhand Timex he'd bought at the Castaway.

"Would it kill us to go one extra second in thinking about Haley Goodman?" Dad said.

"Start!" Mom ordered.

During our sixty seconds, I thought about how pissed I was at Haley. Now there would always be a Before Haley an After Haley. Dad was right; there would be a memory, and it couldn't be unremembered.

Afterward, Sawyer and I leaned against the split rail fence side by side. It was at that instant that our mother decided to grab the cell phone dangling from her wrist and shoot our picture. If this might be the last time she saw us, she wanted us like this, together, on an otherwise perfect afternoon, looking not at her but intently at each other.

3

Dad slouched in an armchair like he owned the place. I stayed standing, wondering what to do with my arms.

We were at Picture This, Mrs. Forest's frame shop on Scrimshaw, where Horton came to frame its diplomas and first dollar bills and cheesy seascapes.

Though my father seemed to be the only one who didn't have a thing for Mrs. Forest, he saw quite a bit of her. When he went to get the check, he'd gossip about whether our windmill was making people horny. They were reporting multiple orgasms while standing in line at Trader Joe's. The windmill deniers apparently had something against multiple orgasms, which struck us all as hilarious.

Dad had dubbed this Our Year of the Windmill.

"Ace!" Mrs. Forest's actual voice startled me.

"Mrs. Forest," I said, like I was identifying someone in a lineup.

"Suzie, please. Call me Suzie." Her hug was vaporous: an unplaceable cologne and then a bouquet that was simply *her*.

"Mrs. F."

"That's downright lewd!"

My face felt like an electric range as I breathed in her

cigarette laugh. She of all people must have experienced lewd, not just with Le Forest, but with how many others? I knew that Sawyer—in his professional capacity as pedicurist—had made love to her exquisite feet. He was a real draw down at Fabia Fonseca's nail salon.

"The same?" Dad said, all business. "You know, I think you could go bigger."

Bigger was not possible when it came to Mrs. Forest.

She was the perfect blank canvas for the masterpiece we'd dreamed up, according to Bill. Mrs. Forest had dyed blond hair and ocean eyes that weren't always the same color. The skin on her upper chest freckled in the sun. She wore black velvet pants and stiff white man-shirts with the collars turned up, fashion scarves, bangle bracelets, cube-shaped earrings.

She was not chiseled, like our beloved Mrs. Robinson. Sawyer and I had streamed the old movie tons of times, on lazy hooky days, blowing off the famous "plastics" line and going for Anne Bancroft and her slo-mo fishnet removal. We'd Googled age-appropriate actresses: Mrs. Forest looked more like the young Catherine Deneuve, Cate Blanchett, Diane Lane.

Dad was interacting with Mrs. Forest like she was the most mundane thing on the planet, like a rock or a tree. "I want to see you full page, back page."

I heard *full-frontal, backside.*

"Way too pricey, Rags. You know that."

"Your ads don't pop. We need to find your niche. Give people a reason to come in that goes beyond picture framing." He turned to me. "Nail the words."

"Like serving caramel macchiatos?" Mrs. Forest said.

"No, but have you ever thought of getting one of those gas fireplaces?" Dad said. "In the winter, it would encourage people to stay and chat."

"And not buy."

Mrs. Forest had nailed it.

We were all born and raised in New England winters, so it was in Dad's DNA to take the sting out of them with fires.

Today, the coast was sharp with the kind of cold that becomes a color.

On the walls of Picture This were right-angle samples of frames and a display of various mat colors, along with Bill's students' artwork. There were no skiffs or lobster pots or Turnerish squalls building in the distance. Theirs were uncontrolled abstracts, set off with words and found objects. In one an actual kebab skewer dangled from a watercolor cabbage.

"Ace could help you with the copy," Dad said.

"Right," Mrs. Forest said. "How's your business going?"

"Sawyer does the graphics. I write the copy, but I'm clueless."

"Ace, you have lots of talents," Mrs. Forest said. "Your dad is so proud of you."

"I think she would make a top-notch journalist," Dad said. "Better use of her verbal skills."

"I'm doing research for Chuck Butten, so Dad thinks I'm Rachel Maddow."

"Chuck Butten could use some research."

I laughed. "Yeah, I wonder what his narrative is."

"He's kind of skeevy," Mrs. Forrest said.

Dad cut in, "I forgot how biting you women can be when men aren't around."

"You're around, Dad."

"I think I disappear into the woodwork around women."

"Not true, Rags," Mrs. Forest said. "And even if it were true, that's not always a bad thing."

Mrs. Forest had a side gig as a real estate agent. This was a joke; no one moved in or out of Horton. There was only one house for sale, the Fonseca mansion, which had belonged to the family of Fabia Fonseca; Fabia owned the nail salon where Sawyer worked. After making their fortune in lobsters and cranberries, the Fonseca dynasty had returned to Lisbon, leaving behind a fantastical "faux Portuguese colonial with Gothic portals, fountains, Manueline windows, balustrades, and twin mermaids guarding the gates," according to Zillow.

Fabia Fonseca refused to have anything to do with her

family's mansion, which was starting to have a life-after-people feel. Little trees sprouted from the corrugated tiles; arboreal animals nested in them.

Fabia, meanwhile, lived in a 1950s ranch in a cul-de-sac on Windjammer Way. A native speaker would have recognized the "No Outlet" sign at the entrance as an admonition. She believed that her "midcentury contemporary" accurately represented the true America. It had a flat roof and a carport, fake bricks and a mauve garage door that opened with electronic eye technology. She lived with an endangered cat, the only reminder of her native country.

Mrs. Forest tried to persuade the few hapless tourists who stumbled into Horton to buy the Fonseca mansion, strolling around the estate, lime skirt-suit, quilted purse on a chain, heels sinking into the untended landscaping, three-ring binder in the crook of her arm. The binder held takeout menus and copies of her kids' medical records, she'd confessed to Bill.

Sawyer and I had a secret fantasy that we would someday live in the Fonseca mansion with our extended family, united against the world.

Now Mrs. Forest held both my hands as if this was a normal way to interact with a human being. "I could use some help from a top-notch journalist." She pressed my palms together like I was praying or applauding. "Soon, sweetheart."

It was settled. I would meet her after hours at the shop, helping her write ad copy for her big, splashy, full-page, back page ad.

I was already hoarding "sweetheart" like a famine victim.

4

Sawyer posed in front of the mirror in his room.

"What do you think?" He was wearing his newest acquisition from the Castaway, a smoking jacket—shirtless, with jeans and motorcycle boots. Sawyer loved vintage shops. "It fits?"

I said that he looked gorgeous, which made him blush. It was easy to find celebrities Sawyer resembled: young versions of James Dean, Taylor Lautner, Liam Hemsworth. He could have been a model, but he wanted to use his brain.

So we'd created Sawyer & Ace Advertising.

I ran my hand across his shoulders. I could feel the wavelike muscle so familiar to me from giving each other backrubs and blasting the Amazons.

"I mean does it *fit* fit," he said, "like, is it from the right era?"

Often a "garment" was so dated that it was contemporary again, like bell-bottoms. This jacket had a water stain hue and was discolored like old paper around the slightly frayed cuffs. Sawyer knew what was authentic.

"It *fit* fits," I said.

Sawyer had a collection of vintage flasks, which he kept filled in plain sight on his windowsill. He selected one like he was selecting wine from the cellar. It was unpolished silver with delicately etched filigree, filled with Johnnie Walker Red. He was pretty much dependent on what our parents had in their liquor cabinet. Neither of us liked Scotch, but we liked passing the flask back and forth in a sophisticated manner. Most times, we didn't actually drink it.

"Dad signed me up to write ads for Mrs. Forest."

"This is your chance. Alone with Mrs. Forest."

"I'm so scintillating with you," I said, "but with her, it's like I'm brain-dead."

"You're good at writing ad copy."

"Not."

Sawyer grabbed an old issue of *Vogue* that was splayed on his messy bedspread. He flipped the pages, licking his finger like an old lady. "Look at this. What you want is phrases like 'Into the Future,' 'Redefines Fashion,' 'Primal Force,' 'Soaring Aspirations,' 'A-List,' 'Panoramic,' 'Beyond Being!'"

"For an ad about picture frames?"

"For an ad about anything. Ads aren't about reality. They're about alternate reality." Sawyer passed me the flask. "Just think of it as the opposite of Scrimshaw Street with all its hokey, ye-olde-crappy shops. Think about the essence of picture frames. Bring Whore Town up to your level."

He turned his Mac toward me. "See? Like this PSA for the turbine. 'Save the Windmill, Save the World.' The assholes on the other side? They're like 'Save our Town. Save our Traditions.'"

Both sides of the debate fought over Don Quixote logos, slogans, and the lyrics to They Might Be Giants songs, the anti's protesting with signs that read "Blow It Out Your Ass," as well as less positive messaging. The pros were hamstrung by wind's invisibility. You had to see it to believe it.

The turbine was like the T.J. Eckleburg billboard looming over the valley of ashes, the perfect backdrop for the vintage/contemporary portfolio Sawyer was developing.

"Aren't you worried I'll be such a good copywriter Mrs. Forest will fall in love with me?" I said.

"I *am* jealous, actually," Sawyer admitted.

"Want to come with me?"

"That would upset the balance."

From the beginning it had been Sawyer and me, wanting to be in the same space, knowing each other's thoughts. Reaching between the slats of our cribs and fumbling to entwine our fingers.

I remember the exact moment when I first knew that we were inseparable. We were about four, eating lunch, perched dangerously on barstools. Eventually we would appreciate Bill and Rags's oblivious and inattentive child-rearing, but that day it could have cut short our life spans.

"What'll be?" Bill said to me, like she was bartending at the Bowsprit.

Immediately Sawyer answered, "She wants cling peaches!"

We'd never uttered the words *cling peaches*, but I'd seen them at the A&P—we'd learned to read logos and labels—and I'd been daydreaming about them. It was clear Sawyer and I shared a brain.

"Where did you get that from?" Bill said. "We don't have cling peaches."

"Buy them next time," I demanded. We knew fruit grew in supermarkets on shiny green plastic, but these cling peaches were better because they were cut up already.

"It's orange like finger paint," I explained, "with the furry skin off."

"Monster skin!" Sawyer said.

Sawyer had gotten so enthusiastic about cling peaches that he'd pitched off the barstool and lost a tooth. Bill said we could glue it back with library paste and raw egg whites.

By the time we were six, we'd made up a brand-new name for our game of crouching naked in the closet: *hide and seek*.

5

Secondhand but Not Second Best

Go Back in Time at the Castaway

Rainy Priest texted Sawyer when an interesting garbage bag had just been tossed onto the front steps of the Castaway. Sawyer was sifting through some recent drop-offs.

The place had the desolate stench of damp wool on an August afternoon. While most everything was secondhand, Sawyer also liked surfing the front racks where a few new items discharged their cheap petroleum breath.

Dad was hoping to get an ad out of Rainy. "Never say die, Dad?" Sawyer said.

"One secret to successful advertising."

"The other is, it's all crap." Sawyer watched Rainy separate and fold. Skeletal in her boyfriend jeans and high boots, she was listening to something on an old iPod someone had left. From behind she looked about twenty years old, like a lot of Boomers, Grandma included. From the front, her varicose skin was stitched, her makeup snagged in the runnels, eyes faded like cloth.

Rainy did not get her clothes at the Castaway. Sawyer was not the usual customer either. Occasionally you'd see a Whore High girl in here looking for someone's great-grandmother's "duster" to wear with combat boots and Spanx. But it was the other Horton—the people who never called it Whore Town; who salvaged from dumpsters, had federally mandated school lunches, kerosene heaters, hand-knit afghans over their knees; whose homes smelled like cat; who ate fattening, un-nutritious food that made the kids seem dense when they were not—who patronized the Castaway.

"Rainy!" Dad called out.

"Hey! What the Frigate you doing in here?"

They both laughed like they'd never heard this before.

As Dad headed over to Rainy's lair, Sawyer held a tiny plaid number to my waist. "Maybe once a year you should wear a skirt."

"What am I, a cross-dresser?" I tossed it at my brother. He didn't catch it.

From the other room we heard Rainy say "sex fiends." When she and Dad came back, after a clearly unsuccessful sales call, Rainy's face was red like a newborn's.

She extended an olive branch. "How's Gretchen?"

"Mom's fine," Dad said. "Thanks for asking."

"Listen, I know your mother's a kook, and I don't agree with anything she says, but I don't wish her harm." Rainy was the kind of person who put the word *the* in front of *Blacks* and *gays*.

"I'll let her know," Dad said. "She'll be up here soon."

On either side of the door, lined up like humans at a soup kitchen, were shoes, battered and misshapen with the ghosts of the feet that had once worn them, bunioned, clubbed, pigeoned; leather soaked in the ocean, dried on radiators, faded by sun, caked with mud. But they were all married, paired with their significant others.

When Dad stopped to inspect them, Sawyer came up behind him. "There are some real finds in the shoe department."

"I can see that." Dad randomly picked one up, holding it

27

to the light, then returning it to its mate. One pair seemed to sparkle in the sun like the Mary Janes little girls used to wear.

They were the kind of man-pumps worn with tuxedos. He hooked his fingers in the heels and removed them from their place in line.

"Good eye, Dad." Sawyer took them. "Sit." He slipped them onto Dad's feet. "Black patent leather pumps. You can wear them to the science center gala with Mom."

"Black-tie?"

"Yeah, Dad, like the one you'll be wearing to the gala."

Smelling a sale, Rainy pulled at the stem of her glasses with her teeth, breathing on the lenses.

Dad examined his feet in the fun-house mirrors that leaned against the walls and made a quick decision: "I'll take them."

Rainy grabbed them before he could change his mind and wrapped them in butcher paper. "They're going to look smashing on you!"

"I know," he said, nearly sashaying out the door. "I buy shoes, you buy an ad," he called over his shoulder.

"Ad, shmad!" Rainy called back, returning to her "office" in the back.

"What's with Dad's new look?" I said. "Patent leather pumps?"

"A trans-parent phase?" Sawyer said.

Not. If Dad wore shiny patent leather pumps like something Mrs. Forest might wear, it was because they existed for him in a patent-leather-pump plane that had nothing to do with the world that had given birth to them. What Dad majorly lacked was context.

6

Sawyer grabbed the 35-millimeter Nikon Dad had snagged at a tag sale. It probably hadn't been used since 1957. The camera sat next to the medicine ball on Dad's top shelf. Rags kept saying he was going to document our family in a slide show. Could a slide show be negative space—capturing us avoiding things?

My brother loved winding the film through the little sprockets. He wanted photos of me for his fashion portfolio. We were going on location to the abandoned Fonseca estate.

Mrs. Forest was at Catboat listening to Bill talk about "creative pediatrics." As we passed through the living room, Mrs. Forest waved, glad for the break.

We were about to order an Uber when Mrs. Forest said she and Bill would drive us.

We all piled into Mrs. Forest's Volvo (which we called her Vulva) and headed out. It was dusk, the best time for picture-taking. Mom grabbed a bottle of wine on the way out.

A thick chain padlocked the big, arched wooden door of the mansion. A perfect backdrop, Sawyer said: things that were off-limits and closed were more creepily beautiful than things that were open and allowed.

Weeds poked up from the stones of the broad front terrace.

The wide, unkept lawn ended in a soggy field of beachgrass and bulrushes; beyond that was the harbor. Even from here you could hear the clanking of stays against the masts that rose like little spires in the distance.

Sawyer had envisioned an incongruous tableau with me wearing winter coats over my bare body. He'd brought some "apparel" in an old square suitcase the color of nicotine stains, with travel stickers all over it.

"Great concept," Bill said when Sawyer explained his plan. She was an artist. "Do it, honey."

"I don't think so, Mom," I said.

"Yeah, Mom." Sawyer indicated Mrs. Forest with his eyes. "Maybe another time."

"Well, someone's got to do it." Mom started to unbutton her cardigan and untuck her shirt.

"Bill, honey," Mrs. Forest said. "No, no, no, I love you, but you should keep your clothes on, baby."

"Why?"

"Sawyer," Mrs. Forest said. "Was that the look you were going for? Your mom without her cable stitches and her stretchy slacks?"

"Uh, that would be a no."

"For once, I'd like to be thought of as a person who disrobes," Mom said. "Suzie, open a bottle."

Mrs. Forest obeyed, clamping the bottle between her knees and twisting the cork from the corkscrew. When she stuck the cork between her teeth, I gasped. Sawyer stopped what he was doing and raised the camera.

"Ace," Mrs. Forest looked right through me. "You would be a perfect model for this, but. . ."

"She *would* be perfect," Mom said. She grabbed a coat from Sawyer's valise and turned to me. "You just have to open the coat a little bit."

Mrs. Forest said, "No, Ace doesn't want to do that."

I mouthed, *Thank you.*

"So who's going to do it?" Mom said.

"Me!" Mrs. Forest said. "I will."

Sawyer had selected a World War II greatcoat the color of baby shit, heavy wool with imprinted buttons and wide lapels. Mrs. Forest wore what she'd been wearing under her skinny jeans and cashmere sweater: a maroon camisole bordered in black lace.

Sawyer's model seemed to know exactly what she was doing. It wasn't just me; Bill couldn't take her eyes off her.

7

Turbine trouble?

By Chuck Butten
Frigate staff writer

It didn't take long for Opposition Wind forces to mobilize in an all-out effort to bring down the turbine. Having lost the battle to install it, the group is now focusing on the Herculean feat of removing it. "We will not give up," longtime resident Doty Cooper told the Frigate.

Frigate Editor in Chief Honor Allerton had no personal pictures in her office. She didn't seem to have anyone in her life, aside from her sister, Amy, who taught Phys Ed at Whore High. Her shelf held an AP Style Book and an adult coloring book featuring Horton's "historic" sites. Her sharpened colored pencils stuck up like little rockets from a coffee mug with pink roses wreathed around her initials. A wood plaque read "Privacy is everybody's business."

"Anything in that rucksack?" she asked me.

Honor's urge to steal food was pathological. All the reporters had learned to cover their lunches, like kids in a big family. If you abandoned a roll, even with a bite out of it, she'd pirate it and slip it in her pocket.

"You mean like weapons?" I said. Honor wore what I'd learned were "wraparound" skirts. Grandma said they were popular in the garden club, perfectly constructed to hold food or a trowel.

"Power bars." She leaned over the desk.

My "rucksack" still had dorky Whore High stickers on it: "Safety Is No Accident!" On the bottom a bunch of sunflower seeds had escaped from a bag of trail mix, alongside gum wrappers, sand, and ink that had leaked from a pen. Most power bars had the consistency of plastic, but Honor had the kind of starvation that wasn't really food-oriented anyway.

"No, sorry."

"Okay." She sat down again and lifted her glasses from the chain around her neck. "Ace." I heard something between exasperation and curiosity. She'd printed out a Word doc. She waved the pages like she was ridding the place of smoke or a fart. "Ace."

"Did I fuck up?" I said.

"In the global sense, maybe." She rested her hands on the desk like she was about to do a push-up. She had long fingers. Everything about her was tall and thin. She wore an L.L. Bean field watch, in case she might have to do some spur of the moment fox hunting.

As EIC, Honor made certain rules clear: She loathed tortured synonyms. She laughed contemptuously when some unsuspecting reporter used a verb other than *said*. "*Explained? Stated? Joked? Enthused?*" She also hated *bravely*s. 'It was all we had,' the victim said bravely."

She loved the word *die*. She'd stand in the newsroom railing against *passed away*, *passed on*, and *lost*. *Passed on* especially pissed her off because of its religious connotations. Where did they go? A *better place*? And you could save *lost* for when you'd misplaced

33

your keys. Where was Grandpa? Between the sofa cushions?

Young, brazen Tadd Trevore, who covered the dead beat, had once erroneously reported the death of one of Horton's most prominent citizens. When the man's wife phoned Honor to complain, Tadd said. "It's her word against ours." Honor was secretly thrilled to have such a smart-ass reporter.

Anyway, death wasn't black-and-white. Plenty of living people were walking around half dead.

"I think you probably know that this is inappropriate for the *Frigate*," Honor said.

"Chuck didn't give me any guidelines."

"Well, the guideline was that you were going to do some research, so he could give more heft to his copy." She eyed the newsroom, which she could see through large glass doors whose Venetian blinds were open. "What I'm about to say may be inside baseball and probably not kosher."

I politely ignored her mixed metaphors.

"Instead of telling stories, Chuck stitches quotes together, terrible for forward motion, and he has no frame of reference," Honor said.

"You could say that." His pages were filled with scattershot data.

"So it's clear to me that he didn't write this."

"Huh, interesting." I pretended to smooth a nonexistent crease in my pants, like I'd seen guys do.

"Let me hum a few bars: 'The wind turbine, like the Washington Monument, ancient Egyptian obelisks, and Masonic imagery, pierces, like the rays of the sun god, the womb of the pyramid, Isis herself amid the pyre.'"

"Well, there's your frame of reference." I crossed my legs, ankle on knee, a confident move.

"Do you really think *Frigate* readers are going to buy this? This . . . ?"

"It might increase visits, beef up the comments section," I said. "Get some hits."

"I'm talking about the print edition. You know that the majority of our readership still prefers the hard-copy version."

Hard copy. It seemed inappropriate coming from this spinsterish editor of editors, sitting across from me with a boatneck jersey that exposed her dead branch clavicles and the bib of skin around her neck.

"Not to mention, you need to work on your attributions, sources, documentation. You can't just copy and paste from 'Sunfire's Weblog.'"

She called Chuck on the interoffice pager. It reminded me of supermarkets. *Chuck to the courtesy booth! Spill on Aisle 9!*

When Chuck saw me sitting with Honor, he put up both hands in the universal sign for *Stop!* He sat on the chair next to mine. "No contest! Sorry, boss." This "boss" was a less than subtle slam. So many women were in charge these days. "I know she was just supposed to do research," Chuck said, "but I was slamming up against the Thursday deadline, and I thought, hey, let her show her stuff, maybe a series in the Weekend Wrap Up."

"In your dreams," Honor said.

"Don't blame her."

"I'm not blaming her," Honor said. "I'm blaming you."

"Fair enough."

"Chuck, you're supposed to mentor her in the basics. And Ace, you're supposed to feed him printable stuff, to contextualize his articles, which can get fluffy."

Chuck was whining like a kid called to the principal's office. "These follow-ups, I mean, they're endless. How many times do I have to quote the Margessons?"

Jake and Eleanor Margesson complained the loudest about the windmill, never missed a meeting, and sent weekly letters to the editor.

We Ragsdales still supported the thing, never mind that we were all sleepwalking around the house at night like Lady Macbeth, a condition allegedly caused by the turbine.

"That's where Ace comes in." Honor stood up, ending the discussion. "Chuck, you can bring in that half sandwich that's sitting on your desk."

8

Fabia's Pedi-Cure

Put Your Feet in Our Hands

For as long as I'd interned at the *Frigate* Sawyer had worked at Fabia's, summers and after school.

The shop had lots of pink and white. One wall was a mosaic of colored polishes. When a client walked in, a chorus of technicians asked, "What color? What color?" The place smelled of chemicals and creams. Sawyer loved to read the women's magazines, not just for the clothing ads but for the educational stories like "Are We Having Sex Yet?" which was about people's sexiest experiences that didn't involve sex.

"Butterflies?" he joked when I came into the shop, holding my hand as if he might kiss it. He knew I was there just for the cutting and filing.

"No stars!" I told him.

It was amazing the paste-on nails women requested: barbells and reptiles and then private imagery, like the secret language of lovers.

"They want spiders?" I said. "You gotta be kidding!"

"Not so loud." Sawyer cut my nails shorter than any other technician; his filing left a fine dust on my skin.

Fabia rested her unmanicured hand on my shoulder. "Ase, you har so lovely today." She had nails like a shepherdess. It was pretty well-documented that her boyfriend was a young trainer at Club YES.

People went to Fabia's because Sawyer Ragsdale was there, removing their sad chipped polish and making everyone who came in feel more satisfied when they walked out, Mrs. Forest included. He was the shop's only male technician.

Women weren't Sawyer's only clients. There were men and old people whose heels were cracked like a parched landscape, gingerroot toes gnarled and misshapen.

Sawyer pulled the hot white towel from what appeared to be an autoclave, wrapped both my hands in it, and massaged them with oil. This was my favorite part.

I let my eyes wander as I luxuriated. The woman in the station next to us had long nails, curved like a scythe. Sawyer discouraged such nails because they could be dangerous in intimate situations.

"Theresa," he called over to the woman, "you need to let Sunny cut your nails shorter, way shorter."

"Why?" No one wanted my brother's disapproval.

"Bowling. They're bad for bowling."

Sawyer's apprenticeship was preparing him for a career in the beauty business. He pushed up my sleeves, so he could massage my forearms. "Or you could be an art therapist like Mom," I said.

"Mom is like, so, she's, yeah, but, I don't know."

Kids at Whore High wanted to be famous in an Ariana Grande kind of way.

"Me?" I said. "Simple A-list celebrity." The word that lodged in my brain was "integrated." I wanted to be integrated like a double-exposed image that gradually comes together on film.

Dad had hoped that Sawyer would do something profitable like pet portraits. Mom was glad he wasn't still in 9th grade.

Sawyer was already attending Massasoit Community College, named for the Great Sachem of the Wampanoags, the buff and shirtless one with feathers in his beaded braids. The Sachem undoubtedly looked better in modern images than he had in real life—like Jesus, a grizzled rabbi schlepping around Palestine in a dirty dress and flip-flops.

The plan was for Sawyer to bide his time at Massasoit until I decided where I wanted to go, and then transfer there. We could be legacy students at NYU, Mom's alma mater, but definitely not at mucky-muck Harvard, where Dad had majored in colonial history so he could pop over to Plymouth Plantation for a sabbatical.

Sawyer had arranged his class schedule so that he could work at the salon. Fabia's was its own kind of university. Each client had a story: so this is how you deal with an abusive boyfriend; here's what you do when your kid is a suburban smack addict.

"Okay," Theresa presented her hands to Sunny like an offering.

Sunny brandished her clippers. "We should go bowling," she said. "Ladies Nite at the Candlepin."

Theresa called over to Sawyer, "I hate the windmill!" A surefire way to get a Ragsdale's attention. Theresa's argument—that it was a socialist plot—was as asinine as the one against same-sex marriage—that the next thing you knew, people would be marrying their parents and their goats.

9

I was alone with Mrs. Forest at her frame shop, for once without Rags Ragsdale bloviating about ad space and promotions.

I examined every sample frame and mat, trying to avoid her. "You have some excellent frames here, a nice assortment. What's the MO?"

I could hear Mrs. Forest noisily doing something in the shop's little kitchen, where she made coffee and chilled booze.

She tapped my elbow with a cold Narragansett, smiling like she knew I was desperate for something to actually do.

I was surprised to see her barefoot. I thought of all the times Sawyer must have held these perfect feet in his hands.

She touched her can to mine. "MO?"

"It's a real art, selecting the frames and the mat and the picture, right? You screw up one, you've ruined everything."

" 'Come to Picture This. We won't screw up!' "

I opened my laptop. "We need to discover the key. Gain entry."

"You're right, dear. Most people don't give a shit. It's like they're blind, picking out combinations that make no sense."

Dear? That was so wrong. It made her seem too old, and me too young. "But that's where you come in. Don't they listen to you?"

"I'm always afraid I'm going to lose a sale." Mrs. Forest sat on a stool, massaging her feet. "Standing up all day."

I looked away. "We need a list of core attributes: quality, wide selection, customer service. That one's important."

"Trust, they need to trust my experience and my eye."

"Mrs. Forest, where did you go to college?"

"I didn't finish college."

"Good decision. College is way overrated."

"How would you know, Ace? You've never been to college."

The repetition of the name, a time-tested marketing tool. I liked the slightly exasperated way she said *How would you know.*

"I was on track to become a physician's assistant," she said, "and then my family ran out of money and to top it off I got pregnant, and then he ran off with another girl."

"Pregnant!" I scanned the room as if Mrs. Forest might have hidden a rather old child somewhere.

"I got an abortion."

"That is *sooo* Planned Parenthood. It's a crime what's happening to them."

I felt the way I'd felt watching Mrs. Forest with Bill, getting wasted in our kitchen. The more traumatic the things she revealed, the more desirable she became. She was old enough to be my very young mother—Bill and Rags had a few years on her—but her abortion was so intimate, so sexual, so painful. I wanted to take care of her.

"Did it hurt?"

"What? The abortion? Yes. I don't advise it, Ace. Kids in your generation are so much better prepared than we were."

"I'm sorry."

"It's not that serious." She put an arm around my shoulder. "It happens. It actually happened again after that."

She was a fertility goddess! "No sex education at your school?"

"I was probably raped."

"*Probably?*"

"An uncle, actually. Everybody got raped back then."

I faced her head-on. "Not everybody gets raped."

"It was a different time, Ace."

"So Bill was raped?"

"It's up to you to ask your mother questions like that."

"Shit." I took our empty cans and headed to the kitchen.

"Ace, when you're with me, only one beer. I know you and your brother drink alcohol and smoke weed, but while you're here, just one, okay? And I know you two hang out at the Bowsprit."

A guy at the Bowsprit had once asked if I wanted to "conversate."

"Aren't you too young for the Bowsprit?"

"I'm too young to *drink* in the Bowsprit. Dave and Dante pour our beers into coffee mugs. Sawyer and me."

"People are so irresponsible."

"Call 911."

What about drugs? I wondered. Was I too young for drugs?

Bill smoked pot while she and Mrs. Forest framed Bill's students' pictures and hung them crazily in the shop.

Pot could knock you out completely, and I knew what some of those pills in Mrs. Forest's medicine cabinet could do. A couple of babysitting nights had been awesomely relaxing, with Sawyer and me crumpling into a life-is-good stupor, eyes heavy, hearts full, world-class appreciation for those assholes on *The Voice*.

"One beer, I'm down for that," I said. "Prudent, very prudent. You too, because you have to drive." I was hung up on the words *when you're with me*—did that mean there would be other times we would have intimate conversations? Or that Mrs. Forest and I would live in a house, go to work, contribute to society?

"What do we have so far?" she asked.

"We have to brainstorm first. Like, what is the essence of picture frames? Like, the picture frames of picture frames?" I was stealing from Plato, but I hoped Mrs. Forest had dropped out of college before getting that far.

"Preservation, artistry," Mrs. Forest said.

41

"Imprisonment." Frames are like the fences that keep murderers and cows from escaping. Abstracts need freedom to go on living beyond the frame, on the wall, across the windowpanes, and into the next room.

Bill and I sometimes "talked art" in the kitchen, feeding each other like birds. A Pollock didn't feel messy; it felt exonerated. I knew people saw me as an abstract. But I felt like a still life, a plucked bird and a vegetable, still, on a plate.

"Imprisonment seems strange coming from you," Mrs. Forest said. "I don't know a family that's more free than yours. You guys talk about everything. No secrets."

"Every person, every family, has secrets." The mystery was whether the secrets were kept, like silent cancers, or revealed, like blazing rashes.

When did a person understand how she fit into the wider world? I'd been maybe seven or eight, older than Brett and Levi Forest, when I intuited how other people saw us—the Ragsdales, both tightly knit and out of the box.

"I know," Mrs. Forest said sadly.

"And I know you know *we* know your so-called secret."

"We knew you kids were eavesdropping on the stairs."

"Dr. Forest is a cunt." I said this so she would feel free to express her anger at him out loud.

Instead, she said, "No, *we're* cunts." The word was muggy and hidden. She lay her cool rice-paper palm on my forehead like I had a fever.

I took her foot into my lap, massaging the gothic arch. "I can't write ad copy with you in the room."

"I know, sweetheart," she said.

She'd known about the blushing and the speechlessness, the watchfulness from places where I'd thought I couldn't be seen.

The memories weren't ghostly, like a face under a frozen pond. They burned.

10

Club YES

Just Say Yeah!

You could do a lot of lying around and eating and texting and writing novels at Club YES, and nobody cared. YES stood for Your Exercise and Sports. You could snore on the banquettes, expressing a nuclear cloud of halitosis, read ratty, bug-infested newsletters from the "lending library," even salivate over half-naked people in the pool—and nothing.

Before I'd meet Sawyer in the exercise room, I'd stop in the Zumba room to spy on Fabia Fonseca and her young mystery man. They were always there at a certain hour. I looked forward to the forbidden thrill of watching them.

He wore a Club YES trainer shirt, had a pop-art jaw, was bald in a good-looking-person way, and he wore a wedding ring. He did everything for Fabia: unbuttoned her coat as if she were disabled, served her breakfast of a halved muffin on a napkin he smoothed flat with his hand. He placed a fold-up chair square in front of the mirrors in the Zumba room and braided her hair.

The age difference and their silence and her faith that she

deserved this man and his blind devotion mesmerized me. They had that filthy look of couples fresh from the shower.

I left before they caught me.

Sawyer lay face up on a Pilates Power Gym. "How was your spying?"

He always let me have the guilty pleasure of observing them without him; I was an atheist praying in an empty pew.

"Fabia's dude falling all over himself is one thing," Sawyer said, "but fucking our mother's best friend? That's monumental. Philosophical, even."

"Yeah," I said, "it's a long shot, but lots of things are long shots."

"Mars colonies, winning the caption contest, but you're talking about . . ."

I pretended to curl three-pound hand weights. "That's crude, Sawyer. 'Fucking' sounds like I just want to fuck her."

"Well?"

"I hold Mrs. Forest in the highest esteem. It's not just about sex."

"What is it about?"

"It's about whatever that thing is when you feel like an ass-wipe around someone." When you feel uncontainable, when regular words aren't enough. "I think it's what dying might be like."

"I'm sorry." Sawyer kept his eyes on the squares of light in the ceiling. "I think I get it. It's like pushing 'send' by mistake."

When a trainer or club member passed, we pretended to spot each other. Sawyer spread his legs in a big Y. "You have to be careful, though—she's twice your age." He arched his neck in fish pose, trying to see my face. "There might be issues."

"You're being ageist."

"You're being politically correct."

"Since when are we not politically correct? 'Save the turbine!'" The three-pound weights were so light they empowered me, like I might fling them across the room, break a mirror maybe, "conk" someone like they do in cartoons.

A trainer walked by, talking on her cell. She gave us a *Just say yes!* smile. "Fuck you," she said into the phone.

"So how do you intend to do it?" Sawyer lowered his legs, his soles touching.

"The usual way."

"Neither one of us has had any real relationships," he said.

"Get to know her in the shop."

Sawyer picked up five-pounders and handed them to me. "You'll need to build up your strength."

"Make myself useful. Get her to depend on me."

"Where do I come in?" Sawyer said.

"One doesn't exclude the other."

"It never works that way," he said, "in reality."

Once, we'd mistakenly clicked on *The Psychology and Business of Clowns,* and learned they had "unsettling familiarity." We knew people thought of us that way, partnered like shoes.

A club member stood near us like someone at a cocktail party, not knowing what to do with herself. She wore tights and a flowing poncho. She was a gorgeous plus-size person, with makeup and dimples. She unleashed a red-carpet smile on us.

Sawyer jumped to his feet. "All yours," he said, a maître d' showing her to a table. Until he flicked his towel like a guy in a locker room.

"No hurry," the woman said. "I've been enjoying watching you two."

"You don't want to overdo it." I wiped nonexistent sweat with my shirttail. "Diminishing returns."

"A sports injury can set you back." Sawyer rubbed his elbow. "Screw up your regimen."

"Moderation is important," she agreed.

We returned the favor, observing her workout. She twisted her body into unbelievable angles. Her movements were fluid, limbs flexible. She was a big, beautiful balloon animal.

"Indigo Mist," Sawyer whispered, wrapping the towel around his neck. "I did her once. Her rings are stuck on her fingers."

Leg skyward, she flexed and pointed, knee perfectly straight.

I stood on tiptoe to kiss my brother on the cheek. "Don't worry, Saw. What are my chances of getting her anyway?"

"Mrs. F., unchartered waters."

I didn't want to correct him. "Precisely."

We could feel the woman's eyes on us as we left, our arms around each other's waists. It was obvious she wanted what we had. Whatever that might be.

11

Turbine supporters fight back

By Chuck Butten
Frigate staff writer

In the ongoing dispute about the future of Horton's wind turbine, Wednesday's council meeting got heated, with frequent meeting attendee Bill Ragsdale speaking for Occupy Wind. "It's a simple matter of economics," she told a half-filled chamber. "Who doesn't want to lower energy costs?" The rhetorical question was answered with a chorus of boos.

Bill and Rags had only one dinnertime rule: full and complete occupation of outer and inner space. Questions asked and answered. We set a place for talk the way the Jews set a place for Elijah.

Our parents didn't even care if we ate what was put in front of us. For years Sawyer ate Froot Loops for dinner, pouring on so much milk that when he was done it looked like Pepto Bismol. As he got older, he started dressing for dinner, wearing incongruous combos like a Castaway foulard and a Kurt Cobain flannel shirt.

"Well!" Dad rocket-launched his opening salvo, flinging a blob of mashed potato onto his plate, like it came from a trebuchet. He'd made them himself, failing to add enough liquid. "Our Ace may have started her career!"

"Don't get your hopes up, Rags," I said.

"No need to have career goals," Bill said. "A career will find you."

I'd been in charge of the frozen peas, which I'd dumped into a colander, followed by boiling water. Occasionally a still-frozen pea found its way to the dinner table. I put my modest pea contribution into an elegant Asian bowl with shards of precious metals embedded in it, no doubt a shameless haul from the Triangle Trade.

Bill and Rags each had inherited a boatload of heirlooms. We were swimming in salt cellars and coasters and candlesticks, table lighters and cigarette cases, mostly silver that no one bothered to polish. We had leather tobacco pouches and pewter plates, which technically you weren't supposed to eat off of. But Sawyer loved them, setting the table like a Henry the Eighth banquet.

"Did a career find you?" I asked Bill.

She sipped water from one of the German tankards Sawyer had set the table with. "I knew I wanted to be involved in the visual arts. I just didn't think that I would be involved in the healing arts."

"Mom, you're the best, but you're in denial. Your students are lunatics."

"Sawyer, that's unfair to your mother," Dad said.

"No, it's not," Mom said. "I love the art part. But my therapy skills leave something to be desired."

"You're good when you're being an amateur," I said. "Everybody's always over here getting your advice and sympathy."

"*Everyone* meaning Suzie Forest."

Dad cut his baked pork chop, pouring copious amounts of applesauce from Grandma Gretchen's mother-in-law's gravy boat. He was the only one who didn't know Bill had just thrown a grenade into the middle of the dinner table.

"Suzie's got to expand her horizons," he said, "spend money to make money."

"Cliché number two, Dad," I warned. "One cliché per sentence."

"Sawyer, terrific job with the pork chops!" Dad yelled. He was so good at ignoring us, sometimes we thought he might be deaf.

"What'd I do?" Sawyer said, using his mobster voice.

"A different ingredient, maybe? Or you just made them nice and crispy on top?"

Sawyer finished his Red Bull. He grabbed my empty can and came back with two more, raising his eyebrows at me as he drank.

I'd told him about my abortive copywriting episode, how Mrs. Forest's inability to focus might signify a long, exciting buildup.

I'd also told him about her abortions. Two of them! She was fertile, fecund, fruitful; we'd thesaurused all the *F* words. We'd researched how to acquire babies for our DIY family: adoption, surrogacy, under-the-table purchases.

You didn't want a Russian baby because Putin might take it away. And white people did not have the cultural competency to be buying babies of color.

"She's got a long road ahead of her." Bill brought me back to the present. Dad was looking at his wife, his head tilted.

"Mrs. Forest," Sawyer prompted.

"It's like the five stages of death," Bill said. "She's in the anger stage."

"How would you know what it's like?" Sawyer said. "Did Dad ever cheat on you?"

"I don't know; did you, Rags?" our mother asked lecherously.

"We got off to a rocky start," Dad acknowledged.

"We were mismatched. We weren't the kind of couple who were introduced by friends."

"So why did you fall in love with him?"

We often talked about Dad as if he weren't in the room.

"He was nice," Bill said, "and I'd gone out with a lot of handsome, disreputable thugs."

"Organized-crime figures?" Sawyer felt protective toward our mother. "Ex-cons?"

"Guys who would not be good fathers. I knew your dad would be a good father."

Sawyer got up and kissed Dad greasily on the lips.

"Plus, he was cute. He was left-handed."

Dad was cutting his meat in such an uncoordinated way that I got a fierce pang of love for him. This was the human condition. People were so inept at survival that you wanted to become their life partners. Mrs. Forest had married the handsome thug, not the one who would love her for her weaknesses. What weaknesses?

"You don't think Dad is handsome?" I asked.

"He had good genes," Bill said.

"Dad, I can't believe Honor lets you go around town like that," Sawyer said. "You look like L.L. Bean if he slept in his clothes. Let me take you to the Castaway. Get something to go with your dancing slippers."

"Okay."

"Okay?"

"Why not? I'm into self-improvement."

"Rags, don't become someone other than the man I married."

I returned us to the subject at hand. "What makes you think Mrs. Forest is angry?"

"The things she says about Lee. She's even talking about abducting the kids."

I knew this. It was thrilling the way she sometimes confessed her darkest thoughts to me.

"Lee's a good guy," Rags said. "We shouldn't judge."

Dad got free sessions at Medical Arts when he hit them up for ads. He had a lingering wrestling injury. Le Forest manipulated his neck like he was assembling components, Dad said. Ethel's ministrations were apparently more like kneading dough, gentle and coaxing.

"Ethel seems like a fine person," Dad said. "She shouldn't be doing what she's doing. Neither should Lee, but they're human. Maybe they're in love."

"Does this Ethel have, like, another name?"

"That's what I mean, Ace. Calling her 'this' is discourteous."

Sawyer was scrutinizing Dad, mentally dressing him. Rags was like a well-regarded outsider in his own family.

"Hooke," Dad said.

"Hook? You absolutely must be one hundred percent kidding."

"Ethel Hooke. Why would I be kidding?"

"Her parents must be barbarians," I said. "Plus, she has her hooks into Le Forest. This is just not credible."

12

You wouldn't throw Great-Grandma's wedding band
into the sock drawer, so why sully her image
with a dime-store frame?

Preserve memories at PICTURE THIS.

"So, how's school?" Mrs. Forest said.

At Picture This, we were attempting to target the local artist demographic.

When Mrs. Forest asked mundane questions, they were heavy, like feelings you can't control.

I tried to hide them with mundane answers. "Teachers, kids, ketamine, the usual."

"That sounds dangerous, Ace." She straightened my collar as if she were about to knot a tie. The intimate gesture, like I was a guy, the proximity; I struggled to contain myself.

I remember the first time I'd experimented with my own agency in Mrs. Forest's presence.

Bill and I had just gotten back from Trader Joe's, and Mrs. Forest was standing on our front steps, not so much waiting as welcoming, like she lived with us on Catboat Road.

That would have been too close for comfort. Mrs. Forest lived *in* you, like an important organ.

I was carrying a bag in each arm, and I was dressed in my usual tight jeans and something ripped and something pierced. Bill and I were finishing the kind of conversation women have.

"Sounds like I'm interrupting something," Mrs. Forest said.

"No, we were just talking about assholes," Mom said. "I thought shopping would be safer than school, given the asshole quotient." She connected with her friend. "To what do we owe?"

"I had to put some stuff in your freezer," Mrs. Forest said. Mom also let herself into the Forests' place on Mill Wheel Lane uninvited. None of us locked our doors. "I hope you don't mind." She aimed this last part at me.

"Suzie, we just bought a bunch of frozen stuff." Mom shoved a bag into Mrs. Forest's midriff. "Where are we going to put it?"

"It's okay, Mom. We can just unfreeze some stuff and eat it," I said. "That's what you do with food." I uncorked a serious smile on Mrs. Forest.

"Not all at once," Mom said. "Like a frozen-food orgy?"

Mrs. Forest returned the smile with one of her own. I couldn't breathe. I was pretty sure she was wearing culottes—I'd have to check with Sawyer. I willed him to show up. Today, he was probably on detention for stealing a quiver from the archery hutch.

"I'm going upstairs," I said abruptly.

"What's upstairs?" Mrs. Forest said.

"Homework?"

Mom laughed. "Ace, honey, what kind of homework?"

"I have to read all of *Walden.*"

"All of it? Jeez, nobody reads all of *Walden.*"

"Speaking of assholes," Mrs. Forest said. "The Scarlet A-Hole?"

It seemed there might be some gaps in Mrs. Forest's schooling.

"Ace, stay with us," she said. "I don't see so much of you anymore." She surveilled me head to toe. "You were shorter last time I saw you. I'm digging the navel piercing."

"Yeah," Mom said, "Rags and I, like, we laid down the law: only forty-five piercings."

Mrs. Forest leaned close. When she touched it, I went instantly wet.

I'd just started to feel quasi-normal in Mrs. Forest's orbit— as long as there were other planets orbiting with me, like Sawyer—but Bill wasn't enough protection. She and Mrs. Forest sometimes got bored with one another, which meant the focus might unexpectedly land on me.

Their default mode with each other was semi-provocative. They both had dudes at home, but they needed female bonding— not just gal pals, more like liquid when it freezes and becomes touchable. Which meant I could concentrate on Mrs. Forest without her noticing. Until I couldn't.

"Honey," Mrs. Forest massaged my mother's skinny shoulders, "don't be mad." She knew her fake-whiny voice would soften Bill up. I could see what Mrs. Forest couldn't: my mother smiling.

I pulled a tub of Trader Joe's ice cream from the freezer, making room. Redirecting their attention, I handed them one spoon. "Here," I said, halfway provocative myself. "You can share and double-dip."

Something prehistoric in me wanted to see them in action.

They obliged, sharing French vanilla and saliva, wiping each other's chins with their thumbs. It was two in the afternoon. They were on their way to a sugar glut that would ruin their dinners with their families: Sawyer, Dad, and me with our required conversation; Le Forest intoning *Firstly* and the word *suboptimum*.

By the time Sawyer came home, Mom was supine on the couch, and Mrs. Forest was sitting on the floor, head resting against Mom's feet, her twin peaks snowcapped with dribbled ice cream.

"I think I might puke," Mrs. Forest said dreamily.

Mom handed her the almost empty ice cream tub.

Back at Picture This, I was too distracted to think. The grapes, the salty snacks, Bill's Carr crackers, the hot and cold beverages—all this further distanced me from the notion of work. Rags said we should have three different ad campaigns. Plus, Mrs. Forest had removed her velvet slip-ons.

She smoothed my forehead with her thumb. "Why so worried?" Luxuriantly, she rubbed her foot against the rough carpet.

"You don't get turned on when Sawyer does your nails?"

"Ace, sweetie, it's nail-filing!"

"Nothing is closer to sex than cosmetology. It's like a brothel in there."

Like every girl, I fantasized more about weddings than about marriages and had envisioned myself walking down the aisle on Sawyer's arm to be delivered like an Amazon package to a divorcée with two kids. Brett and Levi would be the flower boy and ring bearer.

Mrs. Forest placed both hands on my waist as if she were measuring me. "Your brother's all ears; women tell him things."

"What about Le Forest? What is it about him?"

"That's what you guys call him? That's funny." She stopped smiling. "In the beginning, you mean?"

"Yeah, he seems way not good enough for you."

"I know I should be flattered, but that reflects badly on me, like you don't respect my choices."

"Well . . ." I pulled the hair from her eyes, like in a movie.

"On our first date . . ."

"Where? Where was your first date?"

"He took me to an elegant restaurant at a hotel in Boston."

"Hotel?"

"We didn't get a room."

"What was it then?"

"It was when he came to pick me up."

"Flowers?"

"No."

"Tie?"

"Yes, of course. You know how Lee can look. Handsome and smelling of soap or shampoo, something clean."

"So it was the soap and the tie?"

"No, it was that he had shaved himself practically to death, with little bloody nicks. He wanted to kiss me, obviously, but it made him seem vulnerable, which he isn't, of course. He rarely showed that side of himself again."

A fugitive look, a fleeting movement, the way a person kneels to kiss a child: You can be crushed by things people don't even know they're doing. Killing you softly, like in Bill's old song. "Rarely? There were other times when he was vulnerable?"

"When the boys got their glasses, I caught a tear slipping down his face. I loved him for it."

Brett and Levi had the same form of lazy eye. They wore each other's glasses, but their emotional DNA separated them. If you teased Brett, he'd hyperventilate. If you teased Levi, he'd hug you around the knees.

"Are you still in love with him? All his *vulnerabilities*?"

"It takes time to unlove someone."

"Even someone so deserving of unlove?" I was well aware of the double whammy of desire and deceit. We'd learned it in health class, and it was all over the internet, women who stuck with their shitty partners.

"Yes, and the father of my children."

"Would you feel that way about a sperm donor?" When Sawyer turned eighteen, he'd donated sperm to earn $50 for a pair of Depression-era suspenders. It pained Rainy to part with them.

"Depends on whose sperm."

"Is Rags the only person in my family who doesn't have the hots for you?"

"Your mother."

"Yeah, but she does that cheesy, only-you eye-contact

56

schtick, even with you."

"I know."

I kissed her, suddenly. All my life, it seemed, I'd been working up to this moment, and now I kissed her, impulsively, the way you might change your mind about buying something.

She pushed me away, gently, which gave me hope. She might have rejected me with all her mental and motherly strength—I knew how mothers could lift a car to save their children.

The thought crossed my mind, even in my wonderment, that I might need saving. It wasn't just tragedy that you had to survive. Love seemed like something you had to recover from.

When I kissed her again, she pulled me to her. At first, her lips tasted of fresh liquid, then they were loamy and close, unlike all the other kisses I'd known.

I would never get enough of them.

From then on, our work sessions would end in wild make-out episodes: upright against the wall or on the floor under her scarred worktable, stopping just short of scx, as if we were trying to kill each other.

13

Inherit the windbags
By Chuck Butten
Frigate staff writer

Flashing lights, whooshing sounds louder than a jet engine, a blight on the landscape, and a lack of transparency about its risks and rewards are just some of the complaints voiced by residents about the new wind turbine. Some 300 people turned out to sign the huge white blades before the turbine was hoisted. But now it's being blamed for everything from cancer to sexual indiscretions.

"It's a health hazard and an eyesore," complained Bulrush Road resident Eleanor Margesson.

Selectman Doris Wilder said she was happy to hear legitimate complaints but told the Frigate, "We will not and cannot take it down."

Grandma Gretchen stood on our front steps with a duffel bag over her shoulder like a sailor home from the sea. She drove a beat-up military surplus vehicle, parked crazily in the driveway, as if it had come to rest after a car chase. She'd just been sprung from the slammer.

We crowded into her room. "Nice crib," Grandma always said. The Ragsdales had a "guestroom," which was funny, because we had no guests. Sawyer had tricked it out with little amenities from the travel section of CVS.

"You should see some of the cruddy places I stay," Grandma said. "I bunked up in somebody's home during that New Jersey gig, you wouldn't believe it, it was like they were cut off from the march of time: shag rugs, vinyl siding, no rhyme or reason in the urban planning department."

She was fresh off a success in Bayonne, New Jersey, a factory town where the citizens opposed a wind turbine on the grounds that it "altered the skyline." What skyline? The landscape was pill-boxed with oil drums, mystifying scaffolds, and belching chimneys. The cranes of a container port were towering giraffes, keeping watch like moms on the savannah.

Sawyer placed Grandma's duffle neatly on a little foldable stand with fabric straps. "Consider this your second home." He kissed the top of her rusty perm.

"Dinner after you freshen up." Bill pointed to the attached bathroom.

"Who said I need freshening up?"

Rags bent for the mother hug. "You smell fine to me."

Bill went all-out with the store-bought hors d'oeuvres, thrilled that her mother-in-law would soon be taking over town meeting duty.

"Sounds like it's time for some op-eds in the *Frigate*," Grandma said to Bill.

She was one of the few people any of us knew who was born to do what she did. Our parents had fallen into their jobs witlessly like balls rolling off a table, but Grandma's activism was bred in the bones: voting rights, equal pay, marriage equality, whatever.

She turned to us. "Your school into any do-gooding this year?"

"Mr. Prower probably has something up his disgusting sleeve," Sawyer said.

"Our children's ever-so-asinine guidance counselor," Bill said.

"He's always collecting funds for victims of typhoons and earthquakes and draughts and famines," Sawyer said.

We weren't into mass philanthropy. "One fly-infested kid?" I said. "No problem, but it's hard to get all I-feel-your-pain over more than a thousand people at a time."

"I'm no fan of this Stanley Prower character, from what I've heard." Grandma eyed Bill over her beer mug.

"He was afraid Sawyer and I were too close," I said.

"Loving is rarely wrong." Grandma rolled an olive around in her mouth to loosen the pit, spitting it onto a saucer. "That's what I have found. In my experience. In my work."

My first year at Whore High, kids had spread rumors that Sawyer and I might be doing the nasty. Mr. Prower had informed Bill and Rags of our "willful refusal to counter" these rumors and, worse, our "capricious tendency to perpetuate them."

Sawyer and I had been dragged down to Mr. Prower's office. "I just want to head things off at the pass," he'd told us, "now that you two are both at the high school."

"What pass?" Sawyer said.

"I don't need to tell you that your reputations proceed you." Mr. Prower liked to pretend he was friends with students, slapping them around and calling them *buddy* like they were dogs.

"Thank you." I laid my hand on Sawyer's upper thigh.

Most parents would have accompanied their kids to such a meeting, but Bill's favorite mantra was "Fight your own battles."

"We need to disabuse them, your fellow students of . . . of . . ."

Mr. Prower steepled the long womanly fingers he was so proud of.

"Come down to Fabia's, and I'll give you our spa manicure," Sawyer said. "Pick out a nice polish for you."

"I don't wear polish." He examined his nails. "Maybe just clear."

"You'd look good in Fade to Black," I said. "Right, Saw?"

"That or Black Onyx."

"In closing," Mr. Prower said, like he was finishing a speech, "I don't want to have to disabuse students of any notions of . . ."

"Or abuse them?" I said. "Did you mean *abuse*?"

Sawyer had put his arm around my waist. "Notions of what?"

At dinner, Dad was trying to angle the conversation back toward dinner. "Pass the paper towels," he said. Our mother had ordered ribs from a joint in Hull. They were so greasy we'd abandoned the monogrammed napkins Bill had inherited.

"Mom was a rock star," Sawyer said.

Dad's mother handed her son a towel without looking at him. Her gaze was on her grandchildren, her eyes uncommonly wary. "What did you do, Bill?"

"I told Stanley that he should 'correct' the other students."

A word she would never use with us. But you needed to defend the family at all costs, no matter how tortured the defense.

Grandma—uncharacteristically—seemed a step behind what was being argued. "The logic seems right," she said uncertainly.

"Mom put old Prower in his place," I said.

"Salad." Sawyer passed the bowl as if it needed to be classified.

"Well," Grandma said, helping herself to salad. "You are both great-looking kids. You're good people. You need to find some girlfriends."

"In their own good time," Bill said. Our mother sometimes freaked us out. She was like a divining rod.

"I agree," Rags said. "Our kids would be a real coup for someone." Like we were war booty.

61

"Bill, you outdid yourself with the rice!" Grandma yelled. Hanging around so many wind turbines had caused crystals to dislodge in her head, giving her chronic vertigo. Sometimes her world turned sideways, spinning like teacups, and lightning bolts flashed behind her eyes. Other times she just talked too loud, as if she were hearing-impaired.

"It's just rice, Gretchen."

"I can tell this is not Minute Rice. When I try to do the real stuff, it gets super expensive."

"Rice is the cheapest thing around," Bill said.

"That's why starving people eat it," I said.

Rags winced. "That's a little rough, Ace."

"You know, the helicopter comes and dumps a sack of rice?"

"She's right," Grandma said, "but the reason it's expensive is that it sticks to the pan, and I have to throw out the pan."

"Me too!" Sawyer said. "I throw the pans into the special garbage for appliances."

"You're throwing away pans?" Bill was such an indifferent cook she hadn't even noticed.

"Don't throw pans away," Rags advised.

"And pans aren't appliances," I added, irrelevantly.

I could practically see the thought bubble suspended over Grandma's head: Her daughter-in-law was smart, attractive, a bit slack when it came to homemaking and parenting—a good thing—and she could see why Rags had chosen her. Not so much why Bill had chosen him; *consented* was more likely. But their kids were from another planet, or other parents.

It was strange to see Grandma thinking; she was a person who acted. She suddenly pivoted to her son: "How's your neighborhood watch group?"

Our father's face pixilated.

Bill's fork stalled midway from plate to mouth. "Tell her, darling."

"Dad!" Sawyer wiped both hands on the lobster bib he was wearing to protect his shirt.

"I see I've opened a can of worms," Grandma said.

"We live in a dangerous world," Dad started in. "Terrorists, foreign and domestic: kids getting shot up in schools; people getting shot at movie theaters, social service agencies, Planned Parenthood, hazards right here in Horton. I was feeling helpless to protect my family."

Sawyer took aim at Dad with his fork. "From what?"

"Fires, road fatalities, bombings, chokings, you name it."

But what about the hazards that lurked right under our noses? Wasn't homegrown emotion a bigger hazard than Dad's "dangerous world"? Like these terrorists would have some particular issue with the Ragsdales of Catboat Road.

"George Zimmerman was in a neighborhood watch group," I said. "It has a bad connotation." ·

"Your father is hardly George Zimmerman," Grandma said.

"And we're not Trayvon Martin," Sawyer put in.

"There but for the grace of . . ." Dad cut himself off. God was not a particularly good role model for the Ragsdales.

Grandma chucked her rib bones onto an empty plate. "Your dad is nothing like Zimmerman. He doesn't own a firearm, for one thing."

"Look, I don't have a lot of pull in this family," Dad said, "but my one and only job is to make sure you guys make it out of this cesspool of a culture war alive. It's the same instinct Crack has. You don't think if a burglar broke into this house, Crack would defend us to the death?"

Crack was sitting under the table grooming his scrotum.

"Honey," Bill said. "One of the reasons you joined the group was because of the insomnia. Might as well do something useful."

"You can bet that the Opposition Wind crowd is blaming the turbine for all that stuff," Grandma said.

She suddenly veered from wind. "You dating?" she said to Sawyer and me, as if we were one person. "Any nice girls on the horizon? What about that girl who was here last winter?"

Girl? Winter?

"Oh, her!" Was Sawyer stalling, or did he really know? "Our math tutor," he said.

63

I wasn't thinking about Ms. Long Division as a *date;* her genius with numbers had attracted both Sawyer and me. It was a turn-on when a person had so thoroughly cracked a code you yourself didn't understand. Words like *isosceles* rolled filthily off her tongue, which she employed with math-like precision.

"You *both* were flunking math?" Grandma said.

"Yeah, and we were just as bad after Dad refused to pay her any more money," I said. "She left in tears."

"Emily Langmore," Bill said. "You kids were quite fond of her, as I recall."

"She was a math geek," I said.

"I should hope so," Grandma said. "Why else would you hire her, right, Wendall?" Once in a while Grandma fell back into calling her son by his given name.

"She came highly recommended," Dad said.

"By Stanley Prower," Bill said.

"Emily was very cute when she said things like 'to the power of,'" Sawyer recalled.

"She's moonlighting at Ocean Charter," Bill said.

"Babies?" I said. "She's teaching math to babies?"

We'd knocked the math right out of her. When she got it on, her hair, which was ordinarily limp and lifeless, flew around her face, like in *The Exorcist.* She'd wept when Dad fired her, promising that Sawyer and I would get 800s on our math SATs if she were allowed to stay.

Bill and Rags were skeptical; we were still getting D-minuses on our math quizzes. Emily had even offered to cheat for us on our SATs.

Sawyer and I were not into cheating. But she might have made a good surrogate mother, providing the math gene that Sawyer so profoundly lacked, if it weren't for her *Fatal Attraction* gene.

Emily had not been our first threesome. Our first was with Madison O'Malley, our freshman/sophomore year.

Everyone at Whore High had to take Health and Physical Science and try out for something, but no team would have us.

And we didn't want to ruin any team's chances of making the Regionals. That left archery. Bill had strong-armed health and physical science department director Amy Allerton into letting us on the team because Sawyer and I both liked the word *quiver*. Sawyer was so bad they made him manager, but they needed girls, so they took me on.

Maddie had a crush on Sawyer, probably why she gave me extra help, getting way close, her hand over mine as we pulled back the arrow, her sinewy arm gripping the bow. She smelled like the Limited Edition she'd proudly snagged a sample of at Sephora.

The bow-and-arrow hype—Goddess of the Hunt, the one-tit Amazons and the mostly naked Massasoit with his bow hiding his balls—seemed made for me. But I still sucked. When Maddie decided I was ready to go solo one day, all my arrows ended up at the new condos beyond the archery range, where cx hipsters shared space with the woods and wildlife that had been there for millennia. The arrows sailed over the targets, landing like sticks on the hipsters' garden gnomes.

Afraid I might kill a duck or a person, Director Amy Allerton banned me from the range. Sawyer, Maddie, and I ended up in the archery hutch.

Maddie had no Mrs. Forest curves, but I was attracted to her archery skills—she was more or less the coach—and she seemed to like me well enough.

Something about the hutch—cramped, smelling of wood and sweat and synthetics— screamed sex. Being surrounded by weapons at rest also built up a person's confidence: benign and useless, they couldn't suddenly take flight and kill something, until someone like Maddie set them in motion.

We seemed born to the threesome, like with art's triangle and the female sex organ. Maddie brought that squint that archery fiends have to the party. It was like she'd been fucking us with her eyes.

14

Coffee is not just a beverage. It's a state of being.

Experience aromatherapy at Riparian Roasters.

A new name, but the same great Ground Rounds brew.

Senior Eaton strolled around the former Ground Rounds like the proud owner he was. If you were a regular, he'd snap his fingers at a server so you could avoid waiting, even when the line was short or nonexistent.

Fabia Fonseca gave up her place in line to come to my table, charmingly invading my personal space. It was strange seeing her outside her royal fiefdom.

"There's a different energy down at the chop," she said.

"Not a problem, I hope?"

She wore a big wool sweater and Capri pants instead of her fuchsia smock with her initials, *FF*, in flowing cursive on the pocket.

"Sawyer, your brother, there's a flip-flop, the women, he used to make them feel so come-fort-table and now, the women, they're trying to make him more happy!"

"Sends the wrong signal," I agreed. I tried to focus on her

and also watch the door.

"Signal!" Her wispy breaths lifted the corner of my napkin. "Female advize. I should know, I hear it all day, it's not always good."

"I'll drink to that," I raised my water glass.

"You must talk to him. You gize har so cloze. Thank you, thank you, thank you!" She squeezed my arm, not waiting for an answer. "Your pretty lady, she will be here soon!"

When Fabia took her place at the end of the line, Senior Eton materialized at my table "We've gotten some positive feedback," he said. "Except for that guy who complained to the *Frigate*. The name change affected 'quality control'?"

"Bad buzz is better than no buzz," I said.

I often wrote ad copy and did research at the former Ground Rounds. Sawyer and I had advised the Eatons to change the name. "*Ground round* was hamburger. How about *Grand Rounds?*" Junior Eaton had joked, straying into hospital territory.

Senior took a latte and a chocolate biscotti from an incredibly old server. The latte came in a big white bowl; the server carried it like a child afraid of spilling her milk.

Senior delivered it with a simian paw.

Junior stood behind the counter. The Eatons had a gargoyle quality, like they were perched on cornices, watching.

"How are you doing with the laptop-to-latte ratio?" I asked.

The working-in-cafés trend had reached even Horton. Among the students and novelists were solitaire players, the spreadsheet crowd, the agonized emailers, the Olympian thumb-texters. "Capacity, volume, that's important," I said.

Senior was suddenly eyeing the door.

I smelled her before I saw her: Mrs. Forest, filling the space like smoke in an old movie. "Suzie," Senior said. "Welcome to . . . whatever the hell we're calling it now." He turned to me. "Suzie was looking for you the other day." He snapped his fingers for another latte.

"Ace." Mrs. Forest laid her hand on mine. "I'm glad I found you."

"You saw me from the sidewalk?" I always chose the window seat, so I could observe foot traffic and be inspired by the lobster people who did the only real work in town, facing rogue waves, the Perfect Storm even, which was part of Horton's lore. We all took credit, like people in disasters. The real heroes didn't need to take credit.

Mrs. Forest tossed her noisy bag on the seat next to mine. She was all-girl except for her butch way of throwing things. "I thought I might help you with my new ad." She hung her coat on the back of the chair. "Brand," she added steamily, like it was a bedroom word. Her latte arrived, this time from a stunning male waiter who'd lovingly created a heart in her latte foam.

"Thank you, honey." She looked up at him and smiled.

Carly Simon's clouds-in-your-coffee surfaced. Once, I'd received fallopian tubes dissolving into the foam. "The last thing you want to do is frame a real piece of art." I took in the amateurish efforts on the Eatons' walls. "How many more dories tied to how many more floats with how many more gulls soaring overhead?"

"You sound like your mom," Mrs. Forest said.

"My mom?"

Mrs. Forest held the bowl to her lips—two-handed. "Yes. We need to talk about your mom."

"Why?"

"Be on the up-and-up."

"I thought you'd be interested in your branding campaign."

"Oh, I am!" Mrs. Forest peered at my screen. "Are you working on it now?"

I nodded. "Frames are tough, because they're not as important as what they're framing."

"Sometimes the corners of a picture curl up if you don't frame them." She wiped a dollop of foam from the tip of her nose.

I leaned over to dunk my biscotti in her latte. "See? Frames are not like coffee. Coffee has an aroma, a history, an essence. It's organic."

"Gotcha." She removed her compact from the bag that seemed to contain all her earthly possessions. "It tastes really good." She reapplied her lipstick, which had come to live on the rim of her coffee cup. "I still want to help, with the organics and the essences and all, but I just wanted to, I don't know, clear the air," she said. "We should get together."

"We are together."

"I mean all of us, you, me, your mom. It might . . ." She moved so close I could smell fresh coffee on her lips. "Normalize things."

"I don't think we're exactly *normal*."

"I know, but sometimes interacting can bring perspective."

"Should we all play mah-jongg?" I said.

"No, and don't look at me like that. I know what mah-jongg is." (*Use it thrice and make it yours.* Mrs. Carver, first year English.) "It's some kind of Chinese tarot cards."

"Close."

"Dominoes or something."

"You're getting warmer."

"I was thinking you could come with us to the Quaking Bog, for our monthly inspection." She and Bill were co-administrators, saving our primeval swamp from becoming a golf course with condos and a clubhouse and a *Crucible*-sounding name like Goodie Nine Holes.

I was sidetracked by the word *monthly* as it related to Mrs. Forest, the fungus-y high of her blood. "Very educational," I scoffed.

Mrs. Forest took in the art-filled space. "No offense, but your new name for this place is terrible."

"I'm sorry. I was being a shit just then."

"You were. I don't know why you do that."

"To protect myself."

She took my hand. "From what?"

"I guess I'm afraid," I said. We'd progressed to the point where we should have been having sex, but we weren't.

"Of your mom?"

"Of you, of us." It was like whatever we had was too risky for actual sex.

"Me too."

"And you're right," I said. "The new name is precious and elitist."

"Took the words right out of my mouth." Gathering her humongous bag, she leaned across the table and planted a lipstick-latte kiss on my mouth. "Okay, I'll arrange it . . . with your mom."

I watched her leave. So did everyone else.

15

Windmill warnings

By Chuck Butten
Frigate staff writer

A firefighter from the HFD was a guest speaker at Wednesday's council meeting. Bud Andrew Norris warned the council that tiki-torches employed by anti-turbine protesters, dressed as Druids, were dangerous, "especially near the marshes, where cat-o'-nine tails act as kindling."

"Bill," Mrs. Forest said to my mother, "I don't know how you can stand the cold."

The Quaking Bog was laced in a baby's breath of frost. Mrs. Forest's bogwear consisted of a too-tight skirt, a parka and big sweater—under which I knew was a floppy sleeveless number that exposed her bra straps—and inappropriate shoes whose heels caught in the spaces of the boardwalk.

Bill said having an avocation outside your vocation could

give you a sense of purpose, and being in nature could give you a sense of your place in the universe.

Bill and Mrs. Forest knew jack shit about the universe.

"I can't stand it, but this is our job." Bill tugged playfully on Mrs. Forest's hood. "You only like nature when we go to the science center gala."

"Busted," Mrs. Forest said.

They carried little botanical guidebooks and an ancient "cheat sheet" that showed how to identify signs of human interference. I pushed a branch away from Mrs. Forest's face. "No offense, but I don't think you guys are qualified for this job." I grabbed the book.

They didn't know and probably didn't care that we were in a *schwingmoor* with sphagnum moss and sedges in a six-inch undulating mat of wet peat, an antediluvian "bog regime" that could cover an entire bay or inland lake. If all three of us were to die on the spot, our bodies, encased in peat, would be preserved for millennia, like that mummified Scandinavian found 1,700 years after he'd frozen to death in a peat bog.

"I don't see any signs of human intervention," I said.

"Thank God!" Mrs. Forest grabbed my arm. "Let's get out of this sinkhole."

Bill admonished, "Let's at least finish one lap of the boardwalk."

Like we were some kind of track stars.

I wanted to save Mrs. Forest's handprint on my elbow, dust it like evidence. Of what, exactly? That she couldn't stand up without me? "You're right," I said to her.

She turned to face me. "Right? About what?"

"I'm a dick."

"I never said that." Mrs. Forest focused on my mother's back as if it were her horizon.

I took up the rear. Mrs. Forest's little skirt was no match for her ass. "I don't want to be a dick with you," I said.

Bill was ahead of us, loudly expounding on the "ecosystem." A strengthening breeze exposed the backsides of leaves.

"Opposites," Mrs. Forest, said, the word nearly lost as she backed into the wind.

"Opposites attract?" I said.

Mrs. Forest nodded.

Our "lap" of the boardwalk was interrupted by one of our unique Whore Town storms. There were times when Horton was the only town from Boston to Provincetown to experience an atmospheric event: a squall or fast-moving tornado, ice that froze tree limbs, daggers of it hanging from eaves.

What looked like a little cyclone whirled through the treetops. A small bird slammed into an evergreen and stuck to its sappy bark. If the disturbance had lasted more than a minute, we too would have been tossed into the *schwingmoor*.

There was nothing like a storm in a primeval bog to give you that sense of the paleolightning that produced the organic compounds responsible for such biodiverse life forms as John Quincy Adams and Mrs. Forest. Horton's tropical disturbance had sent outdoor furniture sailing into clapboards and shingles. Meanwhile, in Duxbury, Cohasset, Hingham, Plymouth, they were enjoying sunny skies, light breezes, calm seas, and no small craft warnings.

"The murmuring pines . . ." Bill called out.

". . . and the hemlocks," I finished. "Hemlock is poisonous, but deadly nightshade isn't."

"Potatoes are when they grow sprouts," Bill said.

"And I think some grape seeds," I added.

"Mushrooms, too!" Mrs. Forest hollered.

Bill turned to look at us. She suddenly knew: she was like one of those buttons supplied with a new coat.

Spare.

For our next female bonding experience, we tried grocery shopping, the three of us in the Vulva, laughing at the husband requests. Le Forest: "Dried plums are *not* prunes," Dad's "meat" rolling raunchily off our tongues.

"Humans are just meat, after all," I mimicked.

I gave Mom and Mrs. Forest their privacy in the meat department, while I spied on their body language from the dental floss aisle.

They talked like deaf people, their emotions clipped and precise. Mom kept heaving packages into the cart, and Mrs. Forest kept returning them to the shelves. She restored a gigantic turkey to the poultry case.

Customers elbowed them out of the way. "Ex*cuse* us!" Mrs. Forest said.

"Ma'am? Ladies?" A butcher in her bloody apron separated them like boxers.

"Ace, why so much dental floss?" Mom said at the checkout counter. "Do you need to make an appointment with Dr. Mollick?"

"Studies have shown that too many choices can lead to mania in otherwise balanced individuals."

"So you got it all? Waxed, unwaxed, taped, tufted, braided, flavored?"

"I got carried away."

Mom handed half of them to Mrs. Forest. She dropped them into a bag next to the economy-size prunes and the twins' overwrought cereals.

I imagined her flossing, standing in front of the mirror, the Grand Tetons easily scaffolding the salmon towel wrapped around her. She'd be good at it, her coordinated hands reaching way back, spitting bits of meat into the sink that could have gone into the making of Mrs. Susan Forest.

"It seemed like you were arguing," I said from the backseat. "What were you arguing about?"

"Marbled versus lean," Mrs. Forest said.

"You," Mom said.

16

Reprieve for turbine foes

By Chuck Butten
Frigate staff writer

Amid charges that the wind turbine is affecting the health of Horton citizens, opposition forces were given a reprieve. For the last month, the blades have been motionless.

"The turbine experienced sustained lightning strikes in a relatively short period of time," Selectman Doris Wilder explained.

"This may be the first time that getting struck by lightning is a good thing," said Eleanor Margesson, longtime opponent of the turbine along with her husband, Jake.

The turbine was quickly repaired after a new part was delivered by barge from Bath, Maine.

I could hear Sawyer wandering around downstairs. It was what he did when he had insomnia, which might or might not have been caused by our "alternative" energy. This was the word used in *Frigate* stories, as if wind were some kind of additive instead of basic, like fire. Sawyer often rearranged the furniture, usually improving on our parents' arbitrary configurations.

We had frequent headaches, which were probably turbine-induced, though we would never admit this publicly. We took lots of aspirin, which sometimes gave us nosebleeds. We stanched them with paper towels, leaving our bloody evidence in the trash. Bill seemed to buy our stories of knife accidents and hitting our heads on the corners of coffee tables.

I couldn't sleep either, and went down to help Sawyer move the couch, which was now at a crazy angle, nearly blocking the door. Instead of standing back to get a better look, he was slumped on it, his head in his hands.

"Bedhead," I said, tousling his hair. "What's up, bro?"

Bill and Rags kept Bayer in a '40s era silver cigarette case they'd found among Grandpa Gary's "effects." I handed two pills to Sawyer. He threw his head back and swallowed them without water, like a substance abuser.

"Headache?"

"No."

"So why did you take aspirin?"

"Did I? I didn't notice."

"Sawyer! That's dangerous. You could be drug-sleeping. Some people eat entire coffee rings in their sleep. And remember that guy who died driving a front loader during REM sleep?"

"I haven't been myself," Sawyer said.

"No kidding. You've been moping around the house. Bill and Rags ask me what's wrong with you, and Fabia ambushes me down at the Eatons' and wants to know what's up."

"Sorry, I'm just . . . I don't know. Just."

"Just what?"

"Missing you."

"I'm here."

"In body, but everything else is with Mrs. Forest, your mind, your spirit, your libido."

"Sorry. She's, she's . . . I don't know, I want to crawl inside her or something."

"TMI!"

"You know, like when things combine to make something else?"

"No, I don't know." He squinted through spread fingers. "And then there's work. I love Fabia's, but sometimes I just can't take it. They tell me everything and expect me to have an answer. Fibroids and endometriosis, and their kids nodding out and flunking out and their partners cheating and even trying to kill them! Sometimes I'm drowning in a sea of female problems."

"Yikes, Sawyer, I'm so sorry." I patted my lap for him to lay his head there.

"Mrs. Forest tells me things, too."

"I know."

"You don't." He turned to look at me. "She told me she was so turned on by you two not having sex that she was walking around with a hard-on all the time. Le Forest won't have sex with her because he's got some kind of 'exclusive' with Ethel."

"She'd better not be sleeping with Dr. Scumbag."

Sawyer abruptly sat up like they do in movie nightmares. "And that's not all!"

"Keep it down, buddy. The last thing we need is our parental units stumbling down in their nighties."

"I started to understand it, to get it."

"Get what?"

"The worst thing."

The worst thing would be Mrs. Forest dying, Sawyer *and* Mrs. Forest dying. They were alive, so . . . . "What would be the worst thing?"

"If I couldn't have you back, maybe I could control you, half-kill you—that would be the worst thing—like those domestic-violence cavemen."

"Huh?" I tugged my earlobe, imitating Grandma. "Sounds like?"

"Fabia's clients, I just told you, those women with their cavemen."

I laughed. "Hard to imagine."

Sawyer grabbed my wrists, then wrapped his arms around my waist, bear-hugging me. He seemed to be channeling every cop show we'd ever seen, trying to twist my arm behind my back, stopping just short of the murderous chokehold.

I fought back, propelling us both into the coffee table.

Magazines, books, ashtrays, heirlooms flew off it, while Sawyer lay on top of me, pinning my arms over my head.

I kneed him in the gut. He rolled on his side.

We staggered to our feet.

This time, he really had cut himself on the coffee table. He took off his shirt and wrapped it around his head like a wounded soldier. Blood bled into his makeshift bandage.

Like zombies, we moved the couch to a more hospitable position near the fireplace. The couch was back to normal, but what about me, us?

We sat on it, surveying the living room from the new angle. Move a couch, cut down a tree, tear down a building, and nothing looks the same. You suddenly don't know where you are.

My brother still needed to do penance. I could tell.

He didn't see it coming, my flat hand making contact with the rough stubble of his cheek. It was like in movies when the woman slaps the guy across the face, and his head snaps sideways, and he never raises his fists. I loved that.

"I'm sorry." He burrowed into my sleeve. We'd never fought for real, just play. "Did I hurt you?" he said.

"Not really."

"I wanted to. It made me feel . . ."

"Empowered?" I said.

"Alive."

"I get that." I felt it, too. Bodily harm was forbidden and exhilarating. "I forgive you." To prove it, I moved to the arm of the couch, the better to launch into one of our fake-normal conversations. "I told Mom I wanted to marry Mrs. Forest, and she's like, 'Call the caterer!'"

Sawyer lay down, staring at the ceiling. "I'll design your wedding outfit," he said, like 'wedding outfits' were the furthest thing from his mind.

I rubbed my arm. It was sore, and damp with Sawyer's blood. "Mom's getting even more 'whatever' than usual."

"That's just a cover." Sawyer held an empty tumbler like there was something in it. "She wants to pretend this whole Mrs. Forest thing is okay. She's afraid someone's going to get hurt."

"Me?"

"Her. Like she might lose her *Suzie.*"

"How do you know?"

"Rags and Bill, they don't care if you listen to them talk, they don't even need words, they're like, Siamese."

"Mom may just be tired. She could be having one of those late-life pregnancies."

"Maybe Mrs. Forest got her pregnant," Sawyer said.

"It could be the turbine, those flashing lights." I turned toward the window as if I could see them from here. "Maybe we should get away for a while."

"Like we have money and freedom and can sail to the Caribbean like some turquoise ad with humongous turtles and white people." Sawyer dug his toes into my ribs. "Would you leave Mrs. Forest?"

"I don't know. I just don't know anymore."

Sawyer wanted the pre–Mrs. Forest me returned to him, like a lost wallet.

17

The art of healing, the gift of health.

The author of *Thank You for Having Me* will customize

a physical therapy plan just for you.

Visit *drleeforest.com*.

Medical Arts was wall-to-wall mirrors, so physical therapy clients could watch themselves do their "therapeutic stretches."

Dad was admiring his new outfit. "Cliché number one—clothes do make the man," he said.

"Who are you wearing, Dad?"

"Sawyer Ragsdale."

The joke was getting old.

Dad's white highly starched cotton shirts meant a lot of trips to the dry cleaner. Visits to any shop in town could mean more ad money for him. Today, he wore a blue tie, corduroy sport jacket, and well-cut jeans, decidedly not what Grandma called "dungarees." Sawyer had ordered Dad's pricey Italian loafers online.

Bill and Rags had a rule about not criticizing what the other bought.

The receptionist looked up from her screen. "Dr. Forest can

see you now."

Le Forest shook my hand, careful not to crush it, in case I had arthritis or carpal tunnel. He had a cleft chin like Tom Brady. "Ace, so this is your day job?"

Dad sat and crossed his legs, running his hand over the crease of his pants. He used to manspread big time. Bill and Grandma were knowledgeable resources about annoying manspreaders on crowded subway cars. Sawyer and I had done a lot of research on New York City, since we would be living there someday.

"Physical therapy is exploding," Le Forest started in, clasping his hands behind his head. His muscles moved under his too-small polo shirt like little animals under his skin.

"And we have to capitalize on that," Rags said.

"Suzie says that you and your brother have done wonders for her business."

"Mrs. Forest is always very appreciative," I said.

"Well, I was in there the other day, and the improvements were obvious," Le Forest said.

"You were in there the other day?"

"Lunch break."

"Lunch break?" I said.

I could feel Dad's eyes on me. *No sidebars. Stay on message.* "Like *food* lunch break?"

"We ordered in from Uncle Asia's." Le Forest brought his hands back and folded them on the desk. "Brett and Levi are always asking when you and your brother can come over."

"We love them."

"You're good role models."

Dad got us back on track. "We'll need a campaign that targets the changes in the business."

"Ace, are you an athlete?" Le Forest asked.

I shook my head.

"Sawyer?"

"We're not athletic in our family."

"Except for your dad, here. Star wrestler."

"Not a star," Dad said, pleased.

"Anyway, people who are not athletes need physical therapy for things like carpal tunnel, arthritis, baker's cysts, meniscus, fasciitis."

Such poetic diseases!

"We can't get too much in the weeds," Dad warned. "We don't want to lose the audience."

"This is just background," Le Forest said.

"There's also the turbine," I said.

Dad gave me a look.

"The wind turbine has brought in considerable business," Le Forest said. "Physicians, the mainstreamers, they don't want to admit there's a problem."

Le Forest's office had a funereal feel, with gift baskets from grateful clients, plastic wrap stretched tight. There was the smell of fruit beginning to rot; a fly searched frantically for an exit. One of those big horseshoes had flowers on it and a card with a bow. I caught the word *forever* scrawled in red ink.

"The turbine," Dad said. "A lot of folks are blaming it for the kind of ailments that could land a person here. Vestibular issues, migraines," he trailed off. "Violence, sex."

"Testimonials might work," I cut in.

"Right, you have to aim for triumph," Dad said.

A light tap on the door: A woman in baby blue scrubs stood in the doorway, not waiting to be admitted.

Le Forest waved her in. "Ethel, you know Rags. This is his daughter, Ace. She's helping with our ads. I thought you might show her around."

We shook hands. "Dr. Hooke." This was the name of a band that Grandma liked. She claimed to have slept with the guy.

"She's a genius with necks," Dad said.

"Your dad talks about you all the time," Ethel said. "Come on, I'll give you the grand tour."

"My dad?"

I was surprised that this made Ethel laugh. "Yeah, your dad, that handsome guy in there."

"How is he?" I asked.

"There's no need to worry about your dad. Soft tissue, probably. Touch of arthritis, maybe. I doubt there's any disc herniation."

Ethel was completely what she appeared to be. Upright like a sports trophy. "I love that man," she said.

"Dad?"

"Yeah, Rags, he never whines. Some clients, they're like babies, crying when you know they could suck it up and get on with it. He does his home care."

"Like what?"

"Don't you see him rotating his neck? He can do that anytime, at dinner, at work. He absolutely must keep moving. Sitting is the new smoking." She was steering me by the elbow. "Onward!"

We started in the waiting room, where clients pretended to read *Men's Health* and *Eden Foods*, too nervous to concentrate. The ones with crutches looked like young jocks. A senior citizen wore a big boot. A kid stood soldier-straight while his mother smoothed his spine with her hand. The staff behind the counter was courteous, using *Mr.* and *Ms.*

"We're fully automated," Ethel was saying. "Digital records that can network with any doctor, any hospital, any insurance company." We could hear a staff person on the phone. "With the full expectation of privacy."

"Cool."

"And we guarantee, no one waits more than ten minutes to be seen."

On the walls were the obligatory harbor scenes, a comic lobster with a cast on its claw, the usual Matisse print, framed pictures of sports teams.

"Tell me about you," I said.

Ethel Hooke was tall and thin. She'd played varsity volleyball at Springfield and come *this close* to being a Phys Ed teacher. "Too dead-end," she said. "Only a handful of women become elite coaches, and that's where you want to be. Olympics or Division A."

It was like listening to Emily Langmore talk about integers.

"And you?" she asked.

"I grew up in Horton. Horton High. I have a brother."

I was embarrassed at how candy-ass my backstory was. Our rickety little ship had made such a big dent in history that we could all sit on our behinds with our threadbare oriental carpets and tarnished andirons, scorning ostentation, suffocating like bugs in a jar.

"I enjoy the pep squad," I heard myself say.

"That is so important," Ethel said. "Fan support. It can mean the difference between winning and losing."

Ethel Hooke was a winner.

"I wasn't involved in anything formal," I amended. "Just a general appreciation for our sports teams."

The exercise area was equipped like a gym, with miniature stuff for kids. It was sad to see them gravely trying to fix the premature conditions that had hobbled their little bodies. "Physical anomalies in children are often thought to be caused by stress at home," Ethel whispered.

"I like kids." It occurred to me that I could add this to my pathetic CV.

"Lee told me about how much the twins love you and your brother."

Ethel was everything you'd expect from a volleyball player/physical therapist. She had perfect posture. Her hair was short in a practical cut. It shone in the sun. She wore no jewelry except for a Fitbit. Her cross-trainers looked brand-new.

She was also the opposite of Mrs. Forest, younger with no flamboyant curves. Tiny facial scars might have been from chicken pox, or, more poignantly, acne. She didn't try to hide them with makeup. Being a star athlete, she didn't have to.

Hand on my elbow, she guided me down the hallway like I was a blind person. On either side were treatment rooms, their doors ajar. You could see a leg raised at an impossible angle; a person with her head facedown, massage-style; scented steam floated under a door. Dad and Lee were working on his neck. I waved, but they didn't see me.

We took this opportunity to return to Le Forest's office.

On the credenza behind his desk was a framed photo of Le Forest receiving an award, Mrs. Forest at his side. I picked it up. Mrs. Forest looked as if she'd chosen "beaming" from a selection of smiles.

"Dr. Forest has received numerous accolades," Ethel was saying.

"Citations." I scanned the resolutions from the Commonwealth of Massachusetts. "Diplomas."

"Awards," Ethel said.

"And Mrs. Forest?" I asked.

"Suzie?"

"Mrs. Forest."

The tiny craters on Ethel's cheeks were white against her reddening skin. "Suzie is a standout individual."

"In what way?" I said.

"Member of the Chamber? Teacher's aide? School volunteer, maybe?"

"A good businesswoman?" I said.

"That, and mother," Ethel said.

I angled the photo away from the glare of artificial light, and the real light slicing through a high, narrow window. "She's beautiful."

Ethel returned the photo to its home behind Le Forest's desk. "Yes, she is beautiful." She pulled a business card from her pocket. "Call, text, or email if you have any questions at all, anything that could help with your advertisements."

18

Wind in the willows
By Chuck Butten
Frigate staff writer

At Town Hall on Wednesday night, Clam Warden Peregrine White claimed that the turbine's location off Bulrush Road near the transfer station was a "safe distance from residential areas." This comment caused Opposition Wind forces to regroup.

Though there were no blind, deaf, or physically disabled kids at Ocean Charter, the place was set up for a special-needs tsunami: low railings, tennis balls on the doorknobs, spongy, concussion-proof compounds. The school had a registered play therapist. The playground outside had the same safeguards as the sensory one inside. Soon dogwood petals would float over it, with kids yelling, "Pink snow!" The blossoms were pungent, like a sickbed bouquet.

People in this part of the world longed for spring and fantasized about it even when snow still sugar-crusted the streets. We were joyous when ice started weeping from the eaves.

Mrs. Forest would be dropping off the twins soon; they'd be piling out of the Vulva, ready for their numbers class with Ms. Emily.

I was here because I knew she would be and wanted to experience her like a normal person, like a guy, drunk on summer skirts, jacket hooked on one finger, tie blowing over one shoulder, glancing sideways like men do before ducking into cars, worshipping her from across the street.

But before I saw her, I saw Emily Langmore. She was far enough from the red and yellow cinderblock wall of Ocean Charter to be pestling a cigarette into the well-kept lawn.

"Hi," I said.

She was startled. "Hi."

"Long time no see," I said.

"Where's Sawyer?"

Clearly, he was her comfort zone. Ms. Long Division eyeballed me, as if the much taller Sawyer might be hiding, or attached to me—apparently how she viewed the Sawyer/Ace coordinate.

"At Fabia's."

"The geometry seems off," Emily said, trying a joke. "We were always together, the three of us."

I had a moment of empathy, hearing the pained nostalgia coming from this waif of a genius, color rising from her neck like a tide.

"Three points of a triangle?" I recalled the surprising down on her spindly arm. I stroked it to soften the blow.

She nodded. Had I suddenly learned math?

I didn't need to see her to know she was here, in my space, like an aroma.

"Emily, you can go," Mrs. Forest said, with an authority I'd never heard before. Emily watched Mrs. Forest pull me toward her as if I'd suddenly stepped into traffic.

Mrs. Forest glanced over her shoulder at Emily, who was immobilized like Lot's wife, except for the slight lifting of her flowered dress. She was jumping the gun with the dress, though a quilted vest took up the slack. An offshore breeze blew a strand of hair across her cheek, diagonal.

"Swipe left," Mrs. Forest muttered to Emily.

"You're jealous." I was elated. It was like she'd yelled, "I love you!" in a crowded theater.

Mrs. Forest turned to Emily. "Not a triangle," she said, emphatic. "Parallel lines."

Emily headed to the building to teach toddlers how to count, shooting us a puzzled look.

"Parallel lines," Mrs. Forest explained to me. "They don't intersect—ever."

I almost fainted in admiration.

19

I sat cross-legged on the hard foam-rubber mattress, which was covered with a blue-and-white striped fabric. Mrs. Forest had made the little room in the back of her shop into a space for "meetups." There was already a minibar and a microwave, and she'd had Sport Rodgers build a bunk like they have in ships. She'd gone down to Pier 1 for the cushions. For all its permanence, it was really a way to enshrine something that Mrs. Forest herself said could never last.

The tiny room had a nautical motif. It just needed portlights to make it perfect. Port*light* was the proper word, not port*hole*, according to *Caswell's Maritime Handbook*. Mrs. Forest had grabbed one of the seascapes from the shop and hung it on the wall. The cabinet over the sink was filled with the balms and botanicals Mrs. Forest loved.

I could live in here. Which is what I apparently told Mrs. Forest.

"I made it for you, Ace." It seemed like she wanted to build barricades against Long Division.

But I had barricades of my own. "*Dr.* Forest says he comes in here for lunch a lot."

"*Doctor*? I know you're joking, but this 'Dr., Mrs.' crap? I used to think it was charming or eccentric, but now I just see it as a barrier."

"To what?"

"A linguistic barrier that you and your brother use to protect yourselves."

The opposite seemed true with my brother lately—not linguistic, physical. Like men in bar brawls, who wanted to get close.

"At Fabia's, the women commiserate, and they treat your brother like he's Justin Bieber or something. I think it goes to his head sometimes."

But Sawyer was like an X-ray; I could see right through to his bleeding heart.

I picked up Mrs. Forest's foot and held it in my palm. It was petite, puffed like a little bread loaf. "He obviously picks your polish. This, whatever it is, has got your name written all over it."

"Coral Sunrise."

"I don't know how he can look at the entire wall of polishes and pick the right one for every client. The wall, it looks like a Chuck Close painting."

Mrs. Forest Googled him on her smartphone.

Bill called Mrs. Forest *uninformed*, like this would be some kind of deal-breaker for me. But this ad hoc Googling made me love her more. She wasn't unconscious in that way of Whore High kids, Wikipedia fiends, airheads who didn't drill down, using *journal* as a verb and sliding through life on their asses like penguins.

"You tell me you and Le Forest are not together anymore for all 'intensive' purposes, and then I discover he's over here every other minute ordering in from Uncle Asia's, or whatever. You could at least go to a restaurant, a public place."

"*Le Forest* is the father of my children."

"God, I hate that phrase. It's, it's so, so, I can't put my finger on it, pompous in a funny kind of way, like it takes any kind of brains whatsoever to become a father. You can go to a sperm bank. Fuck yourself. That's not creation. That's recreation. Not to mention . . . Dr. Hooke?"

"Ethel?"

"Have you met her?" I said.

"I've seen her at the clinic."

"Then you know."

"Know what?"

"You need to worry about losing the father of your children." I was testing her; what would she say? "I've met Ethel. She's not like the rest of us. She's a normal person."

"Are you attracted to her?"

"She's not good-looking in the usual way. She's like a person who grows on you, not like one you get tired of and throw in the trash."

"Sounds like you're quite taken with her."

"She's sleeping with your husband. Dr. Forest and Dr. Hooke. Hunting and fishing." If our relationship was so fucked up, maybe I should make her leave me, get it over with.

"I don't sleep with Lee."

"You're in the same bed?"

Mrs. Forest nodded.

"Then that's sleeping with him. You do that with my mother, too. Do you know how intimate that is? You're sleeping all over Whore Town—except with me!"

"Ace." She removed her feet from my lap and pulled my head into hers, combing my hair with her fingers. "You're the smartest person I know. And you can't see how complicated this is?"

"Love is not complicated." This wasn't true, obviously. It was just something that people repeat, like it's a line in a movie.

"It is, Ace. You, of all people, must know that."

" 'Of all people'?"

"Your brother?" Mrs. Forest lifted my head. "Can we even talk about your brother?"

Sawyer was like an appendage I was born with.

"I thought so," Mrs. Forest said. "My dear girl."

"Why can't he just *be* with us?"

91

"He's a part of you. What about me?"

It was like she wanted to take scissors to a photo booth picture. "*You're* part of me," I said.

"I know you're not this innocent virgin. That jock at school you told me about—and Emily, and God knows who else. But you're putting me so high you can't reach me, like you'll be safer if you can't. I'm a living, breathing woman, Ace. I have needs."

My tears were like draft spilling over the side of a beer mug. "I thought you wanted to wait."

"It's not so simple." Mrs. Forest used the sleeve of her shirt to dry my cheeks. "With Lee, with others, after a while it was just sex. With you, it would be life. And there's not only your family and mine but the world out there."

"My family doesn't give a shit, and I don't give a shit about the world . . . out there."

"Ace. If you want me too, anything is possible. But I need you to do one thing for me."

"What?"

She held my face roughly with both hands. Her voice came from deep down. "I need you to say my name."

I thought we'd had a meeting of the minds, that she understood that the whole experience of her would disappear if I said her name, like a balloon lifting away from me, silent and on its way somewhere.

20

Bill and Mrs. Forest were in the kitchen again, about to spill their guts out. Sawyer and I were on the stairs, this time passing a flask of Arizona Herbal and sharing a bag of pistachios.

Silvio's antipasto sent its oily, olivey aroma up the stairs. The mood was not somber but hesitant, not exactly tense but almost. Bill sipped her usual Merlot—from a glass. The bottle was still on the counter, like it, too, was a spectator.

Mrs. Forest was drinking beer, my beer. She'd brought a six-pack of Narragansetts, which she left warming on the counter. She waved off the tankard Bill offered her.

"Honey," Mrs. Forest started in. "Bill," she revised, taking a slug. The can, the slug, all of it incongruous with the usual Mrs. Forest stuff: fashion glasses, plunging V-neck, tight skirt, ballet slippers.

Bill waited, making it harder than a friend usually would.

"Cut to the chase," Sawyer breathed, arranging his pistachio shells on the step above. They were in a row like ants on the march. I did the same on the step below.

"I know we need to talk about this," Mrs. Forest said.

"Yes, we do." Bill opened Mrs. Forest's bursting satchel, removing a compact, eyeliner, keys, and an Occupy Wind flyer before finding what she wanted. She lit a Camel with a kitchen match, took a long toke, and handed it to Mrs. Forest. You could tell Bill wasn't used to smoking real cigarettes.

Mrs. Forest exhaled deeply. Smoke ribboned above their heads and knotted under the stove hood. She grabbed a saucer from the cabinet and placed it between them, lightly tapping her ash into it.

"I don't know how it started, exactly," Mrs. Forest said.

Our parents had first met the Forests at a community lobster bake on the beach at twilight. The primal mix of salt and seaweed and ancient creatures hidden miles below the surface attracted and repelled.

One lobster that would never find its way onto a bed of hot stones and seaweed was a 44-pounder, about the size of a little person. He kept surfacing, revealing his brown, barnacled shell. Kids named him Santa Claws. He could often be spotted outside the Bowsprit where diners threw salad and fish into the water. He was also known to eat worms, mollusks, and his own kind.

The Forests and the Ragsdales hadn't just "hit it off." They were infatuated. Bill was bewitched by a woman who would wear sequined slippers, a diamond necklace, and a black cocktail dress to the beach. The dress was one of those numbers where you pull a sash and it slips away, revealing a basic black bathing suit, ill-equipped to contain her.

Our ocean was frigid even in late summer. When Mrs. Forest emerged, her nipples were *en garde*. Bill smelled something commercial coming from her skin.

"My daughter can be quite the enchantress," Bill was saying now.

"Yes, she can be . . ." Mrs. Forest held the can with her thumb and index finger like it was hot to the touch. "I was always vaguely aware of her as part of your family, the kids. And then she was suddenly this grown woman pursuing me, and she gradually became something else to me."

Sawyer and I leaned into their every word. Hearing people you really care about dishing you like you weren't there: Our faces felt singed, like the skin might peel off. Our hearts were outside, like in the Poe story. We were holding our breath, tight-lipped.

The record for holding your breath is twenty-two minutes; we were pushing the limit. The unfamiliar ginseng was earthy, sweet and bitter at the same time.

"She's still a kid." Bill paused to reload. "In some ways. In others not."

"Yes. In others not." Mrs. Forest took a napkin from the stack that came from Silvio's, folding it to her lips.

"She's still *becoming*, by the way. She's not done yet. Marinating." Bill handed the cigarette to Mrs. Forest. "She can be a real know-it-all. It masks her sensitivities."

"I know that," Mrs. Forest said.

"We all have sensitivities," Bill said.

"I know. I was abandoned, too, don't forget."

"Lucky you. He's not exactly God's gift."

"I hate that you and Ace don't respect my choices."

"And now you *have* God's gift?"

Mrs. Forest fussed her sequined slipper against Bill's leg. "It just happened, and now, I don't know, it seems too late."

"Ace doesn't have enough experience to survive being bruised as badly as you could bruise her." Bill abandoned her wineglass as if it was too fragile to hold. "Love is brutal, Suzie, as you well know."

"Not all love. You and Rags?"

Bill spit an olive pit into the ashtray. "Rags is more like an FWB."

"Is he good?"

"He always gets the job done. He's considerate."

"He gave you beautiful babies," Mrs. Forest said.

"My 'babies' are under your spell."

"Sawyer treats me like any other woman at Fabia's," Mrs. Forest said.

Sawyer silently regurgitated his Arizona Herbal into his French cuff.

"It's Ace he worries about."

"That makes two of us," Bill said.

"What do you want me to do?" Mrs. Forest tossed her can into the recycling: *swish*. Perfect basket. "Do you want me to give her up?"

"Yes, and why not give up all the Ragsdales while you're at it: Rags, bullshitting in the shop? Sawyer and his fucking foot-fucking? Throw in the twins for good measure, dump them at a church with notes pinned to their shirts."

"Bill, sweetheart, I'm so sorry . . . honey." Mrs. Forest extended her spangled hand.

Bill gazed at it as if it were an object she had to make a decision about. "There's enough abandonment to go around, *Mrs. Forest.*"

"Do you want to forbid her from seeing me?"

"Sure, then you and I can play tennis all day and start a book club." Bill slipped a greasy roasted tomato into Mrs. Forest's mouth. "I can't—forbid her. She's an adult . . . almost."

Mrs. Forest offered Mom a beer.

Mom shook her head. "If you were having an affair with some guy, some grown man, let's say some customer from the shop, you'd be talking to me about it day in and day out. But now, because it's . . ."

"You're right. It didn't seem kosher to talk about it with you." Mrs. Forest lit another Camel and handed it to Bill without taking a toke. "What if it was Lee instead of me, an older guy, having an affair with your kid, would you be as mamma bear?"

"Worse. She'd want to have his babies, which would repel me."

"I had his kids."

"Different, and by the way, I'm not the only one with beautiful kids." Bill raised the unopened can to her friend.

"Thank God I didn't dump them at Star of the Sea."

"It would have been super easy with the new drive-thru." Bill leaned over and adjusted Mrs. Forest's scarf. "Sorry. Honey. Really, I'm sorry." Bill blew smoke out of the side of her mouth.

"Do you want her hand in marriage?" She laughed, a real laugh.

"We're going to be okay," Mrs. Forest said. "All of us."

"But you have to be careful."

"Of?"

"Teenagers can be thoughtless," Bill said. "They're like amoebas, bumping into things and moving on. Or dangerous like those drops of mercury from thermometers we used to play with, connecting to other drops, merging."

"Merging doesn't sound so bad," Mrs. Forest said.

"Well, it's obvious you've merged with her. *Beer*? You never drank beer before."

"When I taste beer, it's like tasting her."

"Susan!" Bill crossed her index fingers in front of Mrs. Forest's face. "Christ, Suzie, Jesus."

All the *God* words.

"Okay, what else do you love about my daughter?"

"Maybe you don't need to know that, either," Mrs. Forest said.

"If it was someone else, you'd tell me."

"True." Mrs. Forest took the Camel Bill was offering. "She's unpredictable. Not like guys, where you know their every move before they even make a move."

"My daughter is not the opposite of guys," Bill said. "She's unique, a person unto herself."

"Every day is a surprise with her. I like waking up, knowing that my day will be exciting. Different. Alive."

"Protect yourself, Suzie." Bill tried to embrace Mrs. Forest while abandoning the untouched can and reaching for the cigarette.

Our pistachio shells set off a tiny avalanche down the stairs. They sounded like the start of rain.

21

Rags had never had a guy friend like Le Forest, athletic and unafraid of physical contact. No disease freaked Le Forest out.

He'd tried to turn Dad on to tennis or basketball. But as their friendship developed, Dad was more of an influence on Le Forest, taking him to Club YES and showing him some wrestling moves. Le Forest had naturally bought the official "singlet" that made him look like he was on his way to an orgy.

For Dad, wrestling gear was no more provocative than socks.

Now Dad announced that it was no longer "socially acceptable" to cut off such an old friend.

He had invited Le Forest and Ethel for dinner on Catboat. Bill felt we were being disloyal, but she went along with it.

Tonight Mrs. Forest would be alone with Brett and Levi on Mill Wheel Lane.

Why not cocktails instead? Sawyer suggested. Mrs. Forest and the boys could come for dinner afterward.

I helped him rearrange the furniture.

Grandma was present and accounted for. Since she'd been living in Horton, her vertigo had gotten worse, and she'd become wary of anything artisanal, such as craft beers, where you didn't know "what the bloody hell you were getting." She'd taken up

Snapchat and LARPing, and was addicted to clickbait.

Le Forest usually just rapped on the kitchen window, but this time he rang the front doorbell with its five-tone theme from *Close Encounters of the Third Kind.*

"Love that doorbell!" Grandma yelled. She was the one who'd turned Dad on to the old movie. She muttered it a second time. There were pauses in her conversation while she hauled her jerry-rigged sentences to the surface. She never liked to fill empty spaces with nonwords like *umm* or the ubiquitous *like.*

Le Forest cradled a bottle of red in one arm and clutched a bouquet of flowers. Ethel was armed with a Tupperware container.

"Dr. Hooke." I'd rehearsed calling her Ethel, but *Dr.* slipped out because she was dressed in plum-colored scrubs. She wore a turtleneck underneath and a gray cardigan on top.

She extended her hand. "What a lovely home."

It wasn't my home, so I turned to Bill. "You never stop working on a house," she said, accepting Ethel's container. "As you may know."

This was ridiculous; Bill and Rags were extra cheap when it came to repairs, unless the ceiling was actually falling on the dining room table.

"We did some rearranging," Sawyer said with a sweep of his arm, as if demonstrating appliances. Now the couch was to the side of the fireplace instead of in front of it, which was inexplicably important to him.

"Sawyer," Ethel said. It was obvious there'd been some foot action down at Fabia's.

Then again, if your feet hadn't been cushioned in Sawyer's palms, you probably didn't have feet.

Sawyer took her hand in both of his.

"Sorry about the scrubs," Le Forest said, handing the wine to Rags and the flowers to Sawyer.

He wore skinny jeans, pointy loafers, a black muscle shirt, and a sport coat.

"I'm so sorry," Ethel said. "I had a late client and didn't have time to change."

"Excellent color choices," Sawyer said, "and I love the clogs."

"You look classy," Grandma said. Secure pockets were Grandma's signature. Her ramshackle ensembles featured hoodies and workout jackets with zippered pockets, and cargo pants with buttoned pockets. Inside the pockets were the usual stuff: keys, wallet, and cell phone, and then other necessities like tissues, mints, matches, dental floss, teaser comb, and tools such as tiny screwdrivers and a hammer hanging from a loop. She was ready for a date or a maintenance gig. "Did I already tell you that you're a classy broad?"

"This is our grandmother!" I said too loudly. Sawyer and I were proud to have a relative.

Ethel nearly curtsied in Grandma's direction. "Delighted." But she still looked like she wanted to exit the front door and reenter wearing different clothes.

I waited for Dad to say something to Le Forest, like *What the hell, man?* He didn't, so I said, "Dr. Forest, I think Ethel looks really nice."

"Scrubs are the new little black dress," Sawyer confirmed.

"Sawyer should know," Dad, said, buttoning his jacket over his little paunch. He and Sawyer were dressed like they were having a cigar and brandy at a men's club. They were a blur of tweed and leather patches and tassels. They smelled like centuries of smoke. Sawyer had nudged Dad toward the masculine. No scrunched ribbons or pumps.

"Sawyer is a fashionista," Dad said, the word new and hesitant, bobbing in Le Forest's direction. Dad couldn't hide his pride, like he was waiting for Sawyer to have the same belief in his destiny as his own father did—however alien and unknown.

Le Forest persevered. "I like to separate business and pleasure."

"Maybe Ethel doesn't have time to separate business and pleasure," Bill said. "And," dramatic pause, "she still found time to make something for us." She carried Ethel's container to the kitchen as if it were a ring on a pillow.

"It's nothing," Ethel said, her clogs making more noise on the tile floor than she probably would have liked.

"I'm going to put it on our favorite plate," Bill said, as if we had one.

Sawyer rushed to the kitchen, reaching over Bill's head and pulling down the cream-colored platter that Grandma claimed had real gold around the edge.

"Not that one," Le Forest said, peering over the bar. "It's a little classy for cheese dip."

"That's just gold whatchamacallit, buddy," Grandma said. "Gold-plated."

Never mind that she'd told us numerous times that it was the real thing, with real karats.

"I agree with Lee," Ethel said. "It's just a simple dip. Don't you have any Corelle?"

"No, most of our plates were salvaged from the *Speedwell*," Sawyer said.

Ethel was "not from around here."

"You do know the story?" This was Rags, who rarely wore his history-major hat.

"Don't talk down to her," I said.

"Who doesn't," Ethel said, with unexpected sarcasm. I thought she meant, "Who doesn't talk down to her?" until she added, "The boat was too leaky for the voyage, so they had to *settle* for the *Mayflower*."

"Which has more caché? *Speedwell* or *Mayflower*?" Sawyer was already putting the dip in the middle of the plate with the celery sticks lined up like little caskets. I stuck my index finger in the dip.

"All those idiots who say they're descended from the *Mayflower*?" Sawyer said. "What if it was the *Speedwell*?"

"Speedos," Ethel said mistily, which made Sawyer laugh.

"This is delicious." Grandma licked the dip off my finger. "What's in it?"

"Secret recipe," Le Forest said.

"Mayo, catsup, onion, and cream cheese," Ethel said. "That's my big secret."

Ethel pronounced *catsup* the correct way.

Sawyer had positioned the couch and chairs to comfortably fit seven adults around the coffee table, which also held Bill's Trader Joe's *hors d'oeuvres* and the white tulips Le Forest had brought.

I wondered if Le Forest could redeem himself with tulips. The stiff leaves rustled against one another. There was nothing in our color-challenged living room that could clash with them. They arched over the too-short vase like weeping willows, bussing the table, now blemished with salsa and circles of liquid.

Shopping was a loaded word for our Gen X parents. Read: *sex*. One time, after what was apparently very satisfying sex, they'd had a shopping orgy at Building 19 and came back with multipack paper products, giant boxes of cereal with handles, big plastic clips to keep your potato chip bags tightly sealed, and things we would never need, like electronic sandwich-makers, cake decorators, and a dartboard.

They'd apparently had sex this afternoon.

Sawyer poured drinks with a white linen dishtowel folded over his arm.

"Gretchen, I hear you're here to save the turbine," Lee started in.

"Buncha reactionaries. Next thing you know we're going back to coal hods."

"Well, you're doing Medical Arts a big favor," Le Forest said.

"How's that?"

"They're getting a lot of patients down there complaining of turbine-related conditions," I said.

"How can sick people be a good thing?" Grandma asked.

"The health of our medical institutions depends on it," Le Forest said. "Thank God, there will always be new diseases."

Grandma pulled a pipe from one of her pockets and knocked the bowl against the table. "Did you leave your ethics at the door?"

"Sanctimony, Mom," Rags warned. Tonight, a stiff neck kept

him from addressing people head-on.

"Trust me, I love your beloved windmill too," Le Forest said, "but you don't really think that one stupid turbine is going to stop climate change, do you?"

"You don't think that one stupid windmill is going to keep you guys in business, do you?" Grandma turned to her grandchildren. "Must be hard to create an ad campaign around this stuff."

I observed my brother, who was in servant mode. If he could prostrate himself in front of someone, he would. He'd lit a late season fire.

"Ethel is a star athlete," I said, attempting to paper over the scrubs fiasco.

She seemed to respond well to flattery. "Taking up a sport under the guidance of a knowledgeable coach can solve a lot of psychological problems," she said.

"Ace and I want to participate in athletics," Sawyer said.

"Your dad and I approached Amy Allerton about getting you guys on the archery team, remember?" Mom said.

Amy wore men's wingtips with a "steel shank." She believed that a strong body started with a good foundation, like a plinth or a launching pad.

"We were not qualified to be handling arrows." Sawyer looked meaningfully at me.

"I nearly killed some people over at Colonial Condos," I said.

"Massasoit's bow was carved and had turkey feathers on it," Sawyer said. He'd seen a replica on manyhoops.com.

"Your bow and arrows are in the garage, with all the other sports equipment we never use." Dad turned to Ethel. "Feel free to pick through it if you think your pediatric clients could use it."

Ethel thanked him with her hands in prayer.

Eventually the coffee table was a disaster area of empty containers, plates scraped clean, dollops, and crumbs. Crack was staggering under the table, farting and belching. Having dinner after hors d'oeuvres was starting to seem like the worst idea ever.

I seemed to be the only one worried about Mrs. Forest bursting through the door. Ethel was sprawled on the kilim. Mom and Le Forest were dancing to "Shake It Off." Grandma was repeating, "You bet," and lighting a bowl. Sawyer was laid out next to Ethel on the carpet.

Dad and I were the most clearheaded. "What should we do?" It was comforting to be asking my own father for advice. "Mrs. Forest will be here any minute."

"Coffee and chocolate," Dad said. "Text the Eatons."

It was one of those stop-action freeze frames: the delivery girl from Riparian Roasters (RIP, Ground Rounds) rang the bell at the exact moment that Mrs. Forest and the twins let themselves in the back door.

Nothing is more isolating than not being wasted like everyone else. Mrs. Forest stood sober and exposed. Her jacket, skirt, and pantyhose; the brand-new ankle boots; the accent scarf and noisy bangles: they reminded me of 9/11 images.

People had dressed as if it were a normal Tuesday. They didn't wonder, *Is this the right man suit for jumping out a 100-story window? Will this look smart covered with ash?*

I put my arm around Mrs. Forest's waist as if she were grieving instead of humiliated. "I'm so sorry, baby."

Brett and Levi rushed over to Sawyer and me, their bright colors like lobster buoys. The coffee girl turned out to be Madison O'Malley, of all people, with her squinty archery eyes. I immediately pictured the tail of an octopus tattoo circling her areolae and the vestigial fur just above her butt.

Dad pulled a silver money clip from the front pocket of his 1940s suit pants, either a gift from Grandma or a Castaway find. He peeled off a wad of bills and handed them to Maddie. "If you could just be our, our . . ." He stopped, not wanting to cast her as a waiter. Horton's class divide was so wide, no one could claw their way out.

"Assistant," I offered.

Had she been a person of color, Dad never would have asked, but because she was white and had a Boston accent, peppering her speech with the word *plethora*, new clothes from the mall, crooked teeth, turquoise eye makeup and a slightly rough, protective carapace, he forged ahead.

Mortified, Sawyer invited Maddie to join us. She pocketed the money, took the box of coffee into the kitchen, laid out the milk and sugar, and poured coffee into cardboard cups. She arranged the biscotti on the *Speedwell* plate, which she'd rinsed in the sink, then yelled, "Come and get it!" like she was the cook on a chuck wagon.

"You shit!" Mrs. Forest said to her husband. Her verbal assaults were soon accompanied by skillfully pitched objects. If she'd hit us with the cast-iron Buddha Grandma was trying to palm off on us, someone could have gotten killed.

Mrs. Forest didn't have it in her to kill; her anger was on hold like an orgasm waiting to explode.

Maddie had cleared the coffee table and brought in the coffee and biscotti. She'd filled the dishwasher and was now collecting the items that Mrs. Forest had hurled around the room.

"This is cool," she said, replacing the Buddha on the mantel.

"Take it!" Grandma spoke for all of us.

Ethel was skilled at dodging missiles; at one point she grabbed an airborne table lamp. "This is so not me," she said. "I've only had relationships with team members. Certainly not with someone else's spouse."

"Must be the turbine," Le Forest said.

"I'm leaving." Ethel grabbed her cardigan. Bill got up to retrieve Ethel's Tupperware.

"You're not leaving," Mrs. Forest said. "You are not to blame. You're just a weak person."

"Like the rest of us," Dad muttered.

"Suzie, please sit," Bill said.

Sawyer again reorganized the furniture, making room for Mrs. Forest. Brett and Levi sat cross-legged on the rug, drinking coffee from miniscule plastic cups.

"You don't have any toys?" Maddie returned from the kitchen with a colander and some chopsticks. The twins seemed pleased with the makeshift plaything.

Mrs. Forest refused to sit. "As I recall, we were invited for *dinner?*"

Sawyer filled a hefty brandy snifter to the rim and handed it to her. She took a gulp—no swirling it around in the glass.

"Suzie, we obviously don't have dinner." Bill knew enough not to touch Mrs. Forest, indicating the sofa with her eyes.

"I don't think these children should be drinking coffee," Maddie said.

"I'll fix them a smoothie," Sawyer said.

Maddie followed him to the kitchen. Like married foodies, they got out the blender, throwing in powdered Gatorade, milk, honey, and sodium-free kale chips.

"Bill, I didn't expect this from you." Mrs. Forest finally sank into the sofa. She appeared small and beaten-down. Her eyes took in Sawyer and Maddie with their domestic dry-humping.

"I'm so sorry," Bill said.

"Me too," I said.

Mrs. Forest fixed her attention on me, finally.

I led her up the back stairs to my room. My laptop, clothes, earphones, and even shoes were on the bed; I hadn't had a chance to put stuff away. Things hanging out revealed more than any pathetic revelations I might say out loud: my copy of the photo Dad had in his office, Sawyer and me leaning against the fence near the seawall.

Mrs. Forest wandered toward it, caressing it with two fingers.

You never knew what it smelled like in your own den, probably old sneakers and old pot smoke, not-too-clean sheets. I didn't possess any of the lotions that Mrs. Forest loved. The only smell beyond my own, whatever that might be, was hair gel, worming slowly out of the open tube onto the dresser, which was covered with flash drives and cables.

The shades were wide open, letting in the way bright light from the porch across the street. The only illumination inside was my *Dora the Explorer* nightlight.

I swept everything off the bed and pulled Mrs. Forest onto

it, kissing her and ripping the buttons off her shirt.

"Ace, I know I said I want this, and I do, but not tonight." She lightly moved me away. "What happened down there took everything out of me." She removed her shoes. "Tonight I want to give you what *you* want." She turned down the bedspread. "I am so tired, darling." We faced each other, so close I got the delicious high of brandy on her breath. "I want to sleep with you." She pulled me to her. "The whole night, side by side." She cupped my handful of breasts. "*Sleep* sleep."

Just as we fell asleep, she whispered "pistachios" in my ear. "You need a quieter snack, darling."

But we didn't make it 'til morning. We didn't make it to the next ten minutes. Le Forest was silhouetted in the doorway, his shadow stretched menacingly against the wall.

22

I had been saving her; Mrs. Forest was right. I was afraid of devouring her. If you devour something, it's gone, and I couldn't imagine life without her. Now, I wanted her. I played out the scene in my head, how I would show my passion by tearing off her clothes—in a respectful way, of course. I was turning myself on just thinking about it: the way her breasts released, as if they were glad to be free, her coifed patch, wet through.

I entered the shop, flipping the sign on the door from "open" to "closed." But she was buoyant, not seductive. She wanted to tell me about a new "marketing" idea.

She held both my hands, arms outstretched. "Darling." A 1940s screen idol.

"Salons!" She exhaled her *S*'s in a gauzy breath.

"Like the Steins?"

"Whatever. We have wine and cheese. They look at art, and talk about books . . . current events, wind farms."

"That might be a little incendiary."

"Okay, right, so we have point-of-purchase displays, accentuate the frames as well as the art. Offer specials." Again with the *S*'s. "Promotions. We get local stores to kick in the food and beverage."

"I like it."

"Don't patronize me."

"I do! I really do." I squeezed her hand. "It's time."

"Yes, it's time I—we—you and I, we need to start thinking about best practices."

"Cement our partnership."

"Oh, Ace, yes! We're in this together. I'll do the business part. You're the creative arm."

"Speaking of creative arms." I pulled her to me.

"Sweetie, I'm not done yet." She loosened my grip. "There's a reason we need to try new things, hold special events."

"Grow sales," I said. "We don't want you, us, to tank."

"Not just that." She grasped both my hands. "We have to ingratiate ourselves with the community."

"Wow, that's serious. Why?"

"People are talking. You know that."

This was the word *talk* in all its gory small-town majesty. Sawyer and I were used to it at Whore High, and Bill knew how to defend and deflect, marching confidently down the corridors, nodding to students and bringing doughnuts and hermits to the teachers' lounge, staying above petty infighting, and pitching in with PTO and union activities. All this, despite the fact that her own children were the worst students ever.

She was grateful that we weren't sociopaths.

But Mrs. Forest seemed unprepared. "Yeah, people talk," I said. "So what?"

"They talk like I am at fault. Like, what is this older woman doing with this teenager?"

"Good question. What are you doing?"

"Don't start, please. You're ruining my good mood."

"I don't want to wait anymore. You're the one who said I was saving you. I don't want to save you. I want to have you. Now. I'm starving for you."

"Baby, please. You're being a drama queen."

I grabbed her by the collar and pulled her to me, kissing her closed lips, forcing her with my tongue. She tried to pull away.

I tied her scarf tight around her neck. Struggling for breath, her eyes went wide. I took in their sea blue.

I tried to see outside myself, be in two places at once. If I saw myself as another person, maybe I could stop tightening the knot of her scarf. But it was me, just me, hungering for her, like prey. I was stronger, but she was better coordinated. Nearly breathless, she grabbed a frame; its sharp edge grazed my face. I finally released her and dropped to my knees, breaking the zipper of her pants. She pushed me so hard I fell against something solid. I struggled to my knees and wrapped my arms around her body, trying to love the life out of her.

I finally let go. Through one swollen eye, I glimpsed her leaning against the wall, then sliding down it, sitting on the floor, head on knees, arms crossed, my blood on her torn shirt, one bra strap slipping off her shoulder.

Blood ran down my cheek and into my mouth. Delicious, because she'd caused it.

23

The atmosphere in the Catboat kitchen was grim and subdued as I delivered a toneless version of events. I'd decided to face the music with my family so Mrs. Forest wouldn't have to face it with hers, with custody of her children hanging in the balance. For me, there would be no I-ran-into-a-door excuse. Lying could not contain it.

We sat on chairs in the kitchen, not on stools bellying up to the bar but like we were setting up for a home movie. Sawyer held a raw steak to my eye, the artisanal remedy, handed down from our ancestors. The smell of the bloody slab made me retch. Dad quickly grabbed it and threw it into a frying pan, "for later."

Mrs. Forest had no cuts, at least, no bruises or broken bones she would have to explain to her spouse. (*No biggie, just a violent altercation with my teen crush.*)

It was the unseen psychic pain that would kill you. Women rejected the crime-of-passion defense because it was a crime of power. You paid for your crime with a loss of your own life. I'd already lost mine, because I'd squeezed the breath out of her.

She *was* breath.

My family didn't want to judge; I watched their contortions from on high. "Who among you," as Jesus would say.

"I punched someone once," Sawyer waded in.

As far as I knew, my brother didn't even know *how* to punch. Maybe guys punched in the same antediluvian way they protected their balls. He hadn't punched me in our little battle, which we kept silent between us. That hadn't been about hurting but about holding on.

So was this.

Bill came to life. She'd been somewhere else—she was as fearful for her friend, I knew, as she was for me. "Sawyer, who did you punch?"

"A professor at school," Sawyer said.

"Jeez, Sawyer!" Now Dad was fully engaged. "What the hell happened?"

"It was a mistake."

Grandma had pulled a rocking chair into the kitchen to prepare for the long haul. "I've heard that one before."

"Well, she . . ." Sawyer said.

"*She?*" Dad said.

"Our performing arts teacher," Sawyer said. "She's really big. She used to wrestle in the WWF. You guys of course know that professional wrestling is all about performance."

"Yeah, we know, Sawyer, don't change the subject," Dad said.

"She was showing us how to stage fight scenes. She threw a punch at this guy, who ducked, so the punch landed on me, and instinctively I punched her back."

"Not your fault," Grandma said. "That was the testosterone kicking in."

"Well, maybe I punched her again," Sawyer said. "It's like a shark getting a taste for blood."

"Christ, what a shitty school," Bill said. "Even at Whore High, you can't beat up staff and still attend class."

"I was acquitted of all charges, but I had to do a week of anger management and community service."

"Which consisted of what, exactly?" Bill said.

"Tutoring Photo Shop, InDesign. No-brainer."

The package of frozen peas Dad had applied to my eye was

beginning to thaw. He grabbed it and put it in a colander. "For later," he said, returning with a package of frozen fishcakes. It smelled like it had been freezer-burning for millennia. He inspected the cut on my cheek. "I don't think it will leave a scar."

"I was hoping for a scar," I said.

"So you can sashay around luxuriating and basking in your own martyrdom and suffering?" This barrage of poetry came from Bill.

"It's too easy," she went on. "Is anyone thinking about Suzie over on Mill Wheel alone with a husband who doesn't give a shit and babies who don't know shit from Shinola?"

"I am," I said.

"Maybe you should have thought about her before you got into a physical brawl that redounded all its glorious bounty to you. What happened to your vaunted verbal skills?" Bill took in her rapt audience. "Does this family need a talk about the obvious repugnance of violence?"

"I could write a book on it," Grandma said. The rocker, unused until now, contributed an irritating squeak.

"Mom, stop rocking." Dad was uncharacteristically annoyed.

Grandma pulled a tiny tube of 3-in-1 oil from her cargo pants. "Talk about violence." She'd been billy-clubbed, tasered, maced, water-cannoned, and dog-attacked at peaceful demonstrations "all over this nation, and internationally," she said, "not to mention what happened right here in town since I've been on this blow job."

"What happened?" Bill asked. "Right here in town."

"Tires slashed, but the favorite thing of this anti-wind crowd is to throw their little bags of dog shit at my person." She shook her head. "These people, they can get super cross."

"Why didn't you tell us, Gretchen?"

"Not news, as far as I'm concerned."

"It is around here," Dad said. "We could have put Chuck Button on it."

Grandma snorted.

"Dad, what about you?" Sawyer asked.

"What about me what?"

"Have you ever punched anyone?"

Dad paused, seeming to weigh the consequences of truth-telling. "I misjudged a client once. I was arguing against the turbine, just to brownnose, when I should have been arguing for it, standing up for my beliefs."

"What happened?"

"She clocked me."

"Enough!" Bill was doing something she almost never did—cry. "This is not about the bodily harm you all have suffered or inflicted on others." She didn't even try to wipe her tears. Instead, she grabbed her purse. "I'm going over to Mill Wheel."

"Me too."

"Not on your life, Ace." She threw a bottle of Advil at me. "Take two every six hours, and ice your beautiful face."

What Mom would learn from Mrs. Forest is that our "physical interaction" scared her so much that she wanted to "take a break," "gain some perspective," "think about her actions," "weigh her options."

It's this last that scared *me* to death.

24

Create community with the *Frigate*,
your one-stop resource for news, sports,
and offline connections.

Bill was in her room flipping through mail like maybe she could throw away the bills and keep the circulars from Supreme Meats. *Mail* seemed a pretty ridiculous concept these days. She set aside what appeared to be a wedding invitation, and *The New Yorker*. Everybody but Rags fought over the magazine before it was abandoned in the half-bath and stained with coffee. We liked its shiny paper, reflecting light in a way that made it hard to read, and its stray spot illustrations.

I sat on the edge of my parents' bed. The bedspread was white with little knobs, like the hobnail jar on Bill's dresser, handed down from someone who'd used it for hairpins and bobby pins. There were no makeup bottles.

The room had the musty odor of familiarity. Rags's side of the bed was an eclectic mix of boxes for specific purposes, and Bicycle cards. His books held the latest on U.S. politics and history.

My mother's nightstand had a shaky stack of self-help books and novels. Fiction made her feel balanced: She was probably leading a more orderly life than the whacked-out psychotics in these books. A Hanes high-waist was draped over a lamp.

Whatever sex that took place between these sheets was easier to take for Sawyer and me than the weightier marriage-bed chatter that may have been about us.

"Mom." This was my opening gambit.

She was making a to-do list: food, mood-changers, set goals and meet them, gain control of the Ragsdales. "What, honey?"

She returned a pair of ear guards to the top shelf of the closet where Rags's stuff was—a cardboard box of something, a leather medicine ball that wasn't in the garage because it was beautiful and probably came from his father, with his weakness for useless playthings and fakery.

"Mrs. Forest said I should ask whether you were raped."

"When did she say that?"

"A while ago, before, you know, before . . ."

"Why would she say that?"

"You weren't?" I said.

"Well . . ."

"Well, what?"

"It was a different time," Mom said.

"That's what Mrs. Forest said."

"Women accepted things they shouldn't have."

"Who raped you?"

"Frat guys?" She tried to soften it with Valley girl uplift.

"*Guys?* Gang rape? I mean, Mom."

"Don't take it to heart, Ace. We survived. We all did. Suzie did. I'm here. I became your mother."

"People I love were violated—you, Mrs. Forest. How am I supposed to deal with that?"

"*Violated?* Those kinds of abstract words make it even worse."

"Sexual intercourse without your consent."

"Better."

"I don't want to ever violate Mrs. Forest," I said.

116

"I doubt you could, honey."

"I could, Mom. I almost did. I tried."

Bill sat next to me on the bed, which raised me above her. She reached up to pull imagined hair from my face. "Honey."

"I didn't come in here to talk about rape, but when I saw you looking so innocent wandering around in that Skrillex T-shirt, I don't know, something just, something, like—"

"I'm hardly innocent."

"I don't mean that kind, I mean vulnerable. Like someone not prepared or expecting to be assaulted. Like Mrs. Forest."

"We're here for you, darling." She held both my hands. "Do you want to talk to someone?"

I sobbed into my mother's skinny chest.

25

Three Sheets to the Wind.

For all your sailing needs, visit us at Horton Wharf.

"Your parents tell me that you're catatonic and hobbled by crying jags." My new doctor read from notes on his phone.

"They gave me some background on you. I tell you this in the interests of full disclosure."

I wasn't sure if I was supposed to answer something that wasn't a direct question.

We'd all agreed that my therapist had to be a guy, preferably an old one, like Freud himself. With a woman, even if she looked like Mitch McConnell or Yasser Arafat, I'd still fantasize about her half-clothed, sitting there with her pad and pen, legs crossed, cork sandals pumping— nylon briefs, taupe bra, a slip even—not the Blanche Dubois kind but a baggy one "showing" beneath her tweed skirt—waiting patiently for me to free-associate myself back into sanity.

He also had to be an under-the-radar freelancer, no one connected to Medical Arts, or even South Shore Outpatient. Mrs. Forest's privacy had to be maintained. Le Forest would pounce on the tiniest infraction to portray her as an unfit mother.

Dad surfed harvardalums.com for classmates or other likely prospects. The guy was twenty years ahead of him and semiretired, taking on just a few cases "to keep his hand in the game."

But Bill and Rags chose him not only for his résumé, which was "indeed stellar," but for his amazing proximity. He lived in a weather-beaten cottage on the point near the Coast Guard station.

The good news is that I could go by launch from the public landing and wouldn't have to endure awkward parental car rides. Viewing its ruined aesthetic from the harbor, you'd think his place was an old fishing shack.

"Catatonia is related to schizophrenia, which I doubt you have," the doctor said.

"How do you know?"

"I watched you walk in here. You don't bounce on your toes. Schizophrenics generally do."

"Thank God for small favors."

He was an experienced ignorer.

"Your records from your primary care physician indicate that your name is Candace Minter Ragsdale but that you like to be called Ace; Ace it is then."

Dr. Philip Knowlton—Dr. Know—was old, with burnt umber readers and a gray G-string. I'd never seen an old guy shave that way. Sawyer said it took a lot of time, and there wasn't a big cost-benefit ratio. The hair on his head was straight and went sideways in both directions, like maybe he stood in front of a mirror to make it happen. What I couldn't place was his ethnicity.

He had beautiful light dark skin as if he might have been part Portuguese, with maybe an Anglo dad.

He wore jeans and Docksiders without socks, revealing the tongue and groove carpentry of his ankles. When I first arrived, he was wearing an apron, not a butch kind of blacksmith, husband grilling on the deck apron but the kind stereotypical grandmothers—nothing like mine— wear to bake brownies. He slung it over the back of his chair.

"Ace . . ." He leaned back instead of forward, no ostentatious eye contact. Like he was relaxing after a busy day of tying lobster buoys to his faded red shingles. "Why are you here? And be as precise and direct as you can."

I paused to take in his home, a diversionary tactic. The room was finished in an artful way. There was a mind behind it. Gooseneck lamps arched downward, casting indirect light.

It was spare, no musty books or rugs. A few minimalist pieces were offset with clashing fabrics.

Through the window, a sandy path was visible. Too narrow for a real car, it led to the cliffs, then down a steep, winding road, across the causeway, past Star of the Sea and on to Scrimshaw. A well-kept parasail, protected by a makeshift lean-to, occupied a warn patch on the leeward side of the cottage. Grass couldn't grow there. The yard was all rocks and sand. Weeds survived.

"I see you don't have a box of tissues handy," I said.

"Are you planning on crying?"

I couldn't answer.

"See those dishtowels?"

I nodded. They were stacked neatly on the coffee table between us. "I'm supposed to cry into a dishrag? That's very sustainable."

"They came with the house, and I didn't know what else to do with them." He seemed willing to talk about his dishrags, though I was pretty sure that shrinks weren't supposed to disclose personal details.

"Dry dishes?"

"How many dishes can one person dry?"

Now, it seemed 50/50 whether or not I would cry. "I beat up my girlfriend."

He gently lobbed a dishrag at me. It was white with the layout of a room printed in black, with a library and a conservatory. Colonel Mustard might appear at any minute.

"What method did you use?"

"Method? I didn't know you could have a method."

"You used the term 'beat up.' That implies fists." He was like a court reporter who typed without looking. He would never be the kind of distracted pedestrian who would get killed while texting.

My hands were folding and refolding the dishtowel as if they didn't belong to me. "Strangulation."

"I didn't think you beat her up."

"Why?"

"Your hand-eye coordination, it's not good. I doubt you would have won a fistfight."

"Because I flubbed a dishrag?"

He nodded.

"I didn't win, by the way."

"Strangulation is quite definitive. I've done some work at Walpole. What did you use?"

"Her own scarf."

"So she's older?"

"How did you know?"

"The scarf is an older woman's chainmail, protecting her from the abuse society heaps on her."

"She's not that old. Besides, how do you know it wasn't the kind of winter scarf you wear outside?"

"I'm guessing this altercation didn't take place on the street."

Through a large bay window, the windmill was visible from an angle I'd never seen. A photo of it hung over the mantel.

"You like the turbine?" I ventured.

He followed my gaze. "It's beautiful."

"And you support it?"

"Fossil fuels are like typewriters."

I scanned the walls. "No clock?"

"I'm not a movie shrink."

"So you will tell me when the session's over?"

"No. You'll tell me."

"What if I stay all day?"

"You won't. It's like water seeking its own level."

121

"I thought I was supposed to answer questions, not ask them."

"You're on unfamiliar ground, so you're like a bitch sniffing her territory." The proper use of the word startled me. He checked his phone. "And you work at the *Frigate*. Reporters have a natural curiosity."

This misconception could come in handy, so I let it go. But there was also something about this man that made me want to lie honestly, if I was going to lie.

"I'd best be going." Where had that come from? On the rare occasions when our parents had left us with a sitter, Rags's parting admonition was, "You'd best be good." I knew Dr. Know and I had just scratched the surface, so this was a test to see what he'd do. What he did was stand and switch on the ringer to his phone. He didn't walk me to the door. I was his patient, not his guest.

I sat on his float, waiting for the launch. Dr. Know had a graceful pulling boat with a tiny outboard. He'd tied the dinghy expertly to the cleat and flemished the extra line on the dock. He was either a boatman or anal-retentive.

26

"Ace, it's ludicrous for you to sit in the backseat when it's just you and me in the car."

"I don't want to break the pattern," I told my mother as we drove through the leafy streets and winding roads of Horton.

She glanced in the rearview mirror. "The one where I'm your chauffeur?"

"That very one," I said, lying down, my muddy Timberlands pressed against the window.

"Are we all out of Windex?" she asked.

"Like we ever had Windex in the first place." Treetops spun into the blue. "Careful around the corners, Mom. These roads are treacherous."

Soon the shade and SUV-ed driveways gave way to the light and clamor of Route 53, and the trashy splendor of the mall.

Mom and I held hands, swinging our arms. An overall sheen of fresh plastic dazzled. Old people race-walked right at us. The burnt-cheese smell of Panera lingered. The din seemed to originate in our brains.

"Your dad is so hard to shop for."

"Let's not get him anything."

"*Birth*day?"

"I love Dad, but he's not like a gift-type person. He's like if you wanted to make a dad robot, like, what would you buy, economy-whatever, batteries? And then you bake a cake, and he cries and says all he needs is his family, and then Sawyer contagious-cries, and it's all for shit."

Mom paused at a kiosk with sunglasses and chain-link jewelry.

"Let's go in here." I stopped in front of the breathtaking windows of Victoria's Secret, strawberry vapors wafting out the door.

"Ace? Really?"

"Maybe this lingerie will remind us of something Dad really needs, like an axe or something."

Mom succumbed to its salacious marketing. I followed her in. "Let's buy a foundation garment for Mrs. Forest."

"Since we're here?"

Its aura of satin and S&M was inspiring. "Like a peace offering," I said, about a thousand degrees below what I was feeling.

"Did you bring money?" Mom asked.

I hauled some ones from the pocket of my jeans.

"So I'm going to bankroll Suzie Forest's *foundation garment?*"

I opened her purse. "If you would."

"Ace, you haven't cornered the market on this particular aspect of my best friend."

"Market-cornering, not my strong point."

"I'm serious, Ace. I've sucked butterscotch off her finger!"

"Mom."

She entombed her face in my shoulder, where she couldn't see my own misery. Dr. Know said it's therapeutic to help other people besides yourself.

I was nearly done in by the valiant little part in my mother's mussed hair. "Mrs. Forest . . ." There was no need for me to repeat her name. "She's gone from me, too," I said. "*I* don't even have her anymore."

"Her epic beachwear routine," Mom sniffled.

"Mom, no one can un-experience their own experience," I preached.

"Speaking of which. . . ." Mom disengaged from me and put herself back together. "How is your therapy going?"

"I'm trying, Mom."

"Good, that's all we can expect."

"But relational competency, just so you know, it's a marathon, not a sprint."

"Thanks for that, sweetheart, but just so you know, for your dad and me, it's not the journey, it's the destination." She fondled the vicious lace of a D-cup. "This brassiere racket, it ain't cheap."

"I know."

"Turning yourself on with underwear? Such a cliché, honey. And sooo *Special Victims Unit*." She caressed the butt of a jet-black mannequin.

I couldn't wait to get myself off with Grandma's Connie Francis records. I examined a perky little bra. "Mom, you should get this."

"I hardly need a bra"

"It's the principle of the thing."

Mom's eyes wandered to a red bustier. "Neither do you, by the way."

"She likes ripping it off me."

"God! I'm going to kill myself!"

"Mom, how about this?" A modest box featured three tasteful Mini Sparkle Micro thongs.

Mom read the label, *Three for Thee*. "Your dad would love these."

"For *Dad?* You go, Rags! You've taken it to the next level!" An image surfaced. The nighties, the scrunched ribbons, the pumps, they were mere child's play!

"Easy, cowboy. If you give your father a gift to give to *me?* It's like he died and went to heaven."

"Mom, you're so aspirational."

A saleswoman appeared. "Can I help you?" She wore a shimmery loincloth.

"We'll take it," Mom said. "Please gift wrap it."

"Plain or Erotic Overtures?"

Mom chose plain, "just like your dad, Ace. He's a very special man wrapped in plain paper."

"A surprise inside?"

Mom smiled at the memory of Sawyer and me dumping our Cap'n Crunch on the floor, searching for it.

27

Offshore breezes

By Chuck Butten
Frigate staff writer

In a move that appeared to appease Occupy Wind forces, the leader of Opposition Wind suggested possibly moving the windmill offshore, where it would be "less disruptive to inland residents." But, emphasized OP point person Eleanor Margesson, "this would be subject to Coast Guard, Commonwealth, and OSHA regulations."

Davy Chappell, son of the Coast Guard captain, drove the launch to Dr. Know's.

"The usual," I said.

"Same here." Davy's eyes were glued to the horizon. "The usual Whore Town bullshit."

"You doing the 5K?" I asked.

"Yep. It's either autism or breast cancer, I forget which."

"It's always somethin'."

"Well, I try to give back to the community."

"Me too," I said.

Davy took his eyes off the middle distance long enough to laugh in my face. Politely—he'd been the debut captain of the anti-bullying squad.

I was starting to enjoy these miniscule voyages, which offered a slightly skewed view of the things I saw every day, like the lighthouse, the terrace of the Bowsprit, and the turbine, which looked stately and forsaken. I wasn't much of a nature freak, but I'd watch cormorants diving and terns searching for food, ducks with their little V wakes.

Dr. Know always left the door unlocked. When I arrived, he'd be sitting on his Danish Modern leather chair, phone in hand. The only hints that he'd been doing anything besides waiting for me were the delicious smells coming from his tiny galley kitchen.

"So, you told me what you did, but not why," he said.

"Aren't you supposed to wait for me to say something?"

"I'm not *supposed* to do anything."

"My brother and I, we read your seminal work."

"Language, Dialog, and the Limits of Silence?"

"No. *Happiness Realized and the American Twilight.*"

"You and your brother. . ." He checked his phone. "Thomas. . . ."

"Sawyer."

"Tom Sawyer?" Dr. Know allowed himself a smirk.

"Inside joke."

"You and Sawyer, you need to find some hobbies." He typed something on his phone.

"What did you just write?"

"I don't always disclose that."

"Aren't you going to ask me about my parents?"

"What about them?"

"Electra complex? Oedipus complex? Penis envy?"

"Your girlfriend, why did you pull her scarf tightly around her neck?"

"Did I say that?"

"It's in my notes."

"She wouldn't have sex with me."

"Why not?"

"She wanted to wait."

"Why?"

"Societal norms; she's my mother's best friend."

"Your MILF?" He let himself smile at my look of surprise. Bill had jokingly called Mrs. Forest my MILF, which had to be embarrassingly explained to Rags. "I try to stay current," Dr. Know said.

"MILF doesn't describe the relationship, at all. That makes it sound coarse and reductive, and I have more regard for her than that."

"But you wanted to force her?"

"Yes."

"So why didn't you?"

"I did."

"You didn't. You pulled her scarf tight around her neck. Why?"

"I wanted to love the life out of her."

"You wanted to kill her?"

"Not consciously."

"What, then?"

"I wanted to keep myself from forcing her."

"Forcing her to . . .?"

I reached for a dishrag. This one matched his vegetable apron, which he'd forgotten to remove.

"You're an articulate person, Ace. I'm going to ask you to use your words."

I laughed at this preschool mantra, laughed/cried into the dishrag. I finally understood the words *talking to someone*. No Ragsdale bullshitting; it meant you'd finally achieved psychosis instead of just being a normal fuckup.

"To have sex with me." After I blew my nose, Dr. Know threw the dishrag into the washer, which stood open in the

129

kitchen. He'd obviously had practice.

"You wanted to force her to have sex, meaning . . ." He handed me another one from the pile. "According to societal norms, you wanted to . . ."

"Rape her?" I hid behind the question.

"But instead you tried to strangle her, why?"

"If I suffocated her, it would be just me who would have to live with my actions. If I violated her, she would go through her whole life scarred and damaged, and it would be me who did it, who would be responsible . . . forever."

He nodded, a sign that he was thinking. "Ace, what do you want the outcome to be, with you and Susan?"

"I want us to be together."

"Have you seen her since the . . . the incident?"

"Yes."

"Have you talked about it with her?"

"No, we don't talk at all."

"So what do you do?"

"We stalk each other."

"Hmm, stalk, but not talk. So you've seen her, only in the literal sense, spotted her, let's say?"

Today, the room smelled invitingly of fresh coffee. From my vantage point, I could see just about everything in his house, except the bedroom, which faced the water. You were allowed to use his bathroom, but I was saving that. An espresso machine gleamed on his kitchen counter. "Can I have a cup of coffee?"

"This is not a coffee klatch, Ace. No eating, drinking, and of course no smoking." He glanced over his shoulder. "Not even outside."

Outside was a peeling wooden picnic table.

"Who are you cooking for?"

"If you want to ask me something, be direct."

"Do you have a family?"

"It's normal to want to place a person in the world, but we need to use your valuable time to talk about *you*."

"Sorry."

"Why did you apologize?"

"It was kind of inappropriate for me to ask."

"Another therapist, somebody besides me, might have obliged."

The word brought back memories of Rags taking us around town when we were little kids, leaving each shop with the weird valediction "Much obliged."

"This stalking, Ace, you need to describe it, in detail; start from the beginning and don't leave anything out, no matter how seemingly inconsequential."

He talked like Barack in slow, separate words.

Since I was supposed to be so articulate, I collected my thoughts: I of course knew where to find her: at Ocean Charter, at the shop, on Mill Wheel. I would just plan to be near those places at the right time.

It was hard at the shop because it would be easy for her to spot me walking by. Sometimes, I stood across the street or around the corner, with my phone out like I was waiting for an Uber or about to text someone. I knew exactly when she went to the Eatons' for coffee, and if things were going well, I'd follow her at a distance, like I was a private eye or detective.

"Stalking, what kind of an experience was that?" Dr. Know asked again.

"Being anywhere near her is like nothing you can imagine. I can smell her and feel her even when she's not within eyesight. But seeing her without her knowing, it's like she's revealing her whole self without anything protecting her."

"Do you think she needs protection?"

"Yes."

"From whom or what?"

"Me, obviously."

"Is she usually alone or with someone?"

At Mill Wheel, I'd hide behind the hedge. She'd be flipping through magazines and looking distracted when Brett and Levi tried to talk to her. Except for the twins, I wanted her to be on her own. I wanted her to be lonely without me.

"Was she alone?" Dr. Know repeated.

"No, sometimes Dr. Forest was there."

"What would they be doing?"

"Just sitting on the couch, like normal people, drinking wine."

Or fighting. Once, I watched them fight. It started with words that I couldn't hear, but you could tell by the body language. She wasn't sitting with her legs tucked under her, like she sometimes did, like a teenager. She was standing and pacing, and so was he, like they were weaving around each other like animals marking their territory. She grabbed the wine bottle, threw it against the wall, and used a sharp piece of glass to stab him. Blood seeped into his shirt, slow and bright, and beautiful.

"Ace!"

"What?"

"You were gone there for a moment," Dr. Know said. "Were you hallucinating?"

"No, it was real."

"What was real?"

"Blood, bright white shirt, bright red blood."

"*Your* blood? When you and Susan were fighting?"

"Yes, my blood."

"We can work together on some coping strategies to help you deal with that memory."

"Thank you."

"How did it make you feel when you observed Susan sitting on the couch amicably drinking wine with Dr. Forest 'like normal people'?"

"Like would I want to try and kill her again?"

"Yes."

"No, it would be like *I* was dead. I might as well be dead if she left me for someone else."

"Meaning you would take your own life?"

"Of course not."

"Why is that so out of the question?"

"It takes guts to do that. I have no guts."

"What, then?"

"You can make yourself die without committing suicide. I'm surprised you don't know that."

"I do know that, but I want to know how you would go about doing it."

"You can shrivel slowly from the inside. Like a plant dying, you can, like, not water yourself and let it happen."

"You said you were stalking each other. How do you know she was stalking *you*?"

I would see her, outside Whore High. She'd park her car at the farthest part of the parking lot, like under a tree, at a time when it was busy with school buses and parents picking up their kids. She'd be smoking her butch Camels—she'd never be vaping like kids at school—and leaning against her car. I could hardly breathe watching her watch me. Both of us were doing something dangerous, not the kind of dangerous where you touch something deadly, but the kind like when you eat doughnuts and fries and it's bad for you but good.

"What if it were a one-way street, if you were stalking her, and she wasn't stalking you?" Dr. Know asked.

"I would feel hopeless. Like I was trying to grab something you couldn't grab, the way kids try to grab bubbles."

"Unrequited relationships need to be faced. Unless my patients are mentally ill, let's say in a manner that requires psychotropic medications, I encourage a grounding in reality. You are not here for an endless cycle of psychotherapy. I'm not here to bankrupt your parents."

"I want psychotropic drugs."

"Why do you think she stalks you?"

"To see if I'm seeing someone else."

"Is that the only reason?"

"No."

"What else?"

"To be safe in my presence."

He waited for me to explain.

"If we were together, there would have to be some resolution."

"Ace, what do you want the resolution of this to be?"

"Of coming here? My therapy?"

"No, for you and Susan."

"I want us to be together. Check your phone. I said that 'up top.'"

"You want to be a couple?"

I nodded.

"But you don't think that's possible?"

"Intimate-partner violence, it's a deal-breaker, I thought."

"If there were deal-breakers, you wouldn't be here. Do you understand that, Ace?"

"I guess, but . . . I don't want to get my hopes up."

"You're afraid of failure?"

"Who isn't?"

"Maybe she should come here."

"Here?"

"Yes, here." He waited in case I had a response. "You seem possessive of *here*. You don't want her to come here? Invade your space?"

"She might not want to come."

"You'd have to present it in a positive way."

"And if she did?"

"We could talk instead of stalk."

"But I would be afraid."

"Of . . ."

"Of her leaving me."

"She's already left you."

"But it might become definite, like death, like real death, like an ending. Final."

28

I had nothing to lose. As Dr. Know had pointed out, she'd already left me.

I didn't stand across the street, staking out the place or lean against the wall, waiting for her to take her coffee break at the old Ground Rounds. A criminal wanting to get caught, I stood in plain sight in front of Picture This.

I was prepared to go slow, to own her hurt and anger and take responsibility for my actions. But it was as if she'd been waiting for me. "Come in," she said, like I was a guest, her voice between soft and commanding. I walked purposefully to the back room, grabbed a seltzer from the minibar and waited, leaning against the daybed with my ankles crossed.

Hearing how quickly she got rid of a customer heightened my anticipation. "Tuesday, then," the man said, galumphing out of the shop like he was wearing fishing boots. Guys dreamed up reasons to come in here.

It was almost as if she'd been rehearsing. She seemed to be suppressing anything that would betray her. Fear? Hope?

All my life I'd watched women in pain, sitting on floors, leaning against walls, hands clasped over their stomachs. I wanted to share the pain—or to take it from them.

Everything I'd learned about women was in *this* woman, now standing in front of me. I handed her my bottle; it held my fingerprints, my saliva. Her lips covered the place where my mouth had been.

My wild episodes with Long Division and practice sessions with Karen Tilley dissolved. I tried to hide my nerves. I ordered her to remove her boots—I wanted her at eye level. She balanced on one foot, then the other, her hand on my shoulder. After what had happened last time, here, in this place, she seemed to want to be soft and compliant.

I'd been rehearsing, too.

I led her toward the bed, draping her over it, face-up. I massaged her crown, her temples; her eyes closed. I stretched out her arms, Jesus-like. Moving down to her hands, I sucked the rings off her fingers.

All those long-suffering women I'd watched—I'd wanted them to smell of cigarettes and whiskey and to answer me with their eyes. This one was cupping my breast. It was small, and unremarkable, but not, it seemed, to her. Her hand was chapped with experience. I'd fallen in love with the years that had separated us, years during which she'd been sad and joyful in ways only possible before there was me.

I'd watched women in dressing rooms, hips like curio shelves, fashion falling from their bones. This woman dared clothes to protect her.

I didn't want her to love me just for *me*. I wanted her to love the coarseness of my hair, the squareness of my hand. My flat belly. I had a butt you could be surprised by. She'd been surprised early on, bear-hugging me and pressing it to her.

In this moment, we were in a place of our own making, without days or weather. Unbuttoning her shirt, releasing her bra, I lifted each breast to her mouth. She sucked, one, then the other. But she wasn't going to let me be in charge. She sucked my nipples. Moving on, she ran a path downward with her tongue, stopping just above my navel.

Then she lay back, abandoning herself to me.

I lifted her skirt and removed her pants. I massaged the inside of her thighs but kept away from her bush, clipped, not blond, her opening inflamed. She was groaning to be touched—to touch.

I swept her hand away; it was too soon.

Her clit was erect. I licked its shaft, my palm pressing her mons, two fingers hooking the entrance to but not entering her vagina.

She came loudly to a chorus of bells—a customer had just entered the shop—and the chimes of the Star of the Sea.

Sobbing, I let her hand go where it was begging to go.

I waited until we were done to kiss her. I left her with the taste of herself on her lips.

I left her, then went out to wait on her customer. Today it was Junior Eaton who wanted to frame the first dollar he'd made at the newly minted Riparian Roasters.

"What do you think of this?" He pulled the corner of a stainless-steel frame from the wall. I got a whiff of stale milk latte.

"Don't think so." I put it back. "You want something that says coffee, something warm and aromatic." I'd gotten good at being a sales associate.

Junior eyed the door. "Where's Suzie?"

"Trust me. She'd agree. You want this." I handed him a bamboo frame. "Something that says Africa, the mountains of Brazil, Cameroon."

"I guess you're right." He ran his hand over the fake jointed wood.

"And for a mat, burlap." I held the sample against the frame.

Junior handed me the precious dollar that would be imprisoned in bamboo and burlap, the dollar, with its crazy pyramid, the deep, dark female receptacle.

A dollar was a dollar. What difference did it make? I could just as well stash it in the cash register. I flattened it and put it on the counter.

"Say hi to Suzie," Junior said.

Usually I would have engaged him in conversation—I wanted to tell him I was having second thoughts about the new dumb name—but today I hustled him out, claiming that "Suzie" needed my help.

When I came back, Mrs. Forest was exactly where I'd left her, legs wide, head back, eyes closed. I didn't want her to sleep. I wanted her to be alive to the present, to us.

I wouldn't think of touching her. She would be too tender now. Her come was congealed there, cold. I repositioned her on the bed and covered us both with the Pier 1 seahorse blanket. She opened her eyes.

"I'm so sorry. I never meant to hurt you," I said.

"I know, sweetheart. I'm sorry too."

"All this waiting, maybe we were driving each other a little crazy."

"You think?" Mrs. Forest said.

29

There was a time smack in the middle of the afternoon when Sawyer got a breather at Fabia's. He and Sunny and sometimes even Fabia herself relaxed on the electronic massage chairs, switching from *gentle pressure* and *knead* to *pulse* and *vibrate*.

"Perfect timing," Sawyer said when I walked in, pushing aside some *Self*s on the chair next to his.

I leaned toward him. The medicinal smell of polish remover. "It happened."

Sawyer knew right way. "You did her?"

Sunny got up from her chair and returned the magazines to the rack.

"I think we were making love. It was kind of smooth and dreamy, not wild like with Long Division. After . . . everything, I, we, I guess we wanted it to be . . . safe. We're feeling our way, moving slowly."

"I'm glad. I need you to be happy." He pressed our *recline* buttons. "It's like you couldn't really be you without her."

Hearing my thoughts come out of my brother's mouth made them real, like they could walk on their own. "By the way, I don't think *did* her is very respectful," I said.

You *do* someone under a table, or you *have* someone in the

139

backseat of a car, or you *take* a virgin. It's the littlest verbs that could trip you up.

"Sorry," Sawyer said.

"You need to be precise," I said. "Your words need to match your meaning."

"Thank you, Dr. Know Tons."

"He does know tons. You should have a session with him."

I loved Dr. Know. He was teaching me the concept of examining, so I tried to examine the way that I loved him. It wasn't transference; I wasn't *in love.* There wasn't a moment when I fantasized about him naked. It was like with an uncle who wasn't a registered sex offender—I wondered if you could ask someone to be your uncle the way you could ask someone to be your wife.

Not now, of course, because of our professional relationship. But maybe, if I ever stopped being crazy, he could be my uncle.

"Maybe I will." Sawyer gazed at the ceiling. "Have a session with Dr. Know."

Sawyer was on the cusp. There was a time when he would have blown off Dr. Know, that being with me and having dead-end jobs would have been enough. But *my* chance at a future made him think that he could have one, too, that he could express his feelings with a *professional* and have a life partner and a real job.

"I suddenly understand the word *give,*" I said. "It's like she gave herself at that one moment, and I can't . . ."

Sawyer jumped from the massage chair. "Gotta get back to work." There was no one in the salon. Sunny was sanitizing her station, and Fabia was texting.

I *did* girls with or without my brother, partly to learn how to be a good "love mate" like the quizzes in Sawyer's women's magazines. But Mrs. Forest was different. Those rehearsals? I'd been rehearsing for *her.*

I was happy for Sawyer's sake that a customer interrupted us. He nearly ran to greet her, setting her up at his station and pulling out her chair like a date. He was holding both her hands as I got up.

"Something carnelian," I heard him say as I was leaving. "In the amber family. Your skin tone cries out for it."

30

Not in by backyard
By Chuck Butten
Frigate staff writer

Anti-turbine activists Eleanor and Jake Margesson have petitioned the Commonwealth Health Department to step in and remove the turbine.

Meanwhile, Gretchen Ragsdale, point person for Occupy Wind, said she'd camped out under the turbine and felt no ill effects.

Horton Police Chief Nate Carver issued her a summons for illegal camping.

Town Hall sat in the middle of Scrimshaw Square. Large-paned windows offered views of the Shawmut Bank and the cemetery, where acquaintances of famous people were buried.

In a nod to the Vietnam War Memorial, the town wanted to etch the names of the fallen into our monument to King

Philip's War but could come up with only one name, an illiterate *Speedwell* frontiersman who'd frozen to death in the swamps before he'd even had a chance to discharge his musket.

Mrs. Forest wanted to see for herself what all the fuss was about. She also wanted us to do things that other people do, go to public places and "interact."

She came to Town Hall with Sawyer, Grandma, and me, dressed to kill.

"It smells like a rummage sale in here," she said, releasing my hand.

Selectman Doris Wilder called the meeting to order. Back in the '70s, a push to change the title to *Selectperson* had been shot down because the word was clumsy and deemed more exclusive and monarchical than the original.

Selectman Wilder's hair was sculpted into a high wedge like the way some Patriots guys wore theirs.

Chuck Butten sat at the press table with his reporter's notebook, pen with the Rockland Trust logo, and nubby pencil behind his ear.

All eyes were on Eleanor Margesson.

"Madame Selectman, council members, friends and neighbors," she read from a yellow legal pad. She wore a purple warmup suit with lots of diamond jewelry. "As we stand here today . . ."

"*Christ,*" Mrs. Forest hissed.

"As we stand here today, a ten-year-old girl is languishing in Pediatrics at South Shore with a mosaic—and let me tell you, that was her doctor's word—a *mosaic* of conditions and symptoms that weren't evident before the wind turbine and should not be presenting in an otherwise healthy 10-year-old."

"*Presenting,*" Sawyer snorted.

"*These people are freaks,*" Mrs. Forest whispered. Yes, but as Grandma reminded us, they were freaky in a kind of loser way that could make you feel bad for them.

Eleanor's husband Jake wore protective plastic goggles.

"Is he a welder, or what?" Sawyer said.

"Lumberjack," I said. "Cuts two-by-fours down at Ace."

Doty Cooper, resident gadfly, was believed to be mental. She stood on tiptoe to reach the mic. She bought her clothes at Little Songbird.

"You need to interrupt the force field," she said. "Fuck with the blades."

Letter writers to the *Frigate* posited that interrupting the force field by screwing with the blades would be easier than getting rid of the thing altogether.

"Better yet, move the fucker to Dragonsea and see how those uptight faggots like it!" Doty said.

"No racism, sexism, LGBTQ+ phobia, or dirty words," Doris Wilder reminded her.

Doty turned her outsize anger on us. "You two," she said, glaring at Mrs. Forest and me. "You two should keep your dirty laundry at home, not in our sacred Town Hall, of all places, our cradle of liberty."

Grandma quickly approached the mic to a chorus of boos: "Let me remind you that the energy savings per annum with this one little windmill, tucked away near the transfer station where nobody goes anyway, will come to some $300,000. That's enough to buy Obamacare for the lot of you and send your damned kids to college."

Councilperson Browne, who wore a hairpiece that looked like a horseshoe crab, leaned into his mic. "The young couple in the back? I'd like to hear what you think."

Sawyer shot to his feet and jogged to the mic. His motorcycle boots were about two sizes too big. He had no concept of delayed gratification; if he saw something he wanted, he bought it, screw size.

Grandma wore giant red Nikes, bunions like bulbs. The two Ragsdales exuded a clown-shoe effect. Sawyer pulled his phone from his pocket, scrolling to find his place. "Let me remind you," he said, town-meeting delivery creeping into his voice. "When many of our parents and grandparents were born, computers weighed thirty tons. Now just about everyone in this room has a computer in his or her pocket, so let's not be shortsighted about new ways of doing things."

I could hear the name *Ragsdale* being whispered. People were putting two and two together, that Grandma and Sawyer and the absent Bill Ragsdale were part of a left-wing conspiracy to bring Horton into the 21st century.

"And none of you have ever seen the windmill up close," Grandma said. "You're all just bull—"

"Careful," Doris warned.

"BS-ing from the comfort of your own homes."

As we filed out, Mrs. Forest tried playing nice with Doty Cooper. Doty responded, "Fuck you and the horse you rode in on."

Chief of Police Nate Carver always showed up at the end; he knew that these meetings could get rowdy, even violent. He did a mental strip-search of Mrs. Forest.

He'd also instituted a backpack search. He was shocked by what he'd seen in citizens' backpacks—rotting avocadoes, dildos, soiled underwear.

"People in Horton have a lot to learn about personal modesty and hygiene," he wrote in a letter to the *Frigate*.

31

We'd decided to test the theory that fucking with the turbine's blades would interrupt the force field and restore Whore Town's equilibrium. We of course didn't agree with the fascist anti-turbine crowd, but if "restoring equilibrium" could save the windmill, we were all for it.

It was the evening of the vernal equinox. Chippie Holbeck, Bill's art therapy student, would help us by hurling well-aimed baseballs at the blades with his powerful throwing arm. Rags had bought a pillowcase full of them from a tag sale on Route 53, where he'd also found a surfboard, gunny sack, chamois cloth, waffle iron, stereoscope, croquet wickets, a Shelley Berman 78 LP, a wooden tennis racket press, and the 35-millimeter Nikon.

Just before midnight, we went down to the living room, so we could let Chippie in before he woke everybody with the ringing of our *Close Encounters* doorbell.

Bill and Rags were already there, marking the sun's crossing of the celestial equator by rejiggering the furniture and smoking weed. The damp-hay skunk-spray smell of it filled the room, and Bill had that lazy, smiley-mouth pot face. Dulce de leche was melting in a carton on the coffee table.

"Hey guys, have some ice cream!" Dad was wearing his

flannel nightgown with the ratty red ribbon.

"And some pot?" Sawyer picked up the joint from the ashtray, relit it, and handed it to me. He eyed the couch and wingback chair, which were pushed together as if they were for sale in an antique shop. "I'm not so sure about this grouping."

"Are you kids headed out?" Bill drank ice cream from the carton. "Chippie will be here any minute. We're going down to the turbine."

"Celebrating the equinox," Sawyer explained.

Bill and Rags wanted to come. We stood in the driveway admiring Chippie's flatbed rig and his cargo.

"They're so shiny," Sawyer said. "What are they?"

"Toyotas."

"We should get a new car," Sawyer said.

"You kids don't even drive," Bill pointed out.

"Do you think cars are about driving or aesthetics?" Sawyer said.

"You asking me?" Chippie said. "Cars are about transportation."

Our vintage Pontiac, which our parents had bought when we were kids because Sawyer loved the Native American hood ornament, looked like something Chippie's rig might eat for breakfast.

The Ragsdales may have been the only family in Horton with only one car. Rags didn't need one to schlep around town, and Sawyer and I didn't see cars as the ticket to freedom that most teenagers did. They seemed dangerous, and anyway, Bill drove us places. We'd sit in back, talking to each other. She was our chauffeur and, like all servants, deaf to the spoken word.

"It's nice to see you, Mrs. Ragsdale." Chippie's polite Mike Tyson tenor broke the silence. He sat up front with his knees jammed against the dashboard.

Chippie's defining feature was his man-bun. He had no idea that it sent a message or that women hated them. He was a little overweight and wore baggy cargo shorts, even in winter, with orange T-shirts. His beard had barren patches, exposing a map

147

of red, speckled skin.

"It's funny to see you outside of art class, Mrs. Ragsdale." Chippie was scripted, as if he'd studied his lines just before coming in the door, which he'd done with right-angle precision.

"How is that piece coming along?" Bill said.

"Piece?"

"The collage with the motherboard?"

"I'm still searching for something."

"Searching is good," Sawyer said.

"Not if you can't find it." Chippie turned to look at the three of us, squeezed in back. "It's nice to see you, too, Mr. Ragsdale."

"The feeling's mutual, Chippie."

Our windmill could vie with the pyramids of Egypt and Mexico, Stonehenge, and other creations that worshipped, defied, or harnessed nature. It rose from the marshes near the transfer station, where garbage trucks were the only vehicles allowed. Bill parked where the grass had worn to hard ground. Crack peed and crapped around the pedestal, marking his territory.

Rags wore a woolen full-length coat, cinched at the waist. It was winter white, inappropriate for trespassing. Chippie carried the sack of baseballs over his shoulder.

We were his loyal fans, sitting in the stands, imitating arm movements and yelling fight songs for the Whore Town Frigates. No face paint. We had our standards, and Sawyer was vain about his looks. To connect with other humans, he and I watched pro sports, and we You-tubed the rules. Chippie idolized Serena Williams. Sawyer and I loved *love* and *sudden death*.

The night was clear, except for a few clouds that cruised past the moon, temporarily blocking its light.

"Cassiopeia," Sawyer murmured, his head hinged backward.

The smell of salt and dead low carried on a light breeze. The marsh was a giant sponge that surrendered easily when you stepped on it. Big osprey nests perched on high poles. Tonight the gulls were silent.

"Did you see that?" Bill had gathered Crack into her arms

for warmth. "I thought I saw something moving."

"Crack would have noticed." I watched him snuggle into Bill's coat.

This drew laughter from everyone except Chippie, who had no way of knowing that our beloved dog was as clueless as humans.

"You're right, Mom," Sawyer said. "We may not be alone."

"I never bought that," Dad said. "That we're alone in the universe."

"There might be a new planet that takes ten thousand years to orbit," Chippie said.

"It's lurking behind some dark matter," I said.

Bill scanned the immediate area, her neck extending like a periscope. There was a parenthesis of moonlight.

The shaft of the turbine shot upward, its crown blinking red and white and green like airplane lights. There was just enough wind for the blades to make the incessant whirring sound the Margessons had complained of.

Chippie's missiles soared over the turbine, presumably splashing into the water or coming to rest on the marsh, or maybe even onto Bulrush Road.

Bill was pathetic, her elbow at an acute angle, the ball rolling along the ground, where Chippie scooped it up like a grounder.

"You gave it a good try, Mrs. Ragsdale."

"Yeah, nice try, Mom," Sawyer said, warming her up with a brisk back rub.

Mine landed a tenth of the way up the shaft, bouncing back to us. Sawyer picked it up and threw it a little higher, but not much.

Dad had retained an institutional memory of competitive athletics. His baseball bounced just below the blades and landed in a stand of scrub pine. In the process, he nearly dislocated his shoulder. He grimaced and rubbed it, his left arm hanging limply at his side.

Bill put her arm through his. He leaned down and kissed her wetly on the mouth. Sawyer watched, smiling. When she came up for air, Bill said, "We need to tell the council meeting about this."

"About what?" Sawyer said. "That you two need to get a room?"

"About the turbine. People complain about it, but they never get close to it." She seemed to be warming her hands on Dad's buns. "But I want Gretchen to go to the meeting. She'll be more credible."

Our parents wanted the night to end in a crescendo of shopping. Nothing was open on Scrimshaw, so we ended up at the Texaco across from the old Zayer's, which had a 24/7 convenience store. "This is exactly the kind of place that gets held up at gunpoint," Sawyer said.

Neon signs at the Drive Buy blinked "Coffee, "Open," and "ATM." The florescent lights gave everyone a brutish tint. Dad carried a shopping basket over his arm, like a handbag. I brushed hair out of his eyes before he could do it himself.

The beverages in the overly lit refrigerated cases looked like the Terracotta Army, lined up, ready for battle. If you poured enough light into this place, there was nowhere for evil to lurk.

Bill was scooping up Advil, Tums, Dayquil, K-Y Jelly, a kaleidoscope of legal remedies for ailments you thought you had and things that you wanted to prepare for: hard stools, sore gums, joint pain, flat feet, dry vaginas. Just about everything came in gummy form. Rags was loading up on nonperishables.

Chippie ordered an enormous electric blue Slushie and two smelly hot dogs from a slowly revolving spit, a roller coaster in low gear. One was for Crack, who was sleeping in the car. If you were going to eat this food, you would need at least some of the drugs Bill had grabbed off the shelf.

Sawyer's eyes were glued over our heads, like a Secret Service agent. "*That guy over there?*" he hissed, gesturing with his head. "That guy has a knife in his belt."

A youngish skinny white guy like the kid in *Breaking Bad* had a handful of candy bars and celebrity magazines and a plastic package of batteries. His knife was enclosed in a very attractive leather sheath.

The cashier, who appeared to be Indian or Pakistani, wore a shirt that said *Texaco* on the pocket. His sparkly jewelry was the kind women wear. He eyed us warily.

Unbelievably, this kid did whip out his knife, holding the batteries in his left hand, the blade gleaming over the incredibly hard to open plastic package. Sawyer knocked the knife out of his hand, and Dad trapped it with his Adidas.

Package-opening averted!

We all spoke at the same time, apologizing to both the cashier and the customer.

"You people are not balanced," the kid said, in an even tone. "I'd recommend professional help." He paid for his purchases, thanking Sawyer for returning his knife.

The cashier spoke as if his tongue were glued to the top of his mouth. "He has a walid point," he said, ringing up our hefty tab.

When we went out to the car, we had a ticket on the windshield for "leaving an unaccompanied animal in a vehicle."

32

Dad stood beside Sport Rodgers in the driveway, staring at the garage door, where *Breaking Wind* had been spray-painted in big, surprisingly well-executed letters. Dad was trying unsuccessfully to put himself on equal footing with Sport, who was like Barnwood Builder.

Sawyer walked up to the paneled door and raised his shades. "The font," he muttered. "American Bubblegum."

The fresh paint smell could give you a high like glue in a rumpled paper sack, like our only homeless person, Jazzy Tucker, held it to her nose, lounging on the steps of the Grange. I must have said this out loud because Grandma elaborated, "We used to use Duco Cement." Sport stared at her in wonderment.

"That's a little off point, Mom."

"We're going to have to pressure-wash it with a solvent." Sport shook his head. "If you guys would keep your nose clean, this kind of stuff wouldn't be happening."

"Nothing toxic," Grandma reminded him. "This is my fault, and I don't want to cause any more trouble."

"It's not your fault, Gretchen." Bill knew that Grandma knew it wasn't her fault. "You should be able to express your views without fear of retaliation."

"But it's not *my* garage door," Grandma said.

"So they should spray-paint your pipe collection?" Sawyer said.

"Or your shell art?" I leaned against the Pontiac, unconsciously imitating Sport crossing his Rosie the Riveter arms. "Who's *they*, anyway?"

Bill looped a curl behind her ear. Her still-youthful self blew another strand upward. "Of course, it's all those opposition nuts at town meeting, the anti-windmill crowd."

"I didn't take them for the spray-painting type," Grandma said. "That takes originality."

"Who *is* the spray-painting type?" Rags had moved physically—and psychically—a few steps to the left of Sport. Keeping our noses clean didn't advance society or challenge children to be their best selves.

Police Chief Nate Carver had already been here with a volunteer investigator who'd watched an incredible amount of *CSI*; he'd taken pictures, dusted for fingerprints, and checked for tire treads.

It was unlikely that anyone around Horton had a rap sheet.

Sawyer photographed the message before Sport could obliterate it. "Garage-door art. I wonder why they used yellow?"

"What would be better?" Dad said. "Red?"

"Well, the door is a kind of gunsmith green—as you know, Horton has to adhere to historic hues on the color wheel—so I would have said something like a violet or purple."

"Not the right signal," I said. "Lavender Menace, anyone?"

"Betty Friedan, what a jackass," Grandma said. "I met her once. I shouldn't say this, but her face was like a bent pipe."

"No, Mom, you shouldn't say that."

"Somebody should just blow up that blankety-blank wind turbine." Sport's face, which was wrinkled like a dog's, looked as if it might fold in on itself. "Excuse my French." He directed this at the women.

"Blankety-blank is not a swear word," Grandma corrected mildly.

"It's a substitute for a swear word," I said. It was just this kind of patronizing smugness that drove the anti-windmill people crazy.

"So, what's the RX?" Dad interrupted.

"I think a couple of courses of After Blast should do it," Sport said.

"If it's dangerous," Grandma said, "Bab-O could work."

"Well, you don't want to drink it," Sport said. "You need ventilation and gloves."

"We'll have to lock Crack in the house," Dad said.

"I figured you guys were on something," Sport said.

Crack hadn't, in fact, been named for the freebased stimulant but rather for the Crackstones, an entire family who'd made it safely from the *Speedwell* and across the ocean on the *Mayflower*.

"One thing I'd like you all to imagine is Dwight D. Eisenhower on crack," Sport said. "I bet you can't even wrap your arms around it." He swept his dusty work boot across our crushed clamshell driveway. "I can't."

Dwight D. Eisenhower wasn't a guy who fit smoothly into conversations. Though we'd read that they once put him on some money, W and Barack were the only presidents Sawyer and I had any knowledge of. W was a drunk, but Barack? You could just see him and Michelle getting all *Reefer Madness* in the Lincoln bedroom. (Lincoln was his favorite president.) As Michelle Obama recommended, "Go high!"

I had a sudden recovered memory. "Are you Joseph Rodgers? You donated the 'I Like Ike' buttons?"

Sport sprung to life like an overdose on Narcan. "Yeah, and I have bumper stickers, posters, pins, hats, balloons; back then they had stuff you could save in a steamer trunk." He addressed me as if I were a stranger who'd just walked off the street. "Nothing was in a cloud."

"Fifth-grade field trip? Historical Society?" I was laying it on, like you do when you think you can persuade just one person to your side.

Grandma, who had tons of experience with this sort of

154

thing, touched Sport's forearm. "I don't know if I can keep my nose clean, Joseph . . ." Conferring respect with his given name.

"Clouds used to be weather," Sport said mournfully, pulling a handkerchief from his back pocket.

"We're old enough to remember that, Sport," Grandma said.

"These people, your crowd, they're the kind of people who cross their sevens!" Sport sniffled, wiping his nose.

"We're just trying to harness the weather, the wind." Grandma could get poetic when she was talking about wind. "It's not a theory; it's a thing, like that cleaning machine you've got there."

Sport held the hose like he might take a huge piss. "Hydrojet, 750 pounds per square inch."

"Well, there you go, like that," Grandma said. "You may as well commence Hoovering."

In the beginning, Horton Separatists had cut themselves off from an entire country and religion. But now the town seemed to be dividing from the inside, like a cancer cell, from something you couldn't even see. Wind wasn't sharp and flashy like lightning. It didn't exist as a thing. You could only see its effects, like leaves rustling or flags straight out.

Sport stuffed his handkerchief in his back pocket, quickly engaging the noisy pressure washer. We watched the word *Breaking* slip from language, return to paint, and then vanish.

33

Mrs. Forest held me to her chest, her light jacket zippered around us. We sat on the beach, her arms around my waist, her chin on my head. I didn't believe the old wives' tale that excess flesh kept you warm, like we were sea lions or whatever. But everything that made Mrs. Forest zaftig and voluptuous and irresistible apparently also made her impervious to the elements.

It was early spring, but here spring could be cold. We cheered it on by wearing seasonal-appropriate attire, which was never enough.

"Okay, I need to know," I said, "how many besides *Le Forest*, all those dudes who knocked you up, and those Tinder hookups?"

"A lot."

"Do you remember them all?"

"Not really."

"At least I remember mine," I said.

"I've got a few years on you."

In the off-season, there were no rose hips in the dunes, but you could find bayberries in a blue-gray color almost impossible to reproduce. There was the snap of dried seaweed pods. The ocean was so wild, you could feel like you do when standing on the jetty, that you might jump. I said this out loud.

"The French have a name for that," I said. *"L'appel du vide."*

Mrs. Forest pulled out her phone, searching Safari. "Sometimes I don't know what the hell you're talking about, but then again, that's what I love about you. I will never fully understand you."

All this awesome knowledge was just Google and Kindle shit. Sawyer and I were dilettantes in cosmology, cosmetology, and goats (*The Meat Goat Handbook*; we sometimes clicked on the wrong titles when we were high). We ran up big Amazon bills, ordering books, but Bill was happy to pay.

Sawyer clicked on bestsellers he'd heard women talking about at Fabia's. We'd buy political books that were popular down at the *Frigate*. We'd buy how-to books and personal development books, poetry, and classics. We liked fiction that took place in real time: we started *The Lay of the Land* while waiting for the frozen bird to thaw and finished as Thanksgiving weekend reeled out and died.

When we'd over-experimented with stuff from the Forests' medicine chest, we sometimes wrong-clicked on books like *Small-Scale Poultry Flock*. We purposely clicked on *The Real Don Quixote*; *Selected Poems of Stevie Smith*; Plato's "Unwritten Doctrines"; *Boys, Girls, and Pipi Longstocking*; *The Oxford English Dictionary, Second Edition*; *The Great Gatsby*; *Norman Mailer Revisited*; *The Complete Works of John Magee*; *How Proust Can Save Your Life*; "Visual Pleasure and Narrative Cinema"; *A Tale of Two Cities*; *Quotations from Chairman Mao Tse-Tung*; *The Gnostic Gospels*; *The Complete Carpenter*; and *Discovering French*. *Knitting Without Tears* had sent Sawyer down to Madame Defarge's to buy everything he needed to create a line of designer neckwear.

Now Mrs. Forest turned to face the ocean. We were below the dunes, sheltered from the wind, sitting on a Native American blanket she'd bought on eBay.

"Unlike with you, I had Lee figured out that first night he showed up, with his scraped face and his sex-starved eyes."

"Start at the beginning," I said. "Anything besides men?

157

Dogs? Girls? Relatives?"

"Really, Ace."

"Well?"

"Girls, if you can call my babysitter a girl. I guess she was maybe ..." She laughed. "Your age."

"Illegal!" When I turned to look at Mrs. Forest's upturned face, she was smiling.

"It was sweet, really. I'm not sure even now if it was sex. I certainly didn't know then. It was kind of like a full-frontal body clutch."

"Did you come?"

"Yes."

"Did she?"

"It seemed like it."

"Did you have simultaneous orgasms?"

"I didn't even know what that was."

"Should I be jealous or envious?"

"Both."

The fact that Mrs. Forest wasn't doing anything overtly sexual was a turn-on. "Animals?"

"No, I have never fucked a nonhuman. Are you disappointed?"

She used to balk at my questions, question the questions, avoid. Now that she'd opened herself to me, who knew what she might have answered if I'd asked earlier. Did we have a lifetime of questions and answers?

"Family members?"

Mrs. Forest paused. I couldn't see her eyes behind the big sexy fashion shades. "An uncle, remember?"

"Rape is not sex." I tried to pull away.

"Ace, baby, it's okay."

"I know you and Bill talk about all your rapes and everything."

"There's talking, and then there's talking, sweetheart. Only a certain kind of talking involves spilling your guts out to each other."

"Are you and Mom back together? I think you broke up for a while. Ghosting each other?"

"You know it's about you. It would be hard for any mother, even yours."

We covered ourselves with the blanket. It had captured her smell and the smell of her kids and their pet.

"I want that for us, spilling our guts out," I said.

She pulled back her hair with the shades and rested them on top of her head, exposing tiny lines around her eyes.

I spotted a lone gray in her dark roots.

"I wanted to ask . . . you and your brother and Ms. Long Division?"

"That wasn't about sex. That was about geometry. We needed to pass."

"Others?" Mrs. Forest said. "I want to know, Ace."

"Like Karen Tilley? I like her, not love, and with her, it's just externals, like she is so fucking boy-in-a-girl-body, I don't know."

"I have no boy in me."

"That's what I love about you." I handed her a stone. "Except for your throwing arm." I watched her wing it sidearm toward the water. "Where did you learn that?"

"Born with it."

"I love all the stuff you were born with."

No matter what time of year, there were dog walkers, and surfers coming scarily close to the jetty. A race walker with ski poles did an about-face like a soldier and headed in the opposite direction.

I longed for summer when boogie boards made abstract art on the sand. Tropical colors went against our grain. Lifeguards in red with fanny packs stood at the edge, eyes glued to the water.

The lifeguards were mostly kids from Whore High, Karen Tilley included. Next to their tower was a Zodiac, oars at the ready. The perils of the ocean had been drilled into them. In U.S. History, we had a chapter called "Lost at Sea," which catalogued the wrecks that had taken place on our shores, like the *Etrusco*, which had slammed into the lighthouse on March 16, 1956.

"If it was summer, I'd slather your whole body in Banana Boat," I said. "Every inch, and you would squeeze through my fingers."

We were at the end of the beach, where there were houses on stilts that couldn't possibly protect them from superstorms. A small plane buzzed overhead, advertising Happy Hour at Houlihan's. We searched for more flat stones for Mrs. Forest to skip.

"But Karen, this Tilley kid, it's over, right? I mean, she's your age, shared experiences, getting old together. All that good stuff."

Karen and me, we'd had our own sport: practicing oral sex, so we'd be prepared when it really mattered. It was like a basketball drill.

"Nothing to be over. We were just practicing. That's how I learned my technique." I waited for her to laugh.

"Who else?' she asked, as we watched another stone jump and dance across the water.

"A young teacher's aide."

"Illegal!" she mimicked me.

"Yeah, it was," I said. "It was like she was strolling around the classroom, and when she went by my desk, I was on eye level with her girly parts."

We were under the blanket now, like kids reading with a flashlight. I pinned her wrists against the sand, lightly bit her nipples. "Harder," she breathed. One bled into the white silk of her bra. Did she *want* to be raped? By me? There was a difference between rape and rape fantasies.

She was so wet I clenched my hand into a fist, trying to fill her completely. I'd never done that with anyone. I nearly passed out as she closed around me. Imagining all the men who'd felt her muscular grip made me more excited—and somehow proud.

I made her wait for me, guiding her hand between my legs, where I was dripping. We couldn't be silent—didn't have to be. We outdid the breakers, the laughing gulls swooping low over the water. The wind.

Afterward we walked in the dunes, searching for bayberries.

160

She picked a bunch and presented them to me like a bouquet. "Next time, we *make love*," she said, her voice soft.

It was starting to get dark. Sounds were magnified at night—it was as if you heard rather than saw the ocean. Waves crashed or lapped, depending. Wind cut the surface and ballooned our coats. Far off were lights from a tanker; behind us, lights from houses. A car moved slowly across the causeway.

If Mrs. Forest ever were to die, what would I remember about this day? The rough touch of the blanket, the caught zipper of her coat, the trapped smell of her.

The stones we collected for her to skip to the motherland.

Mrs. Forest drove the Vulva carefully over the rutted access road. She was worried about trespassing and having to pay a fine.

"Or, more to the point, explain myself," she said. "Why the hell would I be out here by the turbine with my girlfriend?"

I loved the "girlfriend" part. It was so official, a real label, like when you get a number on your mugshot.

Why were we here? We'd joked about the crazy people who said the turbine was making people orgasmic. We wanted to test *that* theory.

But first a little rock-throwing as foreplay. I loved watching her throw things.

Beach rocks surrounded the base. They often had cosmic designs or were smooth like the ones used for a hot stone massage.

I handed her a volcanic rock with copper-colored stripes. "See how far you can throw this."

It hit an egret off its flight path and into ours. We watched it spiral down, meeting its end in the wiry crotch of a scrub pine.

"Shit. I don't like killing things."

"I don't want to talk about killing," I said. Our "episode" wasn't blurry like Grandma's snapshots. It was sharp.

"That's not what it was, honey." She touched my cheek. "Get

it out of your mind."

Mrs. Forest stepped back to get a better look at the turbine. "It's awesome, the way it rises above everything else."

For my turbine research, I'd clicked on *The Phallic Monuments of the Illuminati*, where it said that any shaft that reaches heavenward, like an obelisk, is a heathen idol, said to be the manhood of Osiris.

"The windmill, it has quiet authority." I pulled her toward me. "Like you."

"Ha! I'm a mess!"

"That's what I love about you."

"Thanks."

"Seriously," I said. "Remember when you told Long Division where she could stick it?"

"One of my finer moments." She stared at the steadily turning blades. "I can hear the whirring that everyone's complaining about. Those crazy people at town meeting? They were right about that."

As if on cue, Chuck Butten arrived, with his reporter's notebook and chewed-up pencil and his man bag dragging on the ground, heaving up the hill with his hands on his knees. How could this man ever play handball?

I cut him off at the pass. "On assignment, Chuck? Finally decided to check it out for yourself?"

"You too, it looks like." He checked out Mrs. Forest. "Unless you two might be up here for some other reason." He leered at us.

"Stuff it, Chuck." Mrs. Forest stepped back from the noxious scent of him.

"Suzie, didn't I see you at town meeting a while back?" He disassembled onto a small mound of dirt.

"Chuck," I interrupted. "I can get you a real scoop on this thing."

"An exclusive?"

"A new angle."

"Spill it." He leaned forward to pull his notebook from his back pocket.

162

"I know a doctor who could give you some really good quotes."

"Shoot."

I wrote Dr. Know's contact info in his notebook.

Chuck visored his eyes from the sun and looked up at the blades. "Well, I'm here, and it's a wind turbine, alright, and the wind is blowing, and the blades are turning. I don't know what else I can get from being up close and personal."

I offered a hand to help him up.

"Thanks for the tip." He doffed his golf cap to Mrs. Forest. "Anon."

"I hope not," she muttered.

We watched him slide on his haunches down the incline and get into his car.

Mrs. Forest muscled me under the turbine. It was urgent, maniacal sex. It wasn't about getting off; it was about surrendering to something uncontrollable.

Afterward, gasping for breath, we gathered our clothes from the bushes where we'd flung them and plucked windblown wrappers from our hair.

Mrs. Forest took her keys from her purse. "Who wants to cure nymphomania, anyway?"

34

Blades of Glory

By Chuck Butten
Frigate staff writer

Opposition Wind forces should not be emboldened by the fact that the turbine blades often remain still, even when the wind is blowing.

That was the consensus at a Wednesday meeting of turbine activists held in the Mark Roundtable Memorial Meeting Room at the Carol Winthrop library annex on New Spit Road.

"What's happening on the ground isn't an indicator of what's happening 300 feet up," said turbine consultant Barry Bradford.

"The fact that we're even meeting about this is

a crock," said Occupy Wind activist Gretchen Ragsdale.

"Ragsdale is a carpetbagger from out of town," claimed Eleanor Margesson, a longtime member of Opposition Wind. "I think she may be from New York, even."

Selectman Doris Wilder once more invoked rules governing name-calling.

"Ace?" Bill vamped my name and grabbed my elbow. "Where you headed?" She sounded like one of her students.

"The fridge."

"Do you always dress up to chug juice from the carton?" Bill pulled on my shirttail. "And smell so delicious?"

"Thanks, Mom."

She put the juice back in the fridge. "How about something stronger?" She grabbed a Narragansett. "Refreshing."

"I have to go out, Mom."

"I know you do, darling." She opened the can. "Tell her something came up." Bill patted the stool for me to sit. "Let's talk and drink and spill our guts out."

I was torn, but drinking and "interacting" with Bill was a surprise gift, like finding money on the street.

She watched me pull my phone from my back pocket. "My Gaawd, such passionate texting!" Mom said.

I sat on the island, legs dangling like a kid.

Bill sat in a chair with her ankles crossed on the island, like one of those *Mad Men* guys at his desk, only she was wearing those fruity Merrills with their girly strap. I could smell the almost pleasant rankness of her socks with the flag motif.

"Sorry I don't have a little flask," Bill said. "You and Sawyer with your flasks. One of your rituals. You and your brother and your big barriers."

165

"You make us sound like a fortress."

"It can be hard for the rest of us, you know, trying to breach the wall."

"You breach, Mom. Trust me, you breach." I leaned down to kiss her.

Now, more than ever, it was a rare occurrence being alone with Bill: the laser eyes, and their opposite, the distracted acquiescence that made our mother our mother. Our parents had once let Sawyer and me nearly float back to England.

We'd had an air mattress in the shape of a seahorse. It was one of those late summer days when the water is as warm as it will get. It was muggy and dead; it was the tide that was taking us out. We lay on our backs, staring at clouds that didn't look like anything but clouds. Sailboats tacked past. Enormous container ships were paper cutouts on the horizon. Bill and Rags shaded their eyes as they watched us, not waving, not drowning.

Someone else clued them in, like elephants, watching out for any offspring, no matter whose. Soon, a Zodiac sidled up to us. Captain Chappell of the Coast Guard and Harbormaster Topher Jones hauled us over the side. Bill and Rags bowed their heads and dug their toes in the sand.

We'd come to appreciate whatever void was in the middle of their parenting.

Today, Mom drank from the bottle, clutching it around the neck in a way that gave me a pang of a memory forming in real time.

I figured I needed maybe two beers to get a good buzz, maybe almost fall from the island and stagger up to my room. I drank the first one fast; I was thirsty.

"I only want you to get drunk on Catboat, with your father and me. No getting drunk out in the world. On Scrimshaw, at the Bowsprit, in a car, for Chrissake."

"Promise." I touched my can to her bottle, then tipped the can to get the dregs. "Sawyer and me, we appreciate your concern and the shitload of opportunities you gave us."

Bill removed her feet from the counter, which brought the

front legs of her chair back on the floor with a thud. She tried to balance a cheese cube on a carrot stick.

"Lol! Whore High? What an opportunity!" Big pause, big swig as Crack scarfed up the food Bill had dropped.

We laughed like girl crews at the mall.

Bill was close enough to the refrigerator to open it without getting up. She grabbed another beer and tossed it to me. I didn't exactly catch it; when I opened it, beer sprayed toward the ceiling.

"Ace, honey, when did this, I don't even know what to call it, smugness? No." She pulled crackers from the cabinet. Easier to eat when you're drunk. "When did this . . ." She took some crackers for herself and stuck one between my teeth.

Already halfway through my second beer, I was high and had to pee something fierce. I crossed my legs.

"No, it's ingratiation," she revised. "I've never heard you or your brother talk about *opportunities* or, God forbid, thank us for providing them."

"We will never forget what you've done for us."

"Don't be cynical." She'd polished off the whole bottle, which dropped from her hand and shattered on the floor.

I watched blankly, broken glass—the vision returned, blood running into Le Forest's white shirt, his mouth open, the slow motion of it. I silently reminded myself not to walk barefoot.

"I mean it, Mom. Sawyer and I, we love you guys and are grateful for what you've provided."

"Like what?"

"Like food, a roof over our heads."

"That's just the unwritten covenant of parenting. If you don't provide that, you need to be locked up."

"Still."

"Ace, I appreciate all these compliments, I do, but you have nothing to feel guilty about, you know that, right?"

"Who said I feel guilty?"

"Oh." Bill stood unsteadily. "I thought . . . I don't know . . . maybe . . ." Her attempt at a kiss dampened my cheek.

A warm, full, man-like stream of urine flowed from my body, onto the island, and puddled on the floor amid the broken glass, which sparkled in the light from the refrigerator Bill had not managed to close.

She picked up Crack so he wouldn't drink the piss or walk on the glass, wobbled into the living room, and fell backward onto the couch.

35

On Mrs. Forest's side of her marital bed was an end table with night creams and British mysteries. But it was the table's little drawers that held the real mysteries, things people hid but wanted to keep handy.

I opened a pink envelope addressed to "Susan" and read the letter inside, written in purple script. I replaced it exactly where it had been.

Thank You for Having Me, Le Forest's self-published book in which he answered made-up questions about his life and work, lay on his bedside table.

Le Forest was a fiend about therapeutic sleeping. If you slept wrong, your spine wouldn't align with your neck, and you'd start walking like a gorilla: "You'll end up with overdeveloped lower extremities, and you'll start carrying your weight in your belly."

"He really talks like that?" I said. Mrs. Forest had emerged from the bathroom to join me in the Forests' king-size bed.

"Only when he's trying to get me into the sack," Mrs. Forest said. I covered my ears.

You could get his book on Amazon. Le Forest had hung anatomy charts on the wall, and he had a real skeleton that doubled as a clothes rack. Today it was wearing a blue blazer with a striped tie. "Does this dude have a name?"

"It's apparently a woman. Can't you tell by the hips?"

"I didn't get that far in biology," I said.

"You guys don't really go to school, do you?"

"How do you think Sawyer got into community college? A high school diploma is a prerequisite." I lay back on Le Forest's therapeutic pillow, which was hard on one side and had ridges like a plowed field on the other.

"And you are on track for that?" When Mrs. Forest lay on her side, her breasts huddled like puppies.

"Even Bill and Rags don't ask stuff like that." I changed the subject. "We should name that skeleton."

Mrs. Forest gazed over my head. "Is Caitlyn too obvious?"

"Brilliant! With those hips and her suits and ties."

"Full disclosure: I think Caitlyn's hot," she said.

"You're making me jealous."

"She wasn't hot as Bruce but definitely as Caitlyn, with her butch voice and sexy dresses."

"Should I get a dress?" I rolled over and headed for the closet. You would expect the Forests to have a walk-in, and they did. On his side were suits neatly hung, shirts still in their boxes from the dry cleaners—the Forests wouldn't think of ironing. His shoes were lined up, the fancy ones with shoe trees, the others a little scuffed, the sneakers a little smelly.

Her side had a messy, T.J. Maxx feel. Her shoes were in order of casual to dressy, with Vans and Converse and sandals on one end, and at the other, something I'd never seen her in: dangerous-looking red stilettos. Slung over a ballet pole were the purses that made me want to protect her.

I chose a short black cocktail dress and red stilettos. Mrs. Forest's eyes went liquid. She pulled me into the bed and ate me alive. She didn't stop even when the stilettos dug into her. She had a gash just below her butt.

I went into their bathroom: his side with razors and shaving cream and tiny specks of beard in the sink like poppy seeds on a bagel; a gray towel to saw himself dry with; her side with "toilet

170

water," an open Pamprin bottle, foundation, and a lavender bra hanging from a light fixture. They had a hot tub with fake gold faucets and water jets that you could majorly turn yourself on with. I grabbed band-aids and gauze and Neosporin from the medicine cabinet.

"Hold still." I cleaned her cut with a "hers" washcloth, rubbed in some Neosporin, topped it off with a Stegosaurus band-aid.

Our athletic sex had prevented us from hearing someone enter the house. Before I could even kiss her boo-boo, Le Forest was standing in the doorway.

"Well, well," he said.

Mrs. Forest pulled the sheet up to her neck like they do in movies. "I'm not dressed, Lee."

He turned his male gaze on me. "But Ace is. You do wonders for my wife's clothes."

"Leave her alone, Lee."

"Black dress, heels, blue-green hair, the way you manage to stay *in* the dress, unlike my wife, who spills out of everything she wears."

"Which is a good thing," I said.

"What cradles might we be robbing here?" He patted the bed for me to sit beside him.

"We're legal," I said. "I did my homework."

"Seems like everything you and your brother do is homework," Le Forest said.

"Where are the kids, Lee?"

"Ethel is downstairs teaching them how to spike a volleyball."

"They're like, two feet tall," I said. "I doubt they're going to be spiking volleyballs."

"I doubt that a delinquent is going to be babysitting my kids."

"Our kids," Mrs. Forest corrected.

"Or that a cradle-robber should even have kids."

"Lee, that's sick," I said.

"No more *Dr. Forest*? You think you're equal to me because you're doing my wife?"

"We were not sneaking behind your back," Mrs. Forest said.

171

"We talked about this."

"That doesn't make it normal. To use Ace's word, it's sick."

"Using your kids as leverage is sick," I said.

"And what does a high school student know about parenting?"

"And what makes you think we're not equal?"

"I have advanced degrees, a career, a successful business, a family . . ."

"A mistress," I said, just as the twins pulled Ethel into the room. "Sorry, Ethel. I shouldn't have defined you by that one word."

Ethel didn't know where to look—at Mrs. Forest who was in the bed, holding the sheet up to her chin? At me, wearing a formal dress and one red stiletto? At Le Forest? What was the male equivalent of mistress? At times like this I longed for Sawyer. I felt half present, only half able to cope.

"You're way more than a mistress," I said to Ethel. "You have a career, hand-eye coordination."

"I should go," Ethel said.

"No, stay," Mrs. Forest said, indicating the bed. "Sit."

"Thit," Brett said.

The twins were just getting over the lisping that was common in toddlers, but they sometimes relapsed when stressed.

"Why are you guys wearing name tags?" I said, making room for Ethel at the end of the bed.

"Ethel dothn't know whoth who," Levi said.

"God, Lee." Mrs. Forest said. "That's demeaning. Hand me my robe, please."

Le Forest headed for the bathroom to retrieve it from the hook on the back of the door.

"I'll get it!" I could hear myself barking.

"No, I'll get it."

We raced each other to the bathroom. I was faster, but he was stronger, trapping me against the wall.

"Boys," I could hear Ethel saying, "Do you want to jump on the bed?"

"Yeth!"

Mrs. Forest consented, desperate to save her children from further trauma. Le Forest bunched the robe into a ball and threw it at Mrs. Forest, who turned her back to the mob in her bedroom, and draped it over her shoulders.

"I'm texting Sawyer to bring over food," I said.

"This isn't a party," Mrs. Forest said.

"It seems like it was a party," Le Forest said. "Play date? Dress-up? You never did that with me, Susan." He addressed Ethel without taking his eyes off his wife. "Can you please take the boys downstairs?"

"Ethel is not your nanny," I said.

Ethel said, "And I'm not just a mistress, either, according to you."

"She's doing it with my husband," Mrs. Forest pointed out.

"And you're doing it with me," I said. "Dr. Forest, you should probably take your children downstairs."

"I need to talk to my wife," Le Forest said. "Alone."

"So do I. Alone."

Ethel picked up the kids and carried them downstairs. "Popthicles!"

"You've unconsecrated our marriage bower," Le Forest said.

"Where are you getting this shit?" I said. "*Thank you for Having Me?*"

"I cannot deal with both of you," Mrs. Forest said. "One or the other of you has got to leave."

"You pick," I said to Mrs. Forest.

"I agree with Ace," Le Forest said. "You choose."

For the briefest instant, I was in a guy club with Le Forest, the shoulder grip and the bear hug, the infinitesimal head nod. *If you don't cross the line, I won't deck you with my fist.*

"Who am I, Meryl Streep?" Mrs. Forest said.

I picked up my clothes and headed for the door, still wearing the dress smelling of Mrs. Forest's half of the closet. I wasn't about to do a striptease in front of Le Forest.

"I love you, too," I whispered to his wife, grabbing Caitlyn's tie.

I left Le Forest standing by the bed, arms crossed, while Mrs. Forest wept into his ludicrous therapeutic pillow.

36

Dear Susan Forest,

This letter to myself is to try to understand this new self and where to go with her. Brené says that writing to yourself can help you embrace the vulnerable person you must be to make the leap into love.

I'm happier than I've ever been. How should I live with that happiness? Is it okay for me to feel this way?

Is it fair to my children?

I only want a more ordered life so that I can embrace the joyous disorder that I feel. Is this fair to the person I love?

She has an entire life ahead of her. Will I smother that life?

But so do I. Will I be a better mother and a better

partner to the person who loves me? Brené asks,
"What is the greater risk? Letting go of what
people think or letting go of how you feel, what you
believe, and who you are?"

I've let myself be weak.

Brené says it's okay to "wake up every day and love
someone who may not love you back, whose safety
you can't ensure, who may stay in your life or may
leave without a moment's notice, who may be loyal
to the day you die or betray you tomorrow."

It felt good to be back on Mill Wheel with Sawyer babysitting the twins, except for our reason for being there.

Le Forest's idea of revenge was a nonconsensual date with his wife. If she refused, he'd file for full custody of his children, whom he would coparent with Ethel Hooke. Not that Mrs. Forest had a problem with Ethel, whose core values kept wiping out her feeble attempts at whoredom.

The Forests' idea of a night out was to go to Boston for a cultural event like the Wang or Amy Schumer, followed by an Olympian ham and cheese sandwich at Jake Wirth's.

Brett and Levi raced into our arms, squealing, while their parents stood in the kitchen. The twins' pet turtle Slow plodded behind them.

"Hello, Dr. Forest," I said, icy. I'd learned this arctic freeze from Bill, who'd mastered the form, especially when she was defending her kids.

"Love your pocket square," Sawyer said. Le Forest had knocked himself out in the sartorial splendor department: dark suit, yellow tie, salacious lupine smile. When the men shook hands, they exuded in- and out-of-the-bedroom competence.

Mrs. Forest stared vacantly at her husband's pocket.

Sawyer stared at Le Forest too. I tried to place this new

scrutinizing. He might have inherited some of Bill's laser-eye schtick. He seemed to be sizing Le Forest up like he might come in handy for something.

The Forests had a kitchen equipped to the hilt, though they weren't cooks. They made simple things involving apple slices and hummus for the kids, and then stood in the kitchen eyeing their cell phones, while Brett and Levi sat at a tiny table with tiny chairs. Among the gadgetry was a wooden knife block with a dozen of the sharpest, shiniest unused knives. Sawyer stowed the block on the top shelf of the closet so the twins wouldn't stab themselves to death.

"Ethel lets us cut meat," Brett said. The name Ethel flitted around the room, coming to rest on the light that hung over the granite counters. Ethel was a name the twins could pronounce without lisping.

"But we like pink yogurt better," Levi said. "We're not lactothe intolerant."

"Slow likes yogurt too," Brett informed us. Slow was stalled on the threshold between the kitchen and dining room.

Mrs. Forest wore a pantsuit, like she was interviewing for HR director. Beige heels clicked on the tile floor, reminding me of Crack's explorations under the kitchen counter. Cubic zirconia caught the light. She was strangely free of instructions regarding the twins. She didn't even bother to kiss the kids goodnight. She kissed us instead, fugitive, freshly lipsticked humid farewells, just missing our mouths.

I followed her out, grabbing her elbow. "I want to be seen with you." I kissed her luscious mouth. "Not just at the shop or the Eatons'. A date."

Her eyes were on her husband, who was striding ahead to open the door to his status symbol, the only Maserati in town, so *outré*. A Volkswagen with a Maserati engine would have been more Whore Town.

"I read your letter," I blurted.

"I knew you'd snoop. Always hunting for *things* that will *tell* you something. I wanted to tell you." She kissed me back. "Yes, baby, a date. I promise."

Babysitting was a chance for Sawyer and me to practice parenting. Not in that desperate way gay people did, making up for millennia of lost parenthood with manic shots at domesticity followed by stultifying successes at it. We wanted to float around society on a cloud of entitlement, no more dysfunctional than anyone else.

"Mrs. Forest said I had no reproductive instincts. Zero."

"Sounds right," Sawyer said.

Who were our models? The Forests were like a movie-star couple, auditioning on camera and then stumbling into the chaos of real life.

Bill and Rags? Who were their models? Dad had Grandma Gretchen, who was a font of unconditional love. His father had loved ducks and boasted a museum quality collection of decoys.

Bill's defining moment was a childhood event that had scarred her for life. A family friend who'd had a quadruple bypass was not allowed physical contact with people outside the family because an infection could kill him. During a Christmas brunch, Bill, wanting to look sophisticated, had thrown her arms around this family friend and kissed him on the cheek. By New Year's, he was dead. His wife blamed Bill. For the rest of her life, our mother was wary of getting close.

After we put the twins to bed, we headed for the couch. I lay my head on Sawyer's lap. "I can streak it myself next time," he said, examining my hair. "Save money. Get some product at CVS."

"I don't know how to say this." I dislodged a Lego from behind the cushion and handed it to him.

"I get it: Mrs. Forest is at that stage where she loves everything about you." He worried the Lego in one hand. "She doesn't give a shit if your hair falls out."

"Something like that." Slow's primordial scent rose from the couch. "Mrs. Forest says she likes me butch."

"She likes me butch, too," Sawyer said. "She thinks women like me because I'm like them. She critiques me during the mani-pedi."

"Because you like fashion and do nails and throw like a girl?"

"Exactly."

"That is so predictable and unsubtle." All the stuff I loved about her.

"And for you, it has to be a woman like Mrs. Forest who you can fantasize about even if she's standing as real as life right in front of you," Sawyer said. "But you might want to start getting real about her."

"Meaning?"

"We don't know what goes on in this house." He panned the room.

I had a pretty good idea of what went on in this house.

"It takes two to tango," Sawyer said. "Le Forest may not be so bad. Maybe she's goading him."

"Goading him? Into what?"

"If he did something really bad, something super illegal, it would be easy for her to get the kids."

"So he's not a cunt anymore?"

"I'm just saying." He scissored my hair with two fingers. "You can't go to college interviews with your hair scraggly and half-dyed, just because Mrs. Forest can't see it."

"She sees *me*."

Sawyer rested his head against the back of the couch. "I know that, but I don't know, it's just ... " I followed Sawyer's gaze. The Forests had track lighting that suited their style, such as it was, but not Horton's. Where were the floor lamps that stood guard near the wingback chairs? "How are your college applications?" he said.

"I'd have to be brain-dead not to get into Massasoit."

"But after that?"

"Start life. How much more school do I need?"

"Hey, community college can be tough. I flunked *Introduction to Human Resource Management: A Survey*."

"What did Bill and Rags say?"

"What they always say," Sawyer said.

179

"'Just don't flunk interpersonal relationships!'."

"'Ethical behavior!'"

"'Treat people the way they want to be treated!'"

Sawyer lit a joint. Grandma encouraged smoking over drinking, though maybe she wasn't the best role model. She said there were mean drunks out in the world. She'd nearly gotten killed by a guy at Max's who broke a beer bottle in her face. You could still see the half train-track scar over her right eye.

"Too bad we can't bring Bill and Rags to New York with us," I said.

When we were growing up, our favorite books were about kids with no parents—Huckleberry Finn, Eloise, Pippi Longstocking. Our parents thought we called them by their first names because we were brash and unruly in ways that made little difference in the long run. But it was because we needed distance.

Nevertheless, it was the safest place to be, with Bill and Rags on Catboat Road, and on Scrimshaw Street with shopkeepers hosing their little sections of sidewalk and goring everyone with small talk while the *Frigate* exposed our broken bonds. But outside Whore Town, we'd be way more exposed.

"Look at the kids who never left." Sawyer blew hair away from my face. "Dave and Dante, Junior Eaton, the Allerton sisters, they all have jobs, they're community-minded."

"And Maddie. She performed well in the archery hutch."

"I liked Maddie," Sawyer said, "but she was just like her name: slightly mad."

"She seemed like the only sane person in the room that night."

"I think her parents were from Billerica," Sawyer said. "That helps, being from away."

If we went to New York, we'd become public transportation fiends, workaholics, people who find ever more industrial frontiers to transform into Brooklyn. "Bill and Rags are okay with us going to New York," I said.

"What wouldn't be okay with Bill and Rags?"

"If we did something to land us on *Forensic Files*?"

"But if we were smart about it, they'd probably say they were proud of us."

"And bring Toll House cookies up to Walpole," I said.

"We can't go to prison! They'd separate us!" Sawyer's Adam's apple rose and fell like a piston. "I always wanted to be in that *Orange Is the New Black* prison, but they'd never let in a straight guy who's not transitioning or whatever."

"We better not commit any major crimes."

"Just quality-of-life crimes," Sawyer said.

"Like Jesus," I said.

37

Harbor Happy Hours
Maritime Mondays at the Bowsprit

The smell of fish hit us the minute Mrs. Forest and I entered the Bowsprit. We'd chosen the most popular place at the most popular time. The point of this date was to be seen.

The Bowsprit's heavy wood door had been salvaged from a hatch on the *Speedwell*, carved with numbers said to be a 17th century bar tab. Just as every strip mall in Vegas had a one-armed bandit, every restaurant in Horton had a lobster tank. That was where the fishy smell was coming from, not the raw bar with its piles of shellfish on little mountains of ice.

"Welcome, ladies." Rainy Priest did double duty as a hostess. The jumbo menus in the crook of her arm made her look even smaller.

No one ordered half the stuff on the menu. Mrs. Forest wore a shawl from Madewell.

"Is that cashmere? You know where to find me." Rainy turned to me. "You're looking pretty sharp yourself, Ace." I was dressed all in black, including a leather jacket borrowed from

Sawyer that was too big in a way that he said "harmonized." My hair was recently spiked, bleached Stevie Nicks blond, with blue stripes. Sawyer had driven Cassandra crazy with his instructions, delivered while looking at himself in the mirror. It was sexy the way stylists held the comb and scissors in one hand.

You could always get a seat at the Bowsprit, except on summer weekends when tourists tied up and headed in for a dock 'n' dine. Paper placemats were printed with the names of shops and jokey swordfish jumping out of the water.

Today Mrs. Forest's expensive shawl, the smell of Ralph Lauren emanating from me, and the general sense of heightened awareness prompted Rainy to give us the best table, which she usually saved for embarrassing celebrations.

Dante came over with the coffee mug he and Dave kept behind the bar for me, filling it with Narragansett from the tap. Sawyer and I could not be seen drinking on the premises.

"Fish stew is hot off the harbor," Dante said.

"We'll have it," I said. "Extra oyster crackers, hold the kale."

Mrs. Forest laughed. "You're ordering for me? What a guy you are."

From every window you could see the harbor with its work boats, yachts, sailboats, and ugly Clorox-bottle cabin cruisers. In the distance was the lighthouse, striped like a barber pole; beyond, the ocean, and then on to Europe.

I sipped from my mug, which was actually Sawyer's. Janie Brewster down at the Pot Shop had made the mugs for Sawyer and me, painting our names on the sides; she'd painted a tiny heart under Sawyer's name.

A guy at the bar bought a drink for Mrs. Forest. Most of the Happy Hour crowd was familiar. Any one of them might take his eyes off the screen, relinquish the field, the rink, the court, to salivate in our direction: Senior Eaton, Nate Carver, Jake Margesson, Stanley Prower, Chuck Butten, even Chippie Holbeck, who hunkered at the end of the bar with the women.

Clam Warden Peregrine White watched himself in the

mirror, sticking his little finger in a beer mug and dampening his sideburns.

Chief of Police Nate Carver gave me a thumbs up. Christ, big Nate Carver with his boots and bowlegs, and armor hanging from his belt? Mrs. Forest acknowledged him with a megawatt smile.

"Nate Carver? What's up with that?"

"I honestly don't know."

"You don't know?"

"You know how men are when they get together," Mrs. Forest said.

"No, I don't."

"I guess you wouldn't." She leaned across the table to wipe my upper lip.

"He's married to my English teacher."

"That will make it very complicated for Nate and me."

"Sorry, I, it's just that I, I don't know, I don't want to ever 'betray you tomorrow.' You laid yourself out there in your letter." More exposed than sex. "Everyone thinks I'm so smart, but I can't even express myself."

"It's alright, sweetheart." She lifted the wine Nate had just bought her. "I think I know."

"You're going to drink that?"

Mrs. Forest shot me an exasperated look.

"If you don't get my humor, it could be a problem down the line."

"I guess I wasn't in a humorous mood. I was more in a romantic one." She raised her eyes. "Those idiots at the bar? They think I'm hot. Big deal. They're men. But what makes me really happy is that you think I'm hot, this smart, sexy young woman likes me, the real me." She raised the glass to Nate Carver. "And I love that you said 'down the line.'"

"You think that because I'm young, I just live for the present?"

"It is a hallmark of youth."

"Where did that come from? I have a sense of my own mortality, just like you."

184

"When I'm with you, I feel like I could live forever," Mrs. Forest said.

"'Loyal to the day we die.'"

We dug into the fish stew, thickening it with oyster crackers and dipping into the other's bowl as if we'd each ordered something different. It was an excuse to exchange fluids and wipe each other's mouths and give the middle finger to those Whore Towners talking behind our backs.

"We need dessert." I motioned to Dave, who had taken over from Dante. They were twins, but they were easy to tell apart: Dave had been born with only one arm.

"Broa," I said. This was Portuguese bread pudding, made with brandy and raisins and served warm with whipped cream.

"Gottit, Acey." Though Dave had had an entire life to practice, he was a one-armed klutz, spilling beverages, dropping plates, and sending entire dinners spinning across the room.

I jumped up. "I'll help you, Dave." I followed him through the swinging door to the kitchen, its portlight, rimmed with brass, salvaged from the *Speedwell*.

"I didn't want Dave to dump our dessert on the floor," I said, serving Mrs. Forest.

"I think if I was born with one arm, I'd finagle it better," she said.

"That's a little rough."

"I don't care about Dave and Dante and those subhumans at the bar. I care about you, us."

"Down the line?"

"Yes, Ace, down the line."

"Can we talk about it later?" I unfolded my napkin, which I'd folded carefully in squares. "I don't want to lose it here in the Bowsprit with all those cavemen staring at you."

She waved Dave over. "Two cappuccinos?"

"Just leave them on the bar," I said. "I'll pick 'em up."

"No way," Dave said. "I am at your service!" The place where his arm wasn't was covered with what appeared to be a Styrofoam cup.

Dave appeared with the cappuccinos, which slid one at a time off his tray and onto the table. The cups managed to stay upright, but coffee sloshed over the rim. I mopped it up with a napkin. "Almost, dude."

When we got up to leave, smoke was funneling through the swinging door to the kitchen. We later read on the *Frigate Breaking News* site that there'd been a grease fire, though they had managed to contain it in the kitchen. Thank God a couple of patrons had saved the swinging door with the portlights from the *Speedwell*.

"Turbine supporters must be living in a cave if they fail to acknowledge these accidents over the past year," Eleanor Margesson told Chuck Butten.

38

Turbine tech tells all
by Chuck Butten
Frigate staff writer

Horton Selectman Doris Wilder on Wednesday evening sought to tamp down turbine fury by inviting turbine engineer Barry Bradford to again address the council.

"Facts are just a smokescreen," alleged Opposition Wind organizer Eleanor Margesson, interrupting Bradford's PowerPoint presentation.

What did we look like to the outside world? Mrs. Forest was too old to be a friend, yet too preoccupied to be one of those aunts of drive-by shooting victims that I'd read so much about.

As we walked to Whore High, she kicked pebbles along the shoulder and held my hand. A bee dive-bombed toward her head. There was the smell of cut grass. Classes just finished. Summer.

I knew that Mrs. Forest had tried on tons of combinations, throwing castoffs on the bed until she'd found the perfect outfit for taking her lover to a meeting with her guidance counselor—all the Ragsdales were at a *Frigate* fundraiser. Mrs. Forest should have worn a different jacket with the skirt. She was dressed like she was going to a job interview. Which, in a way, she was.

"Shouldn't we rehearse?" she said.

"Is there a script for this?"

She sat down on a large rock etched with the words "Donated by the Horton Science Center."

"What dickwads donate a rock?" I said.

She took off her heels. "I should have broken these in first."

I rubbed her feet. "You didn't need to buy all new stuff just to talk to Mr. Prower."

"Your future is in my hands."

"No one's future is in anyone's hands," I said. She was hurt. "Sorry." I kissed her on the mouth. She reapplied her lipstick.

"This is nerve-racking enough. Don't mess up my makeup."

"Just because you're doing something my mother should be doing . . . I so do not want you to be my mother."

"Ace, babe, I don't think I've ever seen your mother with makeup. Does she even wear lip gloss?"

"Jesus, not so literal. You sound like Rags, the way you small-talk each other to death."

"Ace." She kissed me hard. "Do you do that with your mother?"

I fondled her breasts and put my hand up her skirt.

"You're going to have to finish that before we go in to see your guidance counselor." Having sex on the side of the road in broad daylight calmed me enough to stride confidently through the big double doors of Whore High. We breathed in the stench of adolescent locker, ground zero for gangs, hookups, and knife fights.

Trophy cases held Whore High's third- and fourth-place

188

triumphs. On the walls big red diagonal lines slashed through images of the bottle, the needle, the pistol.

High school had not been the life-altering experience for Sawyer and me that it was for most people. We avoided slang because the words changed so quickly, they needed buy-by dates. Bill knew the "lingo," but we stuck to standard words from the OED.

"Welcome!" Mr. Prower extended his hand. His sleeves were too short, exposing bony white wrists. He was tall, with uncoordinated limbs like a marionette. He had a long nose, with glasses sliding to the end of it, and a comb-over. His pants were bunched around his waist. His flat feet stretched his insteps toward the floor.

"Mr. Prower." Mrs. Forest looked like she could use a good squirt of hand sanitizer.

"Stanley, call me Stanley, and you?"

"Susan, Susan Forest."

"The Lee Forests?"

"The Mrs. Forests," I said.

"Dr. Forest does our football squad."

"He does a lot of people," Mrs. Forest said.

"You must be a good friend of the Ragsdales."

"Our families are close," Mrs. Forest said.

Mr. Prower kept his eyes firmly planted on Mrs. Forest's cleavage; she wasn't wearing a shirt under her jacket. Eyes on your own paper, Mr. Prower!

Mrs. Forest could go on the attack with her breasts, or be generous and share.

Mr. Prower opened my file like a doctor and pushed his glasses up his nose with his middle finger. "Ace, it seems like you've had a few problem areas. . . ."

"Problem areas?" Mrs. Forest said. "I don't think so, Stanley."

"Well, let's start with the good stuff. We have Karen Tilley onboard to prep you for the Red Cross exam?"

"Karen thinks I have enough of the basics to keep from drowning," I said.

"That seems like the important thing vis à vis a swimming test," Mrs. Forest said, pulling her suit jacket down so there was even more to see. Her fringe of mauve lace was making me lightheaded.

She'd pronounced *vis à vis* to rhyme with *viz a viz*. I felt desperate to protect her.

"Well, let's hope it goes better than archery," Mr. Prower said.

"Archery is not a necessary skill in the digital age."

"I agree," Mr. Prower told Mrs. Forest's tits.

"Though the bow and arrow played an important part in our nation's history," I put in. "It was the main reason why Native Americans were wiped out by Horton's white settlers."

"It looks like you like history."

"My brother Google-Imaged Massasoit's bow and arrow. It's a work of art."

"How is your brother, by the way?"

Mrs. Forest recrossed her legs, redirecting attention to her come-fuck-me shoes and her skirt, pulled up to her thighs. "Sawyer is doing quite well, as I'm sure his sister will, too, no matter what career she pursues."

"Well, let's get to college first." Mr. Prower turned the page of my transcript. "English! Now there's a subject you seem to have excelled in."

"Excelled?" I said.

"Well, solid Cs all the way through. That's encouraging."

"I don't think English will get you very far in life." I leaned on Mr. Prower's desk, looking him in the eye. His mental undressing of Mrs. Forest was pissing me off.

"Mrs. Carver says here that your knowledge of the material was greater than your 'C' average would indicate. Your problem wasn't in the material but in a 'desultory attitude and an indifference to class attendance and completion of assignments.'"

"What could you possibly do with an English degree?" I turned Mr. Prower's snow globe upside down, which caused a blizzard to obliterate what looked to be baby Jesus and a car.

"Ace, I've always said you could be a writer." Mrs. Forest leaned even closer to Mr. Prower. "She and Sawyer started an advertising agency."

Mr. Prower dismissed this with an effeminate wave of his hand. "Or you could be an English professor in a small New England college," he said, in a trance. This had clearly been his dream job, not shitty guidance counselor at dumbass Whore High.

"English is a fucked-up . . ."

Mrs. Forest's cool hand between my shoulder blades.

"Sorry, English sucks," I revised. Was that Crack shit in the treads of my sneaker?

"No one has a clue what *Beowulf* is about," I started in. "And teachers won't be honest about the 'Pardoner's Tale.' You might actually read Shakespeare if they weren't plays, and epistolary novels if they weren't letters, and poetry if it had plot. And Henry David Thoreau, who people around here think is such a genius? Him and his fancy cabin. He was practically on Scrimshaw Street and pretending like he was in the Gulag or the tundra or some shit. Steinbeck and his useless travels with his dog? He wanted to be home f-ing his wife. *Catcher in the Rye?* What a whiny boy book. All these A-holes with their angst and their sex objects and their egomania? Frost and his 'lovely' woods, what kind of a piece-of-shit word is that? Harper Lee? The best thing about her is her name. Everybody getting so bent out of shape over Shylock? They should actually listen to Portia's speech. It's all a big f-ing plot. That last line of *Gatsby?* Bullshit. If you were going to read just one book? M. F. K. Fisher, she can put your whole life into a trout on a plate."

Mr. Prower closed my file, rested his glasses on top of it, and stared blindly in the direction of Mrs. Forest's chest. "I agree, Ace. English is not for you."

39

Mrs. Forest hadn't exercised her Realtor chops for quite some time. Now she was in full Realtor mode in front of the Fonseca estate: lime suit, citrus spritz, and only a touch of the phony smile common to the breed. The Fonseca mansion was really the only "property" in town. She held her three-ring binder against her chest like a schoolgirl.

"Remember the last time we were here," she said, goosing me in the ribs.

"How could I forget? I nearly came in my pants, and Sawyer was probably hiding half a hard-on."

"Not very successfully," Mrs. Forest said.

"Well, you did look like an Amsterdam sex worker, with that sleazy lingerie and that big coat. I loved it."

Clients Jack and Shirley Robinson appeared on the steps. The Robinsons had arrived by boat. Nothing on the graffitied Horton sign on the expressway would have tempted a motorist to exit, but the harbor offered an historic lighthouse, old homes along the bluffs, stick cottages on the beach, dock 'n' dines at the Bowsprit.

Today our windmill's notorious blades turned drowsily in the distance.

The Robinsons looked shocked.

"What did you have in mind?" Mrs. Forest asked breezily.

"Well, it's so big." Jack looked like Wallace Shawn in *My Dinner with Andre*.

His wife smiled down at him. "Obviously, dear." She was dressed for a tennis match: short skirt, broadcloth shirt, the sleeves of a raspberry cardigan tied around her ropey neck.

"There are certain . . ." Mrs. Forest turned to me. "By the way, this is my partner, Ace."

"Ace?" Shirley scrutinized me. "Partner? You seem kind of young, dear."

"I'm interning with Mrs. Forest for my realtor's license." I stuck out my hand. "Ace Ragsdale."

I wore green slacks and a rose jacket. Sawyer said that rose picked up just a hint of duality in the Anjou pear. "What Mrs. Forest was saying is that there are certain things, entities, in Horton that would not sit well with the zoning board."

"Like?" Jack didn't rake his eyes over Mrs. Forest; he seemed to be one of those men who saved virtual undressing for his wife.

Shirley thrust a bony hip at me. She was a John Updike fantasy woman: freckled, sun-kissed, athletic, an afternoon fucker, ingesting salty snacks and gin and tonics.

"Halfway houses, group homes, youth centers, NIMBY sort of things," I answered. I let my hairline sneer signal to Shirley that I saw her sizing me up.

"That's too bad," she said. "I always think that sex offenders need a second chance."

"We do too," I said, "but maybe not in the Fonseca mansion."

"It's a World Heritage Site." Mrs. Forest opened her binder to a page with the words "Amblyopia, commonly known as lazy eye," the twins' diagnosis so blatantly visible that I reached over and closed the binder.

"In any case, we would just be living in it residentially."

"Do you have a big family?" Mrs. Forest said, diverting Shirley's attention.

"We're empty-nesters," Jack said.

"Could be grandkids," I suggested.

"Ace, very perceptive, only I'm not sure our children are sexual beings."

"Shirley, honey, I don't think Mrs. Forest and Ace need to hear that."

Mrs. Forest stifled a laugh. "We should go in."

A wide white stone terrace spanned the entire front of the mansion.

In the foyer the Robinsons changed their minds about seeing any more of the Fonseca place. There were trees growing on the parapets, kudzu pushing up through the tiles, wildlife taking back what was theirs, but that wasn't it.

Shirley Robinson was apparently phobic about salamanders, a small colony of which were dropping like little snakes from the canopy. She ran down the steps, leaving Jack to blurt his apologies.

"You know how to get back to the harbor?" I said.

"Of course. I can see it from here."

"Just avoid the dead ends and bike paths at high tide." Mrs. Forest handed him a card. "In case you change your mind."

"I'm so sorry," Jack said to me. "My wife, she can be a little . . . I hope you weren't offended."

"Flattered," Mrs. Forest said.

We watched them make their way down the long gravel driveway, with its twin mermaids at the end. One had a broken tail, the other a broken tit.

"I don't mind people ogling you," Mrs. Forest said. "I'm proud, but it was the creepy way she did it."

"But you couldn't blame her for trying," I joked, "residentially."

"Residentially, I'd like to rip off those fruity pants that your brother picked out for you."

"Be my guest."

"You were getting off on her blowing sunshine up your ass. 'Ace, you're so perceptive.' Gag me with a spoon."

"Say that again?" I said. " 'Blow sunshine up your ass?' "

"Sunshine up your ass," she said absently, turning her

attention to the bowels of the mansion. "Wow, we need to get Sport Rodgers in here. Do you think we could get Fabia to sink some money into this thing?"

"Her idea was that the buyers would sink some money into it."

"Maybe a few cosmetic upgrades." Mrs. Forest surveyed the original wood shutters hanging at wild angles from their rusted hinges. "Animal control. We need to get animal control in here, and maybe a tree surgeon."

We got as far as the kitchen, which looked like the one on *Two Fat Ladies*. Sawyer and I had streamed every episode. We'd gotten lost in the flesh of these two lovebirds—never mind their complicated menus, which demanded they motor in their Nazi sidecar and traipse through the weirs, rifles cocked, blowing away guinea hens.

The kitchen's white tiles were now urine-colored. The stove was industrial like the one at the firehouse, where Italian firefighters made their spaghetti with "gravy." The faucet in the soapstone sink was arched in the manner of a swan's neck. High up were casement windows, with hand cranks and the remnants of stained-glass heraldry.

"Sit," Mrs. Forest commanded, indicating the marble counter, veined and cracked. "These pants are ridiculous," she said, pulling them down, her gorgeous face disappearing between my legs. I forced myself to wait, supplying the screams and *fuck me*'s for her climax. They echoed through the empty rooms.

When it was over, I had a cut on my back.

"I'm so sorry, honey." She pulled a tissue from her purse, patting it. "This broken marble, it's sharp."

"I loved it." I kissed her. "I love this place, too."

Maybe I would love anyplace where we were together, even without her face between my legs.

"I do too, but I can't show it again unless we can get Fabia to do some renovations."

I could see beyond the broken-down banisters, the vegetation and scurrying creatures to a fun-filled home, with light and air and loved ones laughing around the banquet table. I grabbed an old coffee can that had been fossilizing near the sink. "We need to catch some of those salamanders for the twins. They'd love them."

"Levi would. Brett will need a little coaxing. It took him a while to warm up to Slow." It was a subtle message: if we were going to be together, I'd have to learn their individual fears and eccentricities.

Mrs. Forest needed some coaxing, too. She was just as freaked out as Shirley Robinson had been, but didn't want to be a wuss in front of me. She helped me corral the beautiful yellow-spotted amphibians.

In the car she said, "You were awesome back there."

"You too."

"No, I mean with those ridiculous Robinson people."

"It's funny how people get off their boats and immediately want to own something here."

She reached across the gearshift for my hand. "I want you to be my partner."

"I am your partner."

"I mean business partners, too. Customers are starting to ask for you at the shop, and we could be real estate partners."

"But wouldn't we need some houses to sell?"

"We could diversify, outside Horton."

At the end of the driveway, I got out and wrestled the broken tit from the mermaid's wounded heart. "A souvenir." I handed it to her.

Mrs. Forest kissed its jagged nipple and placed it lovingly on the dashboard, like a bobble dog.

40

Karen Tilley stood with one hand holding the whistle around her neck, and the other opening the door to Club YES. I ducked under her outstretched arm.

A staffer waved me in. "Hey, girl."

The management had recently given Sawyer and me free passes, wanting us to "drink in the feel of the place," so we could "cement the brand." Today it had an indifferent, ratty energy: ripped T-shirts, baggy sweats, people with no obvious disabilities leaning on claw canes, babies floating like litter in the pool. In the locker room, a *Casablanca* fog escaped from the showers and steam room.

Karen opened the door to the pool. "Personally? I don't think being 'gym-orientated' really matters." She still wore a retainer, which made me think she wanted to smile for sports reporters and say, "We gave a thousand percent."

Karen was a hero. One summer, she'd dived from the terrace of the Bowsprit to save a kid who'd fallen from the launch and was in the path of a speeding Chris Craft.

"It kinda matters to me," I said. "You can't graduate if you flunk the swimming test."

"That's so not correct." Karen had been the first girl to make the boys' wrestling team. Le Forest was their trainer; he wore white pants and an ID around his neck, like he was in the NFL. "Like you have to do the butterfly to be an accountant?"

Karen's thighs bulged from her long Olympics-quality Speedo. Girl jocks were not like the guys, slouched and pigeon-toed, laces untied. Girls were into teamwork and helping others. Karen wore heartbreaking glasses, which she secured with a strap when she was on the field, pulling her baseball cap low over her eyes. You weren't allowed to wear baseball caps in school, but Mr. Prower said yes to nonviolent crimes.

"Nice ink," I said.

"Which?"

Madonna was tattooed on her biceps. "You have another one?"

She had a deflated football on her lower back. "It's a reminder," Karen said. "No cheating."

"What's with Madonna? She's old enough to be your grandmother."

"I like the way she'll tongue-kiss anything. She'd like, kiss a camel if it was on stage with her."

"I admire that."

From the yoga studio we heard lugubrious chant-like Enya music, as an instructor invoked radiant light beaming from their foreheads to the edge of the universe. It made me fantasize about Mrs. Forest and her champion yoga poses. Warrior One: the Amazon, sacrificing her boob to shoot a more deadly arrow.

"If you flunk swimming, it'll be my fault," Karen said. "You have to float for five minutes and swim one length of the pool."

We stood at the shallow end, wearing fluorescent orange flip-flops provided by the club. I tucked my hair under the bathing cap and put on my goggles.

"I need these," I said grabbing a flutter board and a pair of flippers.

"No enhancements! Amy Allerton will never allow that." Karen threw them back on the pile.

I dipped my toe in the water. "It's cold."

"Man up, Acey Decey."

I started with the dead-man's float. The bottom had a Ty-D-Bol feel. Oceans reflect sky; pools reflect phony turquoise paint. I floated on my back for five minutes while Karen timed me using a monster waterproof guy's watch.

I wanted her to support me like Dad used to. His large freckled hand would cover my entire back. I could smell his sweaty, beachy man-smell. A tiny lightning bolt of salt snagged in the stubble of his cheek. I wanted to keep my plastic jellies on. Dad swam out to retrieve them, bobbing on the tide like boats, while ribbons of seaweed snaked by me.

"Okay, time for the lap," Karen said. Because Karen had admired a guy doing the butterfly, I impulsively chose it. The impossible stroke kicked up waves, causing me to take in water and bringing Karen out to save me, with her aptitudes and androgyny. She'd long been certified for a summer on the lifeguard stand at Fifth Cliff.

She muscled me onto the lip of the pool. It started with mouth-to-mouth with her cracked lips and fresh chlorine breath. It was touching the way she removed her retainer first, tucking it in the leg of her Speedo, as we athletically tongue-kissed and more above the begoggled lane-swimmers.

Shit, why had I let this Karen thing happen? I got everything I needed—and more—from Mrs. Forest.

Karen was just *there*. It was life's there-ness that could destroy you.

Afterward, we sat on plastic chairs on the side of the pool staring at the lappers, with their back and forth, like dogs fetching.

Karen draped a towel over my shoulder. "It seemed like you were drowning out there. You scared the shit out of me."

"I got overenthusiastic."

Buying time, Karen turned her attention to a couple sharing a stability ball and texting, as if reclining and typing were sports. "Sorry about that, whatever it was we were doing; it wasn't very professional."

"No, it wasn't."

"Suzie Forest would probably agree," Karen said.

"You call her Suzie?"

"I don't call her anything. I don't even know her, but Dr. Forest is the trainer for all our teams."

"I guess everybody knows about us."

"You guess?" Karen dried her hair with a towel. "She's kinda old for you, no?"

"I never noticed."

"But she is pretty," Karen said. "I'll give her that."

"Pretty?"

"Yeah, pretty," Karen said. "What is this, English as a Second Language?"

"I would never describe her as pretty."

"What then?"

I grabbed Karen's phone from her gym bag, scanning Thesaurus.com. "Delectable," I said.

"That's way sick, Ace."

I couldn't tell if she meant the good or bad kind of sick. "We're partners," I said feebly. I had a model right here at Club YES for this lopsided "partnership"—Fabia Fonseca, who came here daily with her young mystery man.

"You could get hurt," Karen said. "Old people, they're not serious."

"You speak from experience?"

"Soccer coach," she said.

"What happened?"

"She stayed with her husband."

"Shit. I'm sorry," I said.

"For me or for you?" Karen said.

"For me, I guess."

"Well, be careful, is all." Karen's foot whisked my thigh. "Middle-aged people, they think they can have it all."

I contemplated her wide, utilitarian foot. "My brother's handiwork?"

Karen peered at her toes. "If you want to be an athlete, you need to have good nail hygiene. You don't want to be disqualified for injuring someone."

"Are you the only person on the team with, what is that? 'Eggplant?'"

"Periwinkle."

"You're blushing," I said.

"What's with Sawyer, anyway?" she asked.

"Not sure I understand the question."

"Your brother is—I mean, I'm sure you know, like he's—I don't know, not really real. Or something." She absently surveyed the multipurpose lane.

"Most women think he's hot. You don't?" Sawyer never actually got *involved* with women. He danced around them and flattered them, but mainly, he wanted me to think there were other people in his life besides me.

Karen switched to staring at the Club YES pennants strung across the pool. "When you're with him at Fabia's it's like, I don't know. Like he treats you, like the place is filled with people, and he puts you like in this box, like you're protected, and the noise stops, and time stands still, and it's just you and him with your foot in his hand. He smells good."

"Get in line."

"Not interested. I met somebody."

An instructor in a red Club YES robe shooed us away to make room for Aqua Exercise for Arthritis. Old people with their water wings and fringed caps started to assemble. Flesh undulated like bogs. There were thighs like a mackerel sky; skin with discs, moles, scars, lines, folds, and rashes. Arms were chocolate chip cookie dough. Veins were stray threads.

"Bone on bone!" one of them boasted.

The immense glass window that overlooked the pool was like a movie screen. People stared through it as if swimmers and flailers and floaters were the most interesting thing around. Mrs. Forest was no exception. When we started to exit the pool area, she was standing transfixed, yoga mat slung over one shoulder, sports bra and double tank tops keeping everything in place,

201

tight little yoga pants, and flip-flops, revealing toes that had recently enjoyed Sawyer's attention.

How long had she been there?

Karen looked over her shoulder to see if I'd seen what she'd seen, then walked away, leaving me on my own with the pain and rage that Mrs. Forest impaled me with.

41

Mrs. Forest turning up on Catboat Road on a Saturday morning was *not* business as usual. She let herself in through the back door.

"Hello, baby," she said to Sawyer. The greeting achieved its goal; I was jealous and contrite. She'd obviously witnessed my random and meaningless tongue kissing with Karen Tilley. Mrs. Forest couldn't know that Karen was just a habit, not a person.

"Baby," Sawyer repeated hoarsely. Normally I loved it when Mrs. Forest was completely aware of her hold over us; not so much today.

I still wanted to "dress" for her, though she'd seen me in every stage of undress, rank, snot wiped on a sleeve. I wished that I wasn't wearing flannel cowboy pajamas under the kimono I'd stolen from Mrs. Forest, and Bill's horrible Merrills.

Crack stood on his hind legs, paws on Mrs. Forest's knees. She kissed him on the nose and slung her purse over a doorknob.

"Suzie, what a nice surprise!" With morning breath and coffee breath, Bill's air kiss seemed directed at the room as a whole. She handed Mrs. Forest a mug.

"Thanks, I really need this."

"I'll make more," I said.

Mrs. Forest's attention was on me, whether or not she was

looking at me. She was one up on us, clothed, and showered, with her hair squeezed dry. Maybe minutes ago, she'd been nude in that steamy stall of hers, silhouette distorted against the rough glass, skin reddening with the near-scalding water she loved, too hurried with this errand to blow-dry her hair with her precious Bigwig. Among us now, smelling of body wash and shampoo.

"It's always good to see you, Suzie." Rags wore a trench coat over his nightie, as if he'd just that moment thought better of exposing himself. Crack held the belt in his mouth, at the ready. "I'll heat up some pancakes," Rags said. Like pancakes came precooked.

"No!" Mrs. Forest said. "Toast is fine. Toast. Pancakes are too difficult, complicated." I waited for another unnecessary word. "Everything is hard enough." She surveyed the bits of burnt pancake on the griddle. "Life."

I handed her the mug. When there were no Senior Eaton lattes to be had, she liked her coffee black, steam rising from the dark.

"Country white?" Sawyer said, putting two slices in the toaster.

"Seems to suit the occasion," Dad joked.

Barefoot and bare-chested, wearing the Capri pants Fabia had given him, Sawyer looked straight out of *The King and I*. I forgave Mrs. Forest for being unable to take her eyes off the comforting fur that you could smooth like a mother.

Sawyer had grabbed some lemon balm and dabbed it behind his ears when she'd appeared. Why did we have this weird ingredient?

"Sit, Suzie." Bill's moccasins were broken down in back, robe open.

Crack heard what he believed to be humans' favorite word and sat. Rags slipped charred pancake remnants into his mouth.

Our parents—turned on by their shopping exploits—must have been majorly fucking to bring back this bale of paper towels, where Mrs. Forest was now aiming her exquisite backside. The pack exhaled a plastic-y sigh as she sunk into it.

204

"Where are the kids?" I didn't care, but was striving for normalcy. I wanted to turn back the clock to where we were buck-naked in the bed.

She finally had a reason to look at me. "Lee took them to some kind of take-your-dad-to-school event."

"Good for Lee," Rags said, like Le Forest needed to spend more quality time with his kids.

"There're going to be sack races, three-legged races," Mrs. Forest said. "Not Lee's strong point."

"I don't know," Sawyer said. "I could see Dr. Forest doing that, but shit, I wish you would have told me."

"You're not their dad," Rags said, stating the obvious.

"Yeah, but sack races? Three-legged races? I love that shit." Sawyer placed a ginormous box of Cheerios next to Mrs. Forest so she could rest her toast and coffee on it.

"Really?" Bill looked surprised. "We could have provided you with those opportunities if you'd asked."

"Anyway, we're glad you're here," Rags said.

"We don't see enough of you," Bill added, meaning *alone*.

Grandma stumbled into the kitchen like a sleep-deprived teenager. "Mom." Rags pulled her gently by the elbow. "Clothes?"

"Clothes? Shit, I should wear clothes for company, right?"

"For all of us," Dad said.

"Cripes," Grandma said. "I forgot to rinse my delicates."

Dad covered her with his trench coat, but it couldn't be unseen: skin like a too-big sack, bones jostling, tea bag tits, low-tide lines, ghetto patch down there, clam neck of a clitoris, toes crawling over each other like suckling pigs.

Standing in the humongous trench coat, Grandma now looked like a pervert who might open it at any moment to reveal a monstrous dangling penis.

She lurched from one solid object to the next, drinking orange juice from the carton. What the hell was she doing to be so tired in the mornings?

Suddenly focusing on Mrs. Forest, she said, "What are you doing here?"

Sawyer had once pointed out to me that the line "What are you doing here?" appears in almost every movie. I always waited for it now, which made even boring movies suspenseful.

"Suzie doesn't need a reason to be here," Bill said, handing a mug to Grandma.

"I don't see enough of you, Gretchen," Mrs. Forest joked.

Grandma butted her aside, taking a seat next to her. "Ace? You okay with this?" She tilted her head toward Mrs. Forest. Grandma's hair looked like a saltmarsh with barren white estuaries.

"With?"

"With Suzie in the house, and everyone in your family standing around and yakking like this is not super weird or . . ." Grandma trailed off.

"Or what?" I said.

"I know the words, just can't bring 'em up, like something you want to barf but can't."

"*Unique?*" Sawyer tried.

"*Uncomfortable?*" Bill contributed.

"*None of our business?*" Rags said.

"This is not charades!" Grandma pulled on her earlobe. "Sounds like: How do we all *feel* about the woman our daughter, our sister, our granddaughter has chosen for her life partner?" She turned to Mrs. Forest. "Sorry, Suzie . . . shit."

"Gretchen's right," Mrs. Forest said. "Words or no words, she's right."

Bill's voice was shaky. "I don't want my kid getting hurt. She's breakable, Suzie."

"Too bad I'm not here to speak for myself," I said. Sawyer was buttering toast for Grandma; I moved closer to him.

"Put some of that Indian crap on it," Grandma told Sawyer.

"Mango chutney," Sawyer murmured, plumbing the depths of the fridge. "I just want Ace to be happy."

Grandma elbowed Mrs. Forest. "Get up, Suzie."

Mrs. Forest had sunk so low into her nest of paper towels, I extended a hand.

"Ace, Suzie, do you two want to talk here, or do you want privacy?" Grandma gestured toward the back stairs.

"Here," I said. "These people can hear whatever we have to say."

"'These people' being your *family*?" Bill said.

I observed Mrs. Forest, who stood awkwardly like an actor with her hands at her sides.

"You guys just don't get it!" Sawyer carefully lay Grandma's toast on the Cheerios table, which he was calling a "buffet."

"What is it, son?" I'd never heard Dad use this sitcom word, like he was fact-checking the relationship.

Bill, who had been leaning against the island fondling her coffee mug, turned her flaming gaze on me. "Take your lover upstairs." She drained her coffee, plunking the mug on the butcher block. "If you are her partner, be one. You can use our room."

"Why your room?"

"Yours is a mess," Bill said.

"She knows that."

"*She* has a name," Bill said.

I followed Mrs. Forest, who was carefully negotiating the narrow back stairs, as if she were on a ship's ladder. At the top, she stopped. To the left, my parent's boudoir. To the right, my room, where we'd slept and *slept* with each other.

Before I could answer, Mrs. Forest had wandered into Bill and Rags's room, where the busy business of being a couple took place.

The ceaseless pledge drive with Ira Glass and his schoolyard snitching emanated from my parent's Bose Wave radio. I did a quick check for anything parentally embarrassing, like condoms, K-Y jelly, or Viagra. In the en suite bathroom, no caked toothpaste in the sink.

The room had been transformed since the last time I'd been in here, bed freshly made, the smell of Tide in the air. Between the sex and the shopping, there had apparently been the cleansing.

"I'm the *older woman*," Mrs. Forest said. "People look at me like I'm doing something weird, perverted even. I need to organize my life. Get a divorce if I'm going to get one. Sort out the kids. And maybe you need to experiment with people your own age."

"Karen Tilley isn't anything to me."

Mrs. Forest raised her eyebrows. "You could have fooled me."

"And 'sort out'? You don't sort out children."

"You know what I mean. Custody."

"You can't disrupt their lives."

"What about mine, Ace? I'll wait for you. After college or whatever. We can work it out, but we have to do something. You're in this time warp."

"You don't have to give up anything, the twins, me, your life, your best friend."

"Oh, Ace, your youth is showing. How can we do that?"

"I'll show you," I said, gently pushing her backward on the bed.

"Sex is not the answer to everything."

"I know," I said. "I promise I'll change."

It was quiet when we finally descended the back stairs. Saturdays weren't the relief they were to most people. For us, the comfort of the weekly routine was gone: no Whore High, no *Frigate*, no Massasoit; just a string of unruly hours, stretching 'til Monday.

Outside, Mrs. Forest rested a hand on my shoulder while she used a Medical Arts tongue depressor to remove bits of spongy lawn from the soles of her shoes. Her breasts nearly slipped the surly bonds of Earth.

"Ace, we need to separate. You need to show me that you can commit. It will give us both time to think. You need to see if you want to be with someone younger, or alone with your brother. If I lose you, I will have lost fair and square. I can't hold on to someone who drifts away like a kite in the wind."

"Nice image."

She nearly smiled. "I will miss that."

"Don't leave, then."

"And you're right about Brett and Levi," she said. "We can't just sort them out. Maybe we should try being a family again, real parents."

"*We?*"

"You know who."

Mrs. Forest was exactly the same woman she'd been when she was standing in our kitchen a few hours earlier. Same short skirt, same V-neck jersey, same Converse making a crunching sound on the broken shells of the driveway. She had that post-sex mussed-hair glazed-eye look that I knew so well. But she would be gone from me.

The lawn was a mess. It was Sawyer's job to cut the grass, one of his favorite chores. Rags had an old hand mower; Sawyer carefully mowed up and down in even rows. The problem was that he took so much time to do it that he only managed it maybe twice a season.

The flower beds on which our parents practiced their horrible gardening skills were scraggly. Shrubs separated us from neighbors whose names we didn't even know. Beyond that, you could see a sliver of ocean and the ever-present turbine blades turning slowly like the hands of a clock or spinning like a pinwheel.

I navigated Mrs. Forest to the car, my hand on her back. I kissed her through the open window. "Don't go," I said, but she was already gone.

42

Bill and Rags returned from Shaw's or Trader Joe's with their U-Haul of purchases. Plus Brett and Levi.

The twins rushed to hug Sawyer and me. *What the fuck are they doing here?* I mouthed over their heads.

"Suzie and Lee wanted us to watch them for a few hours," Rags said.

"They're having another one of their fucking dates?"

"What the fuck," Brett said solemnly.

"Language," Bill said mildly.

Levi said, "Ace needs a time-out."

"You're enabling them to go on dates? Who goes on dates? What is this, 1953? The military-industrial complex?"

"It's just a couple hours," Rags said.

"She could be pregnant by the time she gets back. Mom, you're supposed to be begging her to take me to college interviews."

Rags eyed the kids. "Who's who?"

"Brett's wearing the wire rims," Sawyer said.

"Well, hello, Brett."

"Hello, Mithter."

"You can call me Rags."

210

"I don't think so," Sawyer said. "We're teaching them respect."

"Hello, Mithter Brett."

"Dad! Don't make fun of them!" Sawyer said.

"You could scar them," I said.

"They might become serial killers," Bill said.

"Cereal," Brett repeated.

"Killers," Levi added.

"Jeez, they're like parrots," Bill said.

"Don't you guys remember having little kids?" Sawyer said.

"It was wonderful," Bill replied. "You were both so beautiful."

"Were?" Sawyer demanded.

"Still," Bill said.

"You played together," Rags went on. "Watched out for one another."

"We didn't need adult supervision?" Sawyer said.

"We'd put you in double strollers and wheel you down Scrimshaw," Bill said.

"We were so proud!" Rags raised his voice to be heard over the radio in the kitchen, which suddenly went from a nearly inaudible murmur to Sarah Jessica Parker's baby voice, pleading for cash.

"Why were you proud?" I said.

"Because you both were beautiful, smart babies."

"That's nothing to be proud of. Making babies takes no skill whatsoever. It's *not* making babies that's hard."

Sawyer squashed his Red Bull can, cutting his finger in the process. "Stigmata," he said vaguely, getting up for a paper towel.

"Band-aids!" Brett yelled.

"We have dinosaur band-aids," Levi said.

"Did you have a boo-boo?" Rags asked.

"Accident," I said. "We're trying to teach them proper English."

"Accident," Levi said. "Daddy put blood on Mommy's nose."

"And she's going out on dates with this guy?" I stopped myself. Who was I to talk?

211

"Le Forest isn't all that bad, but he might not be the best candidate for custody," Sawyer said, wrapping a paper towel around his finger.

"Suzie can give as good as she gets," Bill said. "Remember when she was throwing stuff around the house?"

"Levi," Rags steered the conversation away from blood and violence. "What are you learning in school?"

"Miss Emily does numbers."

My brother averted his eyes. I'd spotted him with Long Division outside Ocean Charter.

"Do you know how to read?" Rags asked.

"Yes."

"What do you read?"

"*Civilization and Its Discontents*!" I said. "Jesus, Dad, they're toddlers!"

Bill got up to forage for dessert. "Pudding pops!"

Soon the twins were asleep, chocolate circling their mouths.

"Dad, give me your belt," Sawyer said, using it to secure Brett to his chair. He removed his own belt with its big Indian nickel buckle to keep Levi from falling out of his.

"No airbags?" Bill said.

"Hey," Sawyer said. "We were lucky to survive childhood, with almost no safety measures whatsoever."

"Whoa," Rags said. "You're here now, aren't you?"

"What about the time Sawyer and I nearly floated to England?"

"To reiterate," Rags said, "you're safe now."

"Safe? You can be rescued, but not completely safe," I said.

"Ace, honey," Bill said. "That's a little dramatic."

Without Mrs. Forest, I felt unsafe—unrescued. "Mom, do you think she'll go to New York with me?"

"I don't know, honey. She said she needed to think about it. What's in it for her?"

"Me."

"She's fragile around you," Mom said.

I no longer wanted to be a fragile-around kind of person—if

I ever had.

"You should think about it too," Mom went on. "How will you feel trapped in a car with someone who's justifiably pissed at you?"

"Like I died and went to heaven."

Sawyer lounged on a massage chair at Fabia's but kept his eye on the door. Fabia had one of those bells that rang like in an old general store.

"What's with Long Division?" I asked.

"You saw us?"

"Yeah," I said.

"She's available, sort of *there*." Our shared brain was in overdrive.

"Are you a math genius now?" I sat on the stool in front of him as if I were going to give *him* a pedicure.

"No, but she might come in handy."

"For solving the Hodge Conjecture?"

"She could be our accountant." He removed his shoes.

"*Our?*"

"Yeah, for Sawyer & Ace."

I was skeptical.

"For Rags and Bill, too," Sawyer said. "They think *Ponzi scheme* is a Netflix series. Ya gotta love 'em."

"How's the sex?" I massaged his foot. I doubted that anyone had returned this favor for him. "Long Division, she's kinda skinny, no?"

"I think you know. . . if memory serves." He leaned back and relaxed. "Not everyone can be a fertility goddess."

I forced the memory to surface. It wasn't Long Division's body. It was her mind. Hers joined ours like a member of a foursome. "That was about passing math, getting out of Whore Town. Now, not so much."

I knew even as I said it that we talked about getting out of Whore Town only because we wanted to *belong*, like other kids.

213

But even New York City was just a big safe GPS destination, not really a place.

We reminded each other of the siblings who'd stayed. "Would you want to be Dave or Dante?" I asked.

"Dave for sure." Sawyer switched feet. "Having only one arm? It would help me design for one-armed people."

"The one-armed-people community is skyrocketing."

"I'd get off on the challenge. Shake things up."

"Sounds like you've already shaken things up." I reached for the foot buffer. "I'm happy for you, Bro."

"It's not like we're getting married, me and Long Division."

I knew that. I'd watched them outside Ocean Charter. She'd flipped her hair, posed in third position; they wove figure eights around each other. The air was electric with their not touching.

43

"It's all yours," I said, like we were in *Storage Wars*. Ethel and Karen stood in front of our open garage door.

"Wow," Ethel said.

She and Karen had fallen in love during Continuing Ed volleyball. So it wasn't just the Forest/Ragsdales who'd driven Ethel away.

Was I missing something by not being a jock?

"If you don't mind me asking," Karen said, "why do you have all this stuff?"

"Our parents thought it might inspire us."

"That is so wrong."

The two were starting their own fitness club with addictive "boutique" services. Karen & Ethel, Inc. would create a whole community of physical psychotics.

Like sanitation workers, they effortlessly heaved bags of baseballs, soccer balls, softballs, tennis balls, and hockey pucks into Ethel's SUV; then bats, sticks, rackets, and my bow and arrow. They probably had giant jars of protein powder lined up like little fat people on a shelf.

Karen mindlessly shot a few swishers into the basketball net hanging precariously from the garage roof. The rim was rusty, the net torn like old fishing gear. She tossed the basketball into the car.

When everything was loaded, we sat in the garage, drinking beer from a moldy-smelling cooler, sitting on mildewed lawn chairs—plaid plastic stretched across bent aluminum. "Ethel, I have to ask you," I said. "Is it hard working with Dr. Forest, now that, you know . . . there's a different . . . zeitgeist?"

Ethel cupped her hand on Karen's knee. "I don't think Karen wants to hear about all this."

"Yes, I do, if there's more to know."

"Lee is really trying to make it work with Suzie," Ethel said. "He's apparently in anger management."

"I can't believe you're telling me this!" I said. "*Suzie?* Isn't that a little . . . a little, like, maybe, is it even completely appropriate?"

"I know this is difficult," Ethel said.

"Do you ever see her?" I asked.

"Why would I see her?" Ethel said. "I broke up their family."

"No, *I* broke up their family."

"Hey, ladies, you both broke up their family," Karen said. I waited for her to blow her whistle, which hung on a homemade gimp lanyard, braided orange and blue, Whore High colors. "Shit, Ethel," Karen said. "You were passionate, reckless even. I don't inspire that?"

"I want a life partner, not angst and turmoil," Ethel said.

There would be kids of course. Ethel was going to be the birth mother. Karen was brave, but not that brave.

Neither was I. I could never do what Mrs. Forest had done to bring Brett and Levi into the world.

"I need her back," I said. Karen and Ethel were like tumbling game pieces that came to rest, touching. Witnessing such newfound soulmates made me miserable. I'd had that, and I'd blown it. "Can I get her back?" I asked Karen.

"Maybe, but there's no messing around." She avoided eye contact. "That thing between you and me, it was mindless. You can't squander her on meaningless . . . activities."

Like our pool kissing was an intramural sport. That was all

it had been.

"If you get her back, you have to cherish her." Karen didn't sound like her usual self.

"And Dr. Forest?" I turned to Ethel.

"That was a blot on my character," Ethel said. "I didn't know myself, who I was. I don't know, I . . . It was . . ."

"Not very therapeutic, doing the boss," I finished.

Karen muscled her partner into the SUV. All they needed were tin cans and streamers flying out from their honeymoon car.

44

Bill and Rags agreed it was time to bankroll extra sessions with Dr. Know.

At first it was like a laundromat: me crying, him washing dishtowels. He opened a dog-eared workbook to the phrase "the peace of perspiration." Physical labor was the first step in cases like mine, Dr. Know explained, so he provided it: We baked bread, sanded the picnic table, tied buoys, mended his sail, and made lattes, using the "9-Bar pressure flow" technique. Decalcifying the espresso machine could lead to "self-actualization."

He didn't think I had a commitment problem. He thought I had a cause-and-effect problem.

He prescribed a therapy usually reserved only for addicts and alcoholics: an intervention. Now I was back where it had all started, when Mrs. Forest had been weeping and wasted in our kitchen. Bill, Rags, Sawyer, and Grandma sat on stools around the island. I leaned against the butcher block, begging.

"Dr. Know said you should intervene," I said.

"That's meddling, honey, the worst possible thing in a mother."

"Meddle, shmeddle," Grandma said.

"Meddle, Mom! You never meddle." I aimed below the belt.

"What kind of parent is that?"

"Careful," Dad said. "I don't know many mothers as open-minded as yours."

"Okay, so maybe Mrs. Forest wouldn't be your first choice for me," I told Bill. "Some loser from Whore High would have been your first choice?"

"You could have found a loser at Massasoit, too," Sawyer added helpfully.

"But Suzie's a good person," Dad said.

No one looked to be in a drinking mood, but Sawyer was practicing for a spot on *Uncorked*. He grabbed the fancy stemware and a bottle of red, doing that twisty thing at the end like a real sommelier.

We all stared like it was performance art.

"We could have done more to dissuade you . . ." Dad stole from Rachel Maddow: "But it seems like that train has left the station."

"That horse is out of the barn?" Sawyer said.

"Any other dumbass clichés?" I said.

"Let's see." Grandma grabbed olives, corn relish, mango chutney, and cream cheese from the fridge. "You're too young to be settling down with one person?"

"That's not a cliché," I said.

"Play the field," Grandma said. "That's what I did."

"So why did you marry Grandpa Gary?" Sawyer pulled down the *Speedwell* platter.

"Like your mother said about your father—genes."

"No disrespect, but that's bullshit," I said.

"I agree," Grandma said. "But heterosexual people have this evolutionary perpetuate-the-species impulse."

"You're not exactly straight," Sawyer said.

"True, since I've been here, I'm a little more gender-fluid."

"Like in 'flugen'?" Sawyer said.

"Just what we need, another dumbass letter to add to *LGBTQ*," I said. "But why not add an *F*? It's all about fucking, anyway." The *Speedwell* platter brought it all home. This was

219

where we all belonged, in this severed backwater. "So who are you being 'flugen' *with*, Grandma?"

"Technically, it's nobody's business," Dad said.

"Dad, that's so bullshit." I said.

"Your dad is right," Bill said. "Who is it?"

"It actually happens every time I get involved in some protest. Especially turbines. It sure as shit isn't the people. You should've seen this dude I got entangled with down in New Jersey."

"Sounds unhealthy, Mom."

"What was unhealthy was his physiognomy. Good God, this guy was butt-ugly, but, boy, he had me laughing. I hate jokes, and I hate stories, but he would just say stuff not trying to be funny, and that's what was funny. You can fall for stuff like that."

"Very unusual in a male," Bill said.

"I'm funny," Dad said.

"You are, darling." Bill let him lick cheese off her middle finger.

Sawyer's face bunched in the middle. "You screwed this guy?"

"*Children!*" Bill was trying out a new word.

"I think Grandma kinda started it," Sawyer said.

"I did, Sawyer. My bad. Like a lot of people without physical gifts, this guy was good."

"Gretchen!"

"And your Grandpa Gary was one of those nice guys who was ignorant in the sack."

"Did he really die in a shooting accident?" Sawyer asked.

"He was such a duck freak, that's what he wanted people to believe."

"He's dead, though," I said, not a question.

"There were some false starts," Grandma said. "It was hard to tell with your grandfather. Many a time I thought he'd kicked, only to find that he was sleeping in that quiet, motionless way of his, or was temporarily unconscious from hitting his head on something."

"What happened to him?"

"He was still using lead paint and turpentine on his decoys—it was before folks knew about stuff like that, and he was pretty much immune to logic, anyway, so he got all kinds of cancer, but mainly lung cancer. He'd been addicted to opioids, and then was abusing stool softeners. He wanted to have one of those still-alive funerals, where he could hear all the nice things people would say about him."

We looked to our parents for confirmation.

"Unfortunately, not many people came to the funeral," Bill said.

"It wasn't that people didn't like him," Dad said. "The decoy community is not as big as you might think."

"We all thought the decoy community was ginormous!" Sawyer said.

"Bigger than the carved-soap community?" Bill said.

This endless sidebar was getting on my nerves. "Who are you screwing?" I asked Grandma.

"Ace."

"It's okay, Rags," Grandma said. "It was the protest gestalt that was starting to float my boat here in Whore Town. Watching these good citizens at town meetings, I was starting to appreciate the feelings on both sides. These people could be sitting home watching *Ellen* or adult-coloring, but they're at Town Hall, fighting for their cause."

"It wasn't Doty Cooper!" Sawyer said.

"Jesus to God, no. That old twat has about as much sex appeal as . . ." She panned the room. "Furniture."

"Selectman Wilder is kind of cute," I said, "maybe not *cute*, but . . ."

"She's got a look," Sawyer acknowledged.

"Eleanor Margesson." Grandma blushed.

I finally broke the stunned silence. "You only did her to get on her good side!"

"Sexual intercourse is not the answer to climate change . . . that's been my observation."

Bill was incredulous. "So what happened?"

221

"Like I said, it was the protest thing. She was so sincere, so articulate, I thought it was just a personality crush. But I was always seated behind her, so I started to develop this attraction to her backside and the way she walked with this self-confident swagger. She was sexy like people who play the piano standing up or put military time in their microwaves. And you could tell there was no way poor old Jake Margesson could keep up. At first I wanted to do one of those Abe Lincoln *Team of Rivals* type of deals—Kearns Goodwin, etcetera, plagiarism shmagerism, what do I care—but then we'd meet at the Bowsprit or whatnot, and one thing led to another. She'd never had an orgasm."

"No!" Bill and Rags said in unison. This was unheard-of in Horton.

"You're a stud," Sawyer said.

I was so gobsmacked by this hookup, I realized I'd lost sight of the intervention. "What's the bottom line?" I said.

"Bottom line?" Bill said. "Your grandmother is a real chick magnet."

"We were talking about me."

I asked each of them to go over to Mill Wheel and plead with Mrs. Forest. After making sure Le Forest was at Club YES for TRX training.

"Bottom line?" Grandma said. "We'll do it."

Dad kissed the top of my head. "We will, honey."

45

Grandma went first. After a typically wild ride in her jeep, I hid in the bushes outside the Forests' bay window. Like the Ragsdales, the Forests were indifferent yard workers, so the privacy hedges were overgrown. I parted them; they smelled of cat piss.

Mrs. Forest engulfed Grandma in a cloud of Ice Blue Secret. I could see a box of Annie's Cheddar Bunnies on the coffee table, the twins in their Stinky & Dirty pajamas eating bananas.

I witnessed lots of comradely touching. At one point, Grandma slammed her big Nikes on the floor and laughed loudly enough for me to hear.

Finally, they stood. Mrs. Forest dabbed an eye with her little finger before they disappeared from view.

The next day was Bill and Rags's turn. From the hedge, I saw the twins watching Bubble Guppies and yogurt-painting on the screen. Bill and Mrs. Forest had the bog binder out, with its minutes and "snapshots" and "clippings." They were probably talking about the "weather event" that had blown off part of the boardwalk.

A kid from Silvio's delivered pizza. He was famous for flunking out of Whore High, an almost impossible achievement.

My parents and Mrs. Forest had that animated look of gossipers or people in agreement. I watched trips to the bathroom and to the kitchen for seconds. The kids had fallen asleep in front of the TV. Rags got up to cover them with his cashmere blazer.

That intervention ended with a group hug.

When it was Sawyer's turn, he played to his audience behind the hedge. I grabbed a survival kit of peanuts, pot, and the kind of camping lighter you flick with your thumb.

The twins hauled out a shitload of stuff for Sawyer to look at. Mrs. Forest looked bored. They finally sat down in front of *Finding Dory*. They knew how to pronounce *Ellen DeGeneres*.

Mrs. Forest lay on the couch with her feet in Sawyer's lap. His attention was on her face, as if her words were physical. He handed her a handkerchief from the pocket of his double-breasted suit jacket, worn with pleated trousers and Birkenstocks.

I couldn't have said how long this scene would have gone on if I hadn't accidentally set fire to the arborvitae with the too-easy click of my survival lighter.

I called the HFD immediately. By the time Karen Tilley arrived, the fire had already moved to the deck and singed the Astroturf. Karen, the only female who'd passed the firefighter test, aimed the heavy hose like a bazooka as she clomped around in gigantic boots. There were smoke tears and ash on her cheeks. She shot me a *What were you thinking?* look.

Karen thought stalking was worse than fire-starting. The hedge was completely destroyed.

This was fine with the Forests' next-door neighbor, who now had an unobstructed view of Mrs. Forest each time she came into the living room—which was often—in the kimono she'd taken back from me. It did nothing to cover her body.

The postmortems took place in the Catboat kitchen.

Grandma's intervention had consisted of Mrs. Forest wanting to know what Gretchen had done to give Eleanor Margesson the first orgasm of her very long life. They'd gone up to the master bedroom so Grandma could give Mrs. Forest a demonstration.

"Not sex, but a tutorial," Grandma emphasized. She'd made use of Caitlyn and Le Forest's anatomy chart.

Mrs. Forest missed me, she'd told Sawyer.

Bill and Rags's intel: She said she wanted me back, but she was afraid of getting hurt.

46

Vacations cure turbine ills
By Chuck Butten
Frigate staff writer

In a stunning blow to activist Gretchen Ragsdale and Occupy Wind forces, a procession of residents testified during the public comments portion of Wednesday's town meeting to "improved health outcomes" while vacationing outside Horton.

"A week in Sandwich did it for me," said Charlotte, who would not give her last name.

"No more restless leg syndrome after a visit to the Glass Museum."

Longtime Horton endodontist Silas Standish told meeting-goers, "When my wife and I were at Tanglewood, no more coughing, urinary tract infections, or intimate . . ."

Frequent town-hall attendee Doty Cooper reported, "Cripes, just going to Edaville Railroad was enough for my moderate-to-severe TMJ to disappear."

A resident who identified himself only as "Chad" said that sitting in an Adirondack chair on Lake Winnipesaukee "took away my acid reflux."

Mrs. Forest's silver-blue Vulva was in our driveway. We all stood next to it.

Bill had apparently convinced Mrs. Forest that driving me to a college interview would give her a chance to see firsthand how much I'd grown as a human being. In truth, Bill knew what she could and could not change and, as the drunks said, she had the wisdom to know the difference. It sounded like the two had disguised the venture as just a high school kid headed to college with all the stereotypical aspirations intact after a very productive meeting with my guidance counselor.

We stood taking selfies, making inane statements.

"A safe car," Rags said, running his hand along the side of the Vulva as if he were thinking of buying it.

"Suzie's a good driver," Bill said.

They were convinced I had a shot at NYU because Bill had "comported" herself well there. I would "knock 'em dead" with a "personal statement." But personal essays left too much room for lying and coloring outside the lines; Sawyer and I scored better with multiple choice.

"Getting away" was the standard remedy for disastrous cocktail parties and bedroom scenes. But anybody could tell you there was no getting away, even if you were vacuum-sealed in the front seat of a speeding Vulva with the person you loved.

Grandma squinted at Mrs. Forest. "That's quite a rack. You might want to throw those boobs around with the guys and gals

227

in the admissions office."

"Mom!"

"Sorry, Suzie," Grandma said. "My filter shorted out there for a second."

"No worries, I don't think Ace needs that kind of help from me."

Bill went to the driver's side and hugged Mrs. Forest through the window. She told Mrs. Forest, "I'll miss you." Mom's eyes went big and floaty, flooding their rims.

What about me? Would she miss me?

Sawyer came to my side and signed, *I heart you.*

Captive with the hurt and pissed-off Mrs. Forest, I was mute. She was a smoker-driver. I watched smoke rings expand and become smoke again. That she knew how to blow them was heart-stopping.

Her skirt inched up her thigh as she drove, open-toed, Sawyer's perfect polish fresh for the occasion.

I watched through the side mirror until the turbine disappeared from view. Taking leave, you felt freed and bereft in the same tangled emotion. Any low-grade physical discomforts started to fall away. I felt cramps coming on. My period had been irregular over the past year, but now this sign that I was a functioning, mammalian female felt empowering.

I spoke. "I'm sorry."

"Don't distract a person when they're driving."

I looked out the window: a water tower or gas station sign above the trees. Walls of rock that had been blasted to make the highway. Goldenrod, broom-dry. Fall was doing its usual death rattle—rough leaves, brittle stalks—before going out with a bang for the leaf-peepers.

On the expressway was a car with its hood up and steam escaping. Someone getting carsick over the guardrail. Drivers lounging from the backseat like homeboys, smoking, drinking from their travel cups, and weaving in and out of lanes. Couples gesticulating. Families with bikes in the back and storage on the roof. Dogs slobbering on the windows. Everyone trapped in speeding capsules. It didn't seem safe.

Mrs. Forest was driving with her arms straight out, thumbs off the wheel, like they were having a tiny conversation.

"*Sorry* is just a word, Ace."

I was startled to hear her speak.

"This trip is for me, too, you know." She stole a quick glance my way. "I have aspirations too, beyond our screwed-up families."

"My family's not screwed up."

"Of course, sorry." She grabbed her sunglasses from the well between us.

"Brett and Levi aren't screwed up," I said.

"Screwed, maybe."

I stared straight ahead at what I imagined was the horizon. If Grandma had been my chaperone, we'd be speeding recklessly in her noisy Army-issue jeep. We'd be stopping for her afternoon beer, and she'd be threatening to break the kneecaps of some poor admissions person.

We took a break at a McDonald's. The smell of fries and special sauce made me think of Mrs. Forest wedged into a stall, the mistress of the silent come.

In the bathroom, I motioned for her to join me. She refused. I made pathetic love to myself, making sure she heard me.

Afterward, we drank fake orange juice at a picnic table out front. "We're alone for an entire weekend," she said vaguely. I gave her my hand. She took it, staring at the braided leather on my wrist, a "good luck" gift from Janie down at the Pot Shop. (*Janie's Clay Creations: Get a Ceramic High at the Pot Shop!*)

"I could have bought this. I wanted to buy you things."

"I'm sorry."

"Sorry isn't enough, Ace. You going to college, maybe that's the best thing, maybe for me, too." She raised her eyes. "Did you enjoy yourself in there?"

"It wasn't the same without you."

Mrs. Forest pushed the leather bracelet up my arm. "I like your tat."

Karen Tilley had gone with me to the Tattler on Scrimshaw.

229

I wanted something that, when I was ninety and they were taking my pulse in the ambulance, would be intact on my sagging skin: a Dali clock. It was already melting; falling from the bone, timeless.

"Thanks." I kissed her on the cheek, like she was one of those aunts I'd heard so much about.

While I waited for a response from her, I watched birds moving vertically like they were on springs, and the real Americans with their clean white sneakers and CAT hats. Though the day was still, they wore windbreakers, pastel like Necco Wafers.

"This is exactly the kind of place that would have domestic terrorists," I said. I watched Mrs. Forest stifle a smile.

Say what you will about Horton, there were no terrorists on Scrimshaw Street. Terrorists only struck national chains like Denny's and Cinnabon.

Back in the Vulva, there would be no sex. We'd done it before, but I didn't want to move too fast. She could spool out any minute, like a roll of crepe paper through the car window.

"Sweetheart, open my bag and light us a cigarette."

Mrs. Forest's "sweetheart" sounded like an unknown language. When we were kids, Sawyer and I thought that adults spoke a different language that had to be learned at an exact age, like driving.

The Vulva had one of those old-fashioned lighters. I'd never seen one and had to be told how to use it, which put Mrs. Forest exactly where she should have been: a friend, doing the family a favor.

After just a couple of drags, she squeezed her cigarette in the ashtray. I dropped her lip-glossed butt into my pocket.

We stopped to change my tampon and to buy two Hess trucks for the twins. I felt smug watching guys eye-bang Mrs. Forest as she pumped gas, with her little skirt and her slingbacks.

Sawyer called it "aesthetic incongruity," like a fish on a chair.

Our hotel had a South Sea Island motif—burning tapers in wicker holders and outriggers in the lobby. The bedroom was tiny, which made the king-size bed look even bigger. To avoid it, we went down to the glass-enclosed terrace for dinner. New York City enveloped us. Car horns, people. "Enrique!" rose above the din.

Our fellow diners were New Yorkers, cradling their helmets like mixing bowls and looking like they'd stepped out of a violent fashion ad.

Mrs. Forest made mega eye contact with our waiter, who was short and ripped like Tom in *Downton Abbey*. *Downtown* to me. "Looks like you've made a friend," I said.

"He's cute."

"Yes, he is."

Would these be the kind of people I would be going to school with? It wouldn't matter, because Sawyer would be with me, and we could do our usual team-up against the world, even this world, which so far was everything I'd imagined.

"That homeless guy?" Mrs. Forest lurched into safe territory. "The one outside the hotel? I gave him some money." She pulled out her phone. "It advises here to 'only give money if the person gives you something in return, like a song, a breakdance, or a gymnastic move.'" The guy had been lying on the sidewalk, bare feet statue-color, large and rough like burnt boards. Something was alive on his body.

Mrs. Forest literally batted her eyelashes at Downtown. "What is branzino?"

He'd been looking over his shoulder at the majestic dark-haired waitress wearing a Lady Liberty crown as she seemed to skate around the dining room. A dancer/model/actress/Amazon athlete of a waitress.

Downtown turned to face Mrs. Forest. "Are you asking me what it is, or how it's prepared?"

"She's asking you how it's prepared," I said. "That goes without saying."

231

Downtown seemed to see me for the first time. "Of course. It's lightly seared, served with carnaroli rice, Parmigiano-Reggiano and arugula risotto with Provençal sauce, caper butter, lemon herb oil, roasted tomato, and garlic."

"That might be a little too precious for you," I said.

"Do you have chicken parm?" Mrs. Forest asked.

"No, but we have a free-range bird that you might like."

Mrs. Forest nodded.

"I'll have the branzino," I said.

He whisked away the menus as if we were thinking of stealing them. "You really don't know what branzino is?"

"I still don't," she said.

"It's fish."

"I've never seen it at the Bowsprit."

"You wouldn't. They only serve fish from our own fleet. Branzino is a European seabass found in the Mediterranean, the Black Sea, and somewhere else, I forget."

"Excuse me if I haven't memorized the Oxford English Dictionary."

"Second Edition."

Mrs. Forest stuck her fork in my branzino, wishing she'd ordered it. Her free-range bird, meanwhile, was one of the best I'd tasted. We lobbed words back and forth like we were backyard tennis players. We eavesdropped on our dinner mates, who seemed to be on a controlled substance that involved manic Friday night restaurant-eating.

Lady Liberty glided over to take our dessert order. Downtown's shift was apparently over.

"Hello, ladies, welcome to New York. Are you in for the drugs?" She was splendid, with large hands and a chiseled face like her namesake, with an Elvis nose and the green tiara from a souvenir hawker on the street, its seven rays the continents and oceans of the Earth.

"Rec pot? I didn't think that was legal in New York." I was pretty sure I'd done my homework.

"Pharmaceutical Expo at the Javits. Your mother looks like a rep of some kind. You're a real cougar, ma'am, if you don't mind my saying so." Lady Liberty's voice was from the pediment of the statue, rumbling from the basement.

"Thank you."

"What can I get you?"

Mrs. Forest turned to me.

"What do you recommend?"

"We have a really fabulous poi, which pairs nicely with a double espresso and a side of pizzelles."

"If you don't have the spumoni, that would work for me," Mrs. Forest said.

Mrs. Forest wanted to stop off at the bar. I wanted to be alone with her in the big bed. I went up without her.

I brushed my teeth, took off my clothes, and felt the cool white percale against my skin. I heard the muffled cottony sounds of people talking. Street sounds wafted up: a whistle like there was a basketball game.

There was the ping of the elevator arriving and a knock on my door. I grabbed the terrycloth robe from the bathroom. Through the peephole, I saw Downtown, still in his wine-dark apron, staring at his feet.

Mrs. Forest came in late, smelling of booze. I pretended to sleep, weeping silently into the pillow.

In the morning, I helped her heave. She'd played beer pong with Lady Liberty, and who knew who else. I steadied her with one hand on her forehead and one on her stomach. Emptying had, for an instant at least, the same effect as entering. The person had abandoned herself to you.

Mrs. Forest, looking pale and anticipatory, as if the slightest movement could make her barf again, sat on the bed watching me dress.

"I've never seen you look like that," she said.

"Sawyer put together an 'interview outfit.'"

It consisted of pants that were too short for me, what he called "highwaters," a man's shirt, untucked, Caitlyn's necktie, a vest, and platform shoes you could fall off of. There was an overarching sense of rattan.

"I wouldn't want you looking that way all the time." She steadied herself on the bed. "Sorry. I know that's controlling."

"No, please, control!" I handed her a ginger ale from the minibar. "Any feeling from you is better than nothing."

"What do you expect, Ace?"

"Was it good?" I asked.

"What?"

"I assumed you had an orgy down there."

"No orgy."

"Lady Liberty?" I prompted.

A slight nod. She was afraid of moving her head. "I was drunk. I don't know what happened, exactly."

"Something."

"Yes, something," she said.

"Why did you do it?"

"You know why. To let you know what it feels like to be with someone who's not trustworthy, not serious."

"Was she good?"

"Who knows," Mrs. Forest said. "The smell and feel and touch of you were with me." She tried a smile. "I'm starting to sound like you."

"Sounds like you had quite the bacchanalia." I hated this ventriloquist's voice, this sidekick who seemed to be standing beside me.

"I needed to get some kind of reaction from you, but I come in, and you're sleeping like a baby."

"Hardly," I said, ordering coffee from room service. "I guess we're even."

Washington Square's *Arc de Triomphe* was exactly as I'd imagined it.

There were still kids with guitars, panhandlers, and a groundcover of pot, like in Bill's day. The Manhattoes were just as chill, selling peyote and tobacco and bartering beads. Grandma's haunts were long gone.

The contact high might make Mrs. Forest feel better—that and the bagel I'd bought her along the way. We shot selfies in front of the arch, both wobbly, she from the hangover, me from Sawyer's Castaway shoes, which were like a curb you could step off of.

Ms. Genevieve Cavali rescued us from a small, dark waiting room with bars on the window. A way random Paris street scene hung on the wall; raspy carpet underfoot. "You had no trouble getting here?"

"Smooth sailing," I said.

Ms. Cavali didn't look like someone who'd just had morning sex. I wasn't envisioning her with her clothes off, or wondering if she had kids who looked like her or a partner whom I'd have to conjure. Her desk was devoid of clues.

"I see here that you don't like to be called Candace. Fair enough. Ace, welcome to NYU. And Mrs. Forest?"

"Susan."

"Susan, then, thank you for coming." Friendly smile. "I understand you're a family friend?"

"Yes. I've known Ace for quite some time."

"We call that the elephant model," Ms. Cavali said. "The herd cares for its young; there's no ownership regarding whose offspring is whose."

We'd had experience with that.

Ms. Cavali looked like her mother had dressed her from the waist up: shell, jacket, glasses slung around her neck. From the waist down, jeans and sneakers, ankles primly crossed.

"I imagine you saw Ace take her first steps, were there for all the firsts: school, menstruation, navigating and negotiating relationships," she said. "Sometimes you don't want to hear about condoms from your own mother."

I watched Mrs. Forest pull herself together. A response coagulated in her brain. "Mrs. Ragsdale is an excellent mother."

"Of course! As a matter of fact, let's talk about Willamena ..."

she opened a file, " . . . Mintner."

I could see that Mrs. Forest was trying to connect this alien name to the Bill Ragsdale we knew and loved.

"Ace, I must tell you that you are here purely as a legacy prospect. There is nothing outstanding in your transcript, but we do give some courtesy and consideration to our alumni. In your case, it would be a chance to live up to Willamena's record."

"We call her Bill," Mrs. Forest corrected.

" . . . or live down her record," Ms. Cavali said.

"NYU has had a history of student deaths," I interrupted, suddenly uncomfortable with where this was headed.

"You've done your homework."

"Ace has memorized numerous reference materials." Mrs. Forest pulled on her suit jacket. I suspected that Grand Canyon cleavage would have no effect.

"Kids throwing themselves over the railing at Bobst Library?" I said.

"As you know, we remedied that with aluminum screens."

"I don't know if you can 'remedy' student angst," I said.

Ms. Cavali closed the folder and—like Mr. Prower—clasped her hands on top of it, like this particular gesture was part of their job descriptions. "You seem a little defensive."

"Not at all! In fact, I wanted to ask if there were any work-study programs. I feel that whatever I declare as a major could be enhanced by real-world experience."

The word *declare* seemed computer-generated, with no context or relationship to lived experience.

Mrs. Forest was finally able to smile.

"Excellent," Ms. Cavali said. "Yes, in fact we handpick professors whose expertise in certain disciplines would launch students into careers, not just scholarship."

"Endless research papers, hanging around in libraries?" I said.

Ms. Cavali was playing cat's cradle with the chain around her neck. "Um, well, something like that."

"Libraries are a valuable resource," Mrs. Forest said.

"I've decided I'm going to be a real estate agent." I watched confusion complicate Ms. Cavali's bland features. High school students could be surprising, but what kind of diversionary tactic was this? "And work in a frame shop."

"Four expensive years at NYU will hardly be required for those pursuits." She swiveled to Mrs. Forest. "I'm afraid you've wasted Susan's time."

"Her time is not wasted with me," I said.

"She also has her eye on journalism and English." Mrs. Forest tried raising her voice, stifling a gag reflex.

I'd absorbed enough at the *Frigate* to pull off journalism and read enough novels to be an English professor at a suffocating New England college. But these careers were so egomaniacal—you couldn't cover a fire or teach *Moby Dick* without sifting them through your own pathetic life story. It wasn't fair to media consumers or students.

"Those are excellent career goals. Ace, it seems like you might be a bit undecided. We often see that in students who are on the threshold of real life. It can be frightening and disorienting."

"We'll continue with the application process," Mrs. Forest said.

The royal *we*?

"Okay, then, the student statement will be your ace in the hole, so to speak . . . Ace. Many students have gained entry to this fine institution on the basis of their written skills alone. You could too."

Mrs. Forest stood. "I'm sure she could."

"I will email you the guidelines, which include a deadline. The degree to which you meet the deadline will be an indication of your maturity and readiness to be an NYU freshman."

Back in the Vulva, Mrs. Forest seemed relieved to be on home turf, hands on the wheel. We started the ride home by doing impressions of the tortured way Ms. Cavali had avoided ending sentences with prepositions. "To whom we are indebted, about which more later!" This kept us friendly between long silences, where we smoked.

I leaned against the door, my breath steaming the window. Reading signs, I wondered about the people who lived in the houses just beyond the tall noise barriers. Any second they could jump in their cars and head out to their manifest destinies. This was America!

We gossiped about our families and people we knew in Horton. Had Le Forest ever hit her? I asked.

She took a long time to answer. Both she and Le Forest had been guilty of "physical exchanges," she admitted. "When I found out about Ethel, I threw a can of Barbasol at him."

"And what about me? Did you fight over me?"

Dr. Forest's blood seeping so prettily into his white shirt; I longed for it to be about me, which was only human, on the very edge of reason.

"Yes," she whispered.

I pulled up Le Forest's self-published book on my phone. "'Physical therapy *can* be addictive in patients with a history of addiction, let's say to sex.'" I lay down, resting my feet on Mrs. Forest's lap. "*Let's say!*"

Mrs. Forest flicked her cigarette out the window and massaged my toes.

At Horton's exit, I was reminded of a recent fatal crash on the ramp. The man who'd died had been lying supine in the middle of the lane. He wore a business suit, arms at his sides, feet in shiny tie shoes pointing left and right. There was no blood, no ripped clothes, no rictus of pain. Shards of glass, sharp as shark's teeth, were stuck to his body. He'd sparkled like an ocean.

Whore Town had been graffitied over the original sign so many times that Public Works had given up.

As we turned onto Route 3, we could see the blades of the turbine over the trees, lights blinking.

We had car sex: toe, finger, tongue.

"It's okay now, baby," Mrs. Forest said.

238

47

Ragsdale kitchen, Ragsdale family: the inevitable postmortem. "What happened to you at my alma mater?" Bill asked.

"I love New York," I deadpanned.

"I heart New York?" Grandma squeezed my hand. "You and your brother can do better than that."

"How was it for you?" I asked my mother. "Did you heart New York?"

"The Village scene was very, I don't, it was . . ."

"It was the cat's pajamas," Grandma said. "Right?"

"Your mother showed enormous promise as a painter," Dad said.

"Suzie told me that the whole New York experience helped her to stop being angry," Bill said, grasping for safer ground. "She thinks you two can work things out, if you can commit."

"Commit! Stop using that word. It sounds like a mental institution." I took it down a notch. "Anyway, I had an epiphany."

"Epiphanies are good," Rags said.

"Super good," Grandma said.

"You guys sound like crazy people!" Sawyer said. "You need

to listen to what Ace is saying!" He threw cans of La Croix at each of us. We all missed, retrieving them from wherever they'd landed.

"Ace, what *are* you saying?" Bill said.

"I'm not going to college." I turned to Dad, who was trying to coax a can from under the counter using a silver martini spoon with a long drill-bit handle.

Our cans were like water pistols. We knew not to open them. "What *are* you going to do?" Dad said.

"Be Mrs. Forest's partner."

"You're going to be a professional spouse?" Mom said.

"Also, I'm going into business with her."

"Wow," Sawyer said. "Good plan."

"Full disclosure," Grandma said, "I never really finished college. Ended up in some sweat lodge in New Mexico with a bunch of 'shroom-eating Manson-type characters, burning smudge sticks and whatnot."

Rags shot his mother a look. "Did you or did you not finish college?"

"I don't remember, Vision Quest maybe."

"Jeez, Mom." Dad turned to me. "Honey, we don't want to pressure you, but if you want to go to college, we want to give you that opportunity. College, it's a family tradition."

"We've been doing it for generations," Bill said.

"Me neither," Sawyer said.

"You neither, what?" Bill said.

"I'm not going to college either."

"You're already in college, unless there's something we're all missing," Bill said. "As you've already demonstrated, it would be pretty hard to flunk out of Massasoit."

Dad was watching his mother for signs of wholesale memory loss.

"I mean real college," Sawyer said. "I'm going to be CEO of Sawyer & Ace Advertising, and design a fashion line. I'm talking to Le Forest about it."

"*Lee?*" Mom said.

240

"Yeah, he has a successful business, and he can wear a pocket square without looking like an asshole." Sawyer attempted to soften the blow. "And Fabia's, that goes without saying. She's going to make me manager."

Sawyer waited for me to back him up. "He's going to be an entrepreneur." I looked from family member to family member. "Like me. Like Mrs. Forest."

"That's the ticket," Grandma said.

48

"Emotional damage is worse," Mrs. Forest said.
We were sitting side by side on director's chairs, a subtle hint that Dr. Know wanted us to be in charge.

"Cheating, frivolous attachments, being buffeted by circumstance, whatever crosses your path." She paused. "It was the infidelities. I could live with our . . . physical altercation."

"I can live with physical altercations, too," I said.

Dr. Know eyed me over his glasses, silently calling to mind our "coping strategies."

White shirt, blood, the color draining from Le Forest's face as he slumped over the coffee table. Nothing's more memorable than a living person *looking* dead with their eyes wide open.

Dr. Know turned his attention to Mrs. Forest. "So the thing that separated you in the first place is not the thing that brought you together today?"

"I don't think we'll be taking restraining orders out on each other," Mrs. Forest said. "If that's what you mean."

"Ace, may I share with Susan your first reaction to the suggestion of couples counseling?" He read from his phone: "But it might become definite, like death, like real death, like an ending, final."

I winced. Mrs. Forest reached for my hand.

"Susan, you said in your written statement that couples counseling 'seemed like an opening . . . I'm too young for a lifetime of yearning and regret.'"

Mrs. Forest nodded.

"The reasons you and Ace agreed to couples counseling seem like competing notions—life versus death. Can they be reconciled?"

The familiar feel and scent of Mrs. Forest's skin made me light-headed.

"Ace looks like she might be feeling ambushed by the question," Mrs. Forest said.

"Ace can handle herself."

"I'm okay," I said. I couldn't believe this old guy living in a shack on the ocean, baking—what was it today? it smelled like pie crust—could strip us so bare. "But I'm not sure she. . . she can answer that."

"She?" Dr. Know prompted.

"She . . ." I tried again. "She . . ."

"Ace, the ancient texts tell us—and this has nothing to do with the deficiencies of organized religions—that naming was the engine that set the world in motion, naming the animals. We need the most basic bedrock of language to understand one another. 'She' . . .?'"

Mrs. Forest's ring cut into my hand. "Susan," I whispered.

Dr. Know handed me a dishrag. Mrs. Forest watched the ritual of me crying and blowing my nose and him tossing the towel into the washer. He turned his attention to her. "What do you want, Susan? What outcome?"

"You asked us about living and dying. I don't want to live without her."

"So you would die without her?"

"Certainly not, doctor. I have twin toddlers."

"They wear glasses," I contributed.

The twins had had to be bribed with hummus and pudding pops and other foodstuffs to set foot in Pearle Vision to buy new ones. I'd seen mothers thumbing crumbs from their kids' faces. But not Mrs. Forest. I watched in awe as she licked goo directly from her children's fiery cheeks.

The twins selected square pink frames with sequined stems. Mrs. Forest said no.

When Brett cried, I lifted him over my head. Mrs. Forest was transfixed as I let his drool yoyo into my mouth.

"Yes to pink glasses with sequins!" I yelled.

Mrs. Forest had given in, not to the twins, but to their nonbiological mom.

"Glasses?" Dr. Know prompted. "They're significant, why?"

"The twins, they need an extra layer of . . . I'm trying to be precise."

"Protection?" Mrs. Forest offered.

"That sounds like condoms," I said.

Mrs. Forest smiled.

I was shocked to see her suddenly stand as if she were leaving a party or nudging a customer out the door. "May I use your bathroom?" she said.

Mrs. Forest was like a camel. I doubted that she needed to pee or wouldn't have wisely peed before she left.

"Of course," Dr. Know said.

"You have some artistic photographs in here!" she called.

"Is she allowed?" I said. "To look at stuff in your house?" I twisted in my chair. "During a *therapy* session?"

"This is not a prison," Dr. Know said. "Of course I allow my patients to use the toilet."

Toilet, not *bathroom?* Freud was into feces. Toilet is definitely a *shit* word. Is that where he was headed with this?

"You should feel free, too," Dr Know said, ". . . to eliminate, evacuate."

Mrs. Forest plumped pillows on the way back and blazed a path with her index finger on a dusty tabletop. I could see that the time away from me had made her stronger.

She returned to her director's chair. "Yes, Ace, I'm allowed," she said. "And so are you. Like partners."

"Susan, what would have to happen for you and Ace to be partners?"

"She has to be responsible for her actions."

I heard her the way you do when you have ocean in your ears. Rags used to tell us to jump on one foot to "open the floodgates."

"I can't be responsible," I heard her say. "It's true how the jailer becomes the jailed."

"She has to earn your trust?" Dr. Know said.

"No, I've made a decision to trust her," Mrs. Forest said. "She has to live with the burden of that trust."

49

"Ace?"

The question—open-ended, hopeful—made me feel briefly important, chosen.

"May I?" Eleanor Margesson pulled out the chair across from mine and raised her hand to Junior Eaton, who was hurtling by with a tray of empty cups. "You gottit, Ellie!"

Ellie? I'd never even called her Eleanor to her face, let alone Ellie. Seeing her here was like being outside school during a fire drill.

"Hi." I half stood, like a guy on a date.

Junior arrived, delivering one of those drinks with swirls and a cinnamon stick poking from a dome of whipped cream.

"When I saw you here, I wasn't planning on approaching you, let alone sitting with you," Eleanor said. "I hope I'm not interrupting."

I closed my laptop. "Not at all."

"You're not expecting company?" She glanced at the door. "Your friend?"

She loaded the word like ammunition. That same-sex person I do unmentionable things with? "She might show up."

"Of course. Listen, Ace, I know our families have been at

odds, but I respect the Ragsdales—as people."

"As opposed to?"

"Socialists." She carefully lay her cinnamon stick on a napkin.

"Can I have that?" I sounded like Honor Allerton.

"This?" She pointed to it. "Sure."

I used it to stir my latte. "I know you've become friends with my grandmother."

Tight mouth, eyes uncertain. "Maybe that's why I'm here talking to you." Pause to pull herself together. "Your grandmother is a fine person."

I searched for signs that Eleanor had a Town Hall self and a macchiato self. In place of the warmup suit were relaxed-fit jeans and a sweater featuring brocade puppies. An impressive diamond hollowed the veins and arthritic bones of her ring finger. Could this be old Jake Margesson's sparkling hardware?

I must have been staring at it because Eleanor said, "I can't even remove it."

"Have you tried soap?"

"Ha. After forty years, they'd have to cut it off."

"Mr. Margesson's?" I said.

She nodded. "He used to be quite the romantic." The plush toys on her chest rose and fell with every breath. "It's hard to imagine, I know, Jake with his goggles and that out-to-lunch look of his." She gazed heavenward. "He was smart and handsome, too."

"I hear he's a whiz with boards . . ."

Puzzled look.

"Sawing two-by-fours? . . . down at Ace?"

"Oh yes, he found his bliss late in life."

I raised my eyebrows as I tried to erase images of Grandma and *Ellie* going at it. Eleanor flushed. "We married super young, the kids, the lying to ourselves, the whole nine yards." She explored the depths of her drink with a straw. "I'd studied to be a lawyer."

"Wow!"

This elicited a smile from Eleanor.

"You would have made a good one," I said, meaning it.

She met me eye to eye, not turning her head. "She's here. Your friend."

"How did you know?"

Eleanor stood. "The look on your face."

50

The crowd spilled out the door of Picture This, where we'd set up a makeshift café on the sidewalk out front. Paper lanterns beamed cones of amber light onto the street.

Nate Carver said it was illegal, but he gave us a one-night variance and instructed the HFD to be on high alert.

The posters Sawyer had created and distributed around town for the maiden voyage of Mrs. Forest's salon read "Art and Energy: Wind and Unrest in an Age of Angst." Selectman Wilder had made an announcement at town meeting. The *Frigate* had posted a breaking news item.

Sawyer and I had copied *catalogues raisionnés* from the Institute of Contemporary Art website. The show's aim was to represent the wind turbine, no holds barred—paintings, abstract or representational; sculpture; photography, collage; video, and performance art—"to mend fences and bring the community together."

Sawyer wore a new suit with a pink tie. Rainy stood on tiptoe, growling about how he could have found something just as nice at the Castaway.

Le Forest was the only other guy in a suit and tie. Though each handshake was bursting with clinical possibilities, it was my brother whom he corralled near the drinks table after he shook Sawyer's young, healthy hand. They looked like networkers at a wedding.

Chippie Holbeck had been deputized to search bags and pockets for box cutters, paring knives and prismapencils, which could deface any art medium. Pat-downs would have been enjoyed by Horton residents, but were not allowed, unless you happened to be an authorized TSA agent. Bottles of booze, poking from bags or tucked under arms, were allowed.

Chippie's massive wood windmill stood like a totem at the entrance. It was profoundly real. Almost nothing about it elevated it to art. He was willing to give it to anyone who wanted a lawn ornament. "It's priceless," he said.

The Bowsprit had sent over a couple of kegs and a pan of broa. From Uncle Asia's came dumplings and spring rolls. The Eatons contributed boxes of coffee and feta olive toast points. Dr. Know brought a homemade mincemeat pie. The new five-star place off Scrimshaw sent over a case of wine and their signature death tarts.

I was covering the event for the *Frigate*. But as a Picture This partner, I had to make sure everything went well, especially during the Q&A, when artists discussed their "work."

Being a housekeeper or busboy was work, not making these self-reverential handicrafts.

Grandma had gone down to the Pot Shop to fashion her tiny clay rendition, obscenely out of proportion, almost all shaft, with blades like insect wings. She'd glued on some shells and painted it madder red.

One photograph, unsigned, was shot from above the turbine. In the foreground, one giant blade severed Whore Town's homes, roads, highways, an occasional steeple and high-rise. Water snaked through the marshes, and the ocean was stop-actioned. The photographer had to be Dr. Know, shooting from his parasail.

Someone had painted an Edward Hopper windmill, capturing the sad aloneness of the thing with imagined scenarios happening off canvas.

In front of a watercolor titled "Human Folly," Eleanor Margesson was holding forth. She'd penned a little essay underneath in the kind of cursive you'd find on your electric bill. Her picture was like a kid's drawing, with the sun setting below a mountain of dark clouds.

One of those "business school elites" the anti-turbine faction had complained about stood on the raised platform Sport Rodgers had built, discoursing on his "oeuvre," which included a multimedia work with sound, video, and a collage of oils and "sustainable detritus." His index fingers and thumbs formed a vagina as he addressed the crowd, which was eating, drinking, gossiping, and only perfunctorily looking at art. "It radically subverts interrogation in a preconceived hierarchy that both engenders and precludes cultural assumptions," he said, "embracing interiority and the void, in an infinite quest for the assumed tension of the final cause."

This man approached the drinks table. "You and your dad," he said to Sawyer and Le Forest. "You look like out-of-towners, too."

Though I was busy with minor details, I always knew where Mrs. Forest was. It was a shared experience, intense in a different way from sex, because we were sharing each other with our friends and neighbors.

One abstract was totally derivative, with Pollack drips, Picasso cubes, Martin grids, O'Keefe vaginas, Ofili *madonnas*. This is what our mother had been toiling over in secret in the mixed media room at Whore High. "Wind Chimes" adhered to the dictates of triangle composition, the subversive female form. Too bad Bill had abandoned her art career to serve disabled students, a loyal husband, and kids who emptied her like that last suck of the tub.

It turned out that Sawyer had FaceTimed the Director of Public Engagement from Boston's Institute of Contemporary Art. She'd found him so engaging that she'd shown up for our "opening." She'd been so taken with Bill Ragsdale's "Wind

251

Chimes" that she offered to include it in a juried show at ICA.

Bill rejected the offers of family members to go with her to drop off her work. She chose Chippie instead. He was her student. He would never get arrested for DUI. They would have unambiguous conversations that didn't involve love or sex or subterfuge. He would drive the rig, drop her off at the museum, deliver his cargo of Honda Accords to a dealership in Dedham, and then pick her up.

Bill said nothing about the transformative moment itself. Instead, she revealed that riding high up in the rig had given her a new perspective on life. She had an unobstructed view of lone motorists. Not all of them were turning themselves on or getting a buzz with beer cans nestled in their crotches. Some focused searchingly on the road ahead.

When she glanced behind her, she was blinded by the light of Chippie's dazzling metallic beasts blazing in the sun.

We didn't know it yet, but Chippie Holbeck's secret fears would do us in. He'd searched rucksacks, briefcases, and man-bags, carefully observing their contents and their owners' demeanors. But women's purses confounded him, with their dark, succulent mysteries. He recoiled from tampon cases, lubricants, single-pack Cialis, Lifestyles, medications for cramps and hot flashes. He let dangerous weapons, like tweezers and nail clippers, pass.

51

Art show not picture-perfect

By Candace "Ace" Ragsdale
Frigate staff writer

Susan Forest, owner of Picture This, held the first of what will be a series of salons at the Scrimshaw Street frame shop.

Local artists were asked to submit works depicting their views—both psychic and literal—of the controversial wind turbine.

Tractor trailer driver Chippie Holbeck's wood sculpture was the largest in the show. "I donated it to the Horton Science Center," he said.

Eleanor Margesson's "Human Folly" represented her long-standing opposition to the turbine. "The title says it all," she told the *Frigate*.

253

The event was marred by an anti-turbine activist who destroyed many of the works, using eyeliner, lip gloss, and teaser combs.

"At least the apparatus itself is still standing," one attendee told the *Frigate*.

Chippie's big wood sculpture welcomed guests to the Horton Science Center gala. Inside, an enormous tree, still strung with Christmas lights, shot up through a skylight. Day-old mistletoe hanging from rafters failed to reignite the holiday tongue-kissers.

A glass case displayed illustrations of "local flora and fauna," including the lovely salamanders and the nightmare water moccasin, seen less often but unwelcome when it was. Pink and yellow lady slippers were hermaphroditic, with their veined sacks.

Mrs. Forest wore the little black dress with the red stilettos. The color would pair nicely with the treasure hidden deep in the pocket of my trousers. The small box was brand-new from Jared's, but inside was Grandma's white gold ring nestling a pair of rubies and two baguettes.

Dad and I both wore tuxedos from the Castaway with contrasting cummerbunds. His was pink with aquamarine *fleur-de-lis*; mine the reverse. He wore his one bow tie and the patent leather pumps.

I grabbed two flutes of champagne from the tray of a passing server. "Maddie!" Madison O'Malley was on the waitstaff with about a half dozen other Horton kids. Some were now raising kids of their own.

"How's your family?" she said with a friendly sneer.

"They're all here." Sawyer, with his weird brown suit, slouching against a fake Corinthian column, encircled by Fabia clients. Bill, wearing something she'd wear to a PTO meeting.

Maddie seemed amazed that we'd survived the episode on

Catboat Road. "Gotta run, duty calls." She dried the empty tray on her behind.

Chuck Butten was attending, now in a new job as my assistant. (Honor had tired of waiting for him to die at his desk.) I watched him ambush Grandma near the bar, bent almost double to hear her, hoping for a "good quote." Everything at the *Frigate* was either a good quote, or a good catch, like when our cranky, embittered copy editor saved us from printing "cock" instead of "dock." She embodied resting bitch face.

Mrs. Forest licked the remnants of a bacon-wrapped canapé from her thumb. The canapés were "locally sourced," with dandelion greens in vinaigrette atop ground and braised mushrooms. I kissed her vinaigrette lips.

The room went quiet as Honor Allerton approached the lectern and raised the mic; she towered over the phragmite expert who'd introduced her. Chippie Holbeck, a burnt-orange bow in his man-bun, helped with her audio/visual aids, a fuzzy collage of humans and animals. As board chair of the Horton Science Center, Honor encouraged donations and thanked "Susan Forest and Bill Ragsdale for their excellent stewardship of the Quaking Bog."

I caught Bill's satisfied slip of a grin. Dad clapped loudly. Mrs. Forest stood straight, yanking her clingy dress. She hated nature.

Sawyer was thanked for his work on the dioramas and glass-enclosed exhibits that lined the preserve. He wore a bolo with a turquoise chevron. When Honor called his name, he pulled it straight. Le Forest, standing next to him, tightened his Windsor knot.

After the speech, Le Forest moved toward Ethel and Karen, who were standing near the Promethean chafing dish, spearing food with toothpicks tipped in red cellophane.

Honor made her way toward Chuck. I heard her say, "Please get some quotes for Ace." She turned to Mrs. Forest. "You look lovely tonight."

"Thank you, nice speech."

"Ugh, no, but thanks."

Honor pulled Chuck aside. "Work the room. Nothing in the realm of 'A good time was had by all!'"

"Shit, but yeah." Chuck had forgotten to remove his handball glove from his back pocket. He seemed relieved that I had taken his old job. "Your Dr. Know gave me some good quotes," he exhaled into my ear.

I pulled my notebook from the capacious inside pocket of my man-tuxedo. "Don't leave without me," I told Mrs. Forest. I was glad to see her laughing and drinking with Bill. And *touching*. I no longer wanted to know the boundaries of their friendship. Whatever it was, it was fine with me, and it belonged to them alone. There should be more of it, people loving, body and soul.

"Hey Chuck," I said. "Did you get this one? 'It's the community spirit here in Horton'?" Chuck pulled out his pen and scrawled it on the back of an envelope.

Mrs. Forest and I moved to the small wood dance floor, slow-dancing to a cover of Elvis's "Can't Help Falling in Love."

I led her to a quiet corner, "Lean on Me" fading into the background. When I knelt in front of her, I was on eye level with the womanly core of her, and the miraculous baby bump.

She said yes, breathing hoarsely, her eyes wet and bright, not reflecting light but creating it.

A slew of little mammals had lost their lives to the fur coat that Mrs. Forest had saved for the gala. It lived in a temperature-controlled vault in Boston. I rescued it from the makeshift "coat check," where Chippie was doing double duty as coat-check girl. I stroked the salmon satin lining before draping it over Mrs. Forest's shoulders.

"Nice." Rainy Priest, who had been surveying the coats, ran her blue hand over the fur. "I'll take that off your hands when the time comes."

Mrs. Forest kissed me behind the ear. "I wear it for special occasions," she said.

I tipped Chippie two dollars, which he said was too much, "considering."

52

We all gathered in front of the Fonseca estate, like we were some kind of celestial choir, Mrs. Forest conducting with her real estate notebook in the crook of her arm.

Other people might escape to new places, new jobs, start new lives, but we leaned in, circled the wagons, became even more of what we were to begin with.

We were all going to buy the Fonseca mansion together.

Karen and Ethel planned to open their fitness/physical therapy center on the ground floor. They would be living in the garden apartment opening onto the pool, overhydrated with grenades of bottled water strapped to their waists.

Le Forest had returned from a Vision Quest Medicine Walk a changed man. It was Grandma who'd advised him that healthy doses of cacti and high colonics could improve parenting and cut back on misogyny. He now had a business throuple with Karen and Ethel.

He and Sawyer had already launched the fashion line, Man Candy Coordinates. There was plenty of room in the mansion for Sawyer's live/work design studio and Long Division's "business center."

Long Division had finally snagged Sawyer and was more

than happy with FWB status. Uncle Sawyer, meanwhile, would be babysitter extraordinaire—from sack races to sex-ed.

The maid's quarters on the top floor would be Grandma's home base, when she wasn't on the road saving the planet. The night of the vernal equinox and the throwing of the baseballs, she'd been keeping watch over us—we'd seen something moving, strips of florescence reflecting starlight. That's when she'd decided not to leave us.

Bill and Rags were moving into an apartment on the third floor. It would be a chance to nip in the bud any hoarding instincts that had begun to flower on Catboat Road. They were looking forward to sitting at poolside with long nets to trap leaves and litter.

Mrs. Forest and I would occupy the second floor with our new baby.

Le Forest had refused to have sex with his wife once I'd "unconsecrated" their "marriage bower," so the baby wasn't his. Despite all Sawyer's steamy pedicures, he would not have slept with Mrs. Forest, and he'd heard from New England Cryogenics that he was shooting blanks anyway.

That left our friends in New York. Downtown had been with me that night. When he'd knocked on the door, I'd said no to sex but yes to drinking and weeping together like grown women, because our lovers were with each other.

Lady Liberty, not yet fully transitioned, had apparently made sweet, gentle love to her stunning drunken cougar, a one-night stand that brought us Emma Lazarus Forest Ragsdale. It was a lot of name for a little girl, but not if you took into account the teeming shore, the tempest tossed, the slamming of the Golden Door.

Brett and Levi could live with us, or with their newly minted father, or choose to live with Bill and Rags, or Karen and Ethel. They had unlimited options.

They would either be well-adjusted kids or candidates for psychotherapy. Dr. Know would be waiting in the wings.

The twins made us promise to give them time-outs in their

new home. An alcove off the foyer held a perfect bench for this purpose, intricately carved and low to the ground.

Though Mrs. Forest and I would try to sell the houses on Catboat and Mill Wheel, it was likely no one would buy them. They'd return to the earth, just as the Fonseca estate had been doing before we occupied it.

53

We moved in on Inauguration Day, which happened to coincide with a weather event in Horton that would be recorded in the Dock Master's log as Typhoon Turbine. The rest of the area got normal weather like that in D.C., where it was rainy and cold. The Fonseca estate's giant flat-screen was tuned to the Inauguration, without the sound.

We watched the Chief Justice of the Supreme Court trembling, a stiff breeze floating his robe over the Home of the Brave. He dropped the Bible. The President-Elect, who would be President in a matter of minutes, picked it up and dusted it off, as if the grounds of the United States Capitol were the dirtiest place on earth. Like all modern Presidents, this one toughed it out hatless, blond hair blowing—the word *carnage* scrolling out on frozen breath. Those in attendance were immobile, fear icing their features.

Here in Whore Town, it was like the tsunami that had hit Indonesia. Before the towering waves overwhelmed the islands of Sumatra and Phuket, the ocean pulled back in a vast, hideous grin. Kids collected sea life. Divers off the coral reefs of the Maldives reported wild currents and eddies. Fish disappeared. Humans would have done well to take their cues from animals.

Fearful and on guard, they made sounds no one had heard before. Birds could have escaped, but some lingered as if to warn their ignorant humans.

Our new home stood high above the harbor. From its ramparts and parapets, we got a map-like panorama. Tributaries cut the salt flats like roads that led places. The wind whipped up frothy swells. In the distance, the ocean lay black and undecided.

The typhoon, or whatever it was, brought a fitting end to our Year of the Windmill.

The storm roared through Whore Town, lifting great blankets of marshland, quilting Bulrush Road. You could hear tree trunks cracking. Branches took flight. Shingles soared from roofs, skimming the beach like laughing gulls. A Foreman grill crashed into Uncle Asia's fish tank. The lighthouse curtain-called into the jetty. Boats came to rest on Scrimshaw Street. Colossal waves breached the seawall.

Though Opposition Wind claimed victory, it was an act of God that brought our struggle to an end.

Crack sang out as we stood on the mansion's eastern balustrade. Like the Royal Family— waving, not drowning—we watched our windmill plunge into the ocean, its huge propeller-like blades powering toward Southampton.

Acknowledgements

My sincere thanks to Elizabeth Andersen, Malaga Baldi, Darrah Cloud; the Bathrobe Babes—Gloria Jacobs and Jeanann Pannasch, Marianne K. Martin, Ann McMan, Alyssa Bredin Quiros, Sandra Shea, Elizabeth Sims, Nancy Squires, Jen Walter, Salem West—and my deepest gratitude to Helen Eisenbach.

About the Author

Kate Rounds is a veteran journalist whose work includes stints as News Editor and Senior Editor at *Ms. Magazine*, Executive Editor and speechwriter to the President of the Planned Parenthood Federation of America, and Editor in Chief of the *Hudson Reporter*. She has an MFA in Creative Writing from Goddard College. She grew up in Massachusetts and lives in Jersey City without a cat.

At Bywater, we love good books, just like you do. And we're committed to bringing the best of contemporary literature to an expanding community of readers. Our editorial team is dedicated to finding and developing outstanding writers who create books you won't want to put down.

For more information about Bywater Books, our authors, and our titles, please visit our website.

www.bywaterbooks.com

9 781612 942452